THE BLOOD OF ILLUCIDIA DUOLOGY
BOOK ONE

IMOGEN KAY

Half Breed

© 2026 Imogen Kay All rights reserved.

This book is a work of fiction. Names, characters, places, and events are products of the author's imagination or used fictitiously. Any resemblance to actual persons, living or dead, events, or locales is entirely coincidental.

No part of this publication may be reproduced, stored, or transmitted in any form or by any means, electronic or mechanical, without written permission from the author, except for brief quotations in reviews or critical articles.

Cover Design: Donn Marlou Ramirez

Edited by: Vicky Skinner, Nora Reed, and Jade Hemming

For permissions or inquiries: www.authorimogenkay.com

Imogen Kay | House of the Black Dragon Publishing

ISBN (Paperback): 979-8-9945121-1-1

ISBN (eBook): 979-8-9945121-0-4

For the ones who were told they were too much, too wild, too soft, or too broken — this story is proof you were always magic.

CONTENT WARNING

Half Breed contains themes and scenes that may be sensitive or triggering for some readers. Please read with awareness of your own comfort level.

This book includes:
- Explicit, graphic sexual content (consensual)
- Violence and mild gore
- War-related themes and magical combat
- Death of side characters
- Mentions of parental loss
- Trauma healing and recovery
- Power dynamics, addressed respectfully

Your safety and reading experience matter. Please take care while engaging with this story.

Illucidia

Enactel

Hunter's Hovel

Wild Lands

The In Between

Fort Fayline

Kenna's Cottage

Fae Realm

Eiradia

Trading Market

Citri

PROLOGUE

MANY YEARS AGO

In the courtyard of Eiradia, the capital of the Fae Realm, music floated gently through the air. Harps, flutes, and the rhythmic pulse of soft drums, each note stitched with threads of enchantment that made the night feel both ancient and newly born.

Moonlight glinted off the silver trim of his formal attire, but King Arrion hardly noticed. His eyes were fixed on the faces moving through the crowd: wide-eyed children clinging to their mothers' hands, elders sipping nectar slowly with worn fingers, nobles and farmers laughing shoulder to shoulder. Fae nobles dressed in silks that shimmered like moonlight mingled freely with common folk who wore their finest garments, simple but lovingly crafted.

The divisions that often defined his realm had faded tonight, at least for a while. Just as he had hoped. The air vibrated with unity, a testament to the enduring bond between Eiradia's rulers and its people.

He breathed deeply. The scent of jasmine, honey glaze, and warm bread mingled with the faint tang of magic; a fragrance unique to Eiradia. Unique to home.

And still, despite the joy, there was a pinch of tension in his shoulders that had not eased all evening. The gravity of preserving his beloved queen's dreams of peace and safety within the Fae Realm overtook much of his mind. The crown sat lightly tonight, but the weight of rule never truly left his bones.

At the heart of it all stood King Arrion and Queen Amabel, moving gracefully through their guests like twin stars orbiting one another. Arrion's imposing figure exuded both strength and warmth; his lilac eyes sparkled with a joy rarely seen in sovereigns burdened by duty.

"Arrion," came the soft voice he could always hear, no matter the noise around them. Amabel.

He turned just as she reached him, the soft glow of lantern light catching in her auburn hair. Her gown shimmered with subtle hues that shifted like dawn across a still lake. She placed a hand on his chest, her fingers warm through the fine fabric.

"You're frowning," she said gently.

He smiled at her in a way he reserved only for her. "I'm thinking."

She raised a knowing brow. "You're always thinking."

"It's a king's curse," he said as his hand closed gently around hers.

"And what burdens you on this perfect night?" Amabel tilted her head to look up at him.

He hesitated. Around them, the music soared, and a pair of dancers twirled past, laughing. Their son, Finnian, stood near the edge of the crowd, watching them both, his posture just a little too stiff. He was so much like Arrion had once been, yet so much yet to learn.

"I keep wondering if it's enough," Arrion murmured. "What we've built. The peace we've kept. Is it strong enough to last when we are no longer here? What if this is all temporary? There's always a chance that your love will be forgotten or those I banished will return..."

Her fingers squeezed his. "This kingdom is not built on stone or spell, Arrion. It is built on the people, and on love, whether it be mine or that of the next generation. That will stand the test of time."

He looked at her then—not the queen, not the realm's symbol of grace, wisdom, and love, but *his*. His compass in every storm. His anchor after every war.

"I will always wonder what I did to deserve you," he said softly.

She smiled. "You made me laugh when no one else could. That counts for more than you know."

"Your Majesties." An elderly Fae woman bowed low before them, her gnarled hands trembling slightly as she held out a small bundle wrapped in delicate cloth. "This is my family's offering for Prince Finnian, a token of our gratitude for all you have done."

Amabel knelt gracefully to accept it, unfolding the cloth to reveal an intricately carved pendant made from an iridescent stone that shimmered with colors unearthly in its beauty. "It is exquisite," she said warmly, her voice lilting. "Please thank your family on my behalf. The prince will treasure this always."

Arrion stepped forward, placing a hand on Amabel's shoulder, not for ceremony, but out of habit. Out of love. "And we treasure you," he added, addressing the woman directly. "Without your faith and support, there would be no kingdom for us to serve."

Another commoner stepped forward—a farmer, broad-shouldered and flushed from drink. Arrion shook his hand.

"We're grateful, Your Majesty," the man said, "for the safety you've given us. After the revolution…"

Revolution. The word hung there, like a cold wind threading through warm air. Arrion's jaw tightened just slightly, but he did his best not to show it.

"I only ever wanted to give our people a place where children could sleep without fear," he said. "Where families could live without looking over their shoulders."

The farmer nodded and smiled. "Thank you to the queen as well. You have inspired so many with your kindness."

The queen nodded her head with a small smile. "It's my pleasure."

"Goddess knows she has inspired me to be a better man," Arrion said fondly. "I wouldn't be half the king I am without Amabel."

As they moved on through the crowd, their love for one another was palpable, not just in their words but in every glance exchanged and every subtle touch shared between them. It was a love that inspired all who bore witness: genuine and enduring despite difficulties faced while ruling together.

Prince Finnian watched his parents from a distance, his heart swelling with pride as he observed their effortless grace. Dressed in royal finery tailored to perfection, a deep amethyst tunic embroidered with threads of silver, he looked every bit the heir to Eiradia's throne. Yet beneath his composed exterior lay a swirling storm of emotions: excitement at stepping into his role as crown prince; trepidation at living up to his father's legacy; and a fierce determination to protect all that his parents had built.

"Standing out here brooding like a tragic poet?" a voice rumbled beside him. Finnian startled slightly as his mother's favorite baker appeared, cradling a goblet of nectar. "Go on, lad. Smile. You've survived your first twenty-five years in one piece, haven't you?"

Finnian huffed a breath of laughter. "Barely."

The baker grinned, eyes crinkling. "Well, you've got their blood. That'll carry you further than you think."

Finnian looked toward his parents again, noting the way his father's hand lingered on the queen's shoulder: gentle, unhurried, reverent. They moved together, seamless in every glance and gesture.

He hoped he'd have that one day. Or at least not ruin it if it found him.

The music slowed. A shift in the rhythm. Arrion recognized the cue and stepped up onto the dais, the crowd quieting in a gentle wave as attention turned toward him. The night air held a reverent stillness, as if even the stars leaned in to listen.

"My lovely people of the Fae Realm!" Arrion boomed; his voice amplified by magic, yet still carrying its natural warmth. "Tonight, we celebrate not only my son's coming of age but also our shared triumphs—the peace we have built together after years of struggle!"

The crowd erupted into cheers so loud they seemed to shake the very ground beneath their feet. Arrion gestured toward Finnian, beckoning him forward as pride shone brightly in his eyes.

"And this—" he gestured to Finnian, who stepped up beside him with hesitant grace, "—as you all know, is Prince Finnian. My son. My legacy. My greatest pride."

Applause broke like a wave over the courtyard, cheers echoing against the columns of the castle.

"Cherish him," Arrion said, voice roughening. "As you have cherished me."

Amabel joined them then, resting her hand at the small of Arrion's back. He turned and pressed a kiss into her hair, letting the scent of her calm him like it always had.

"You and Finnian are my greatest treasures," Arrion whispered to Amabel. "I don't know what I would do without you, my love."

"Let us hope you never have to find out," Amabel said sweetly and wrapped an arm around the king.

He nearly laughed until he saw the servant approaching, weaving through the crowd with purpose etched into every step. The man bent low beside him.

"Sire," he whispered, "there are rumors. Discontent stirring in the northern territories... the Wildlands."

Arrion's jaw clenched. "Who?"

"No names. Just whispers. They speak of old exiles. Those driven out after the revolution."

Arrion's jaw ticked once, twice.

"If they have grievances," he said flatly, "they may come to me directly. I'll hear them, but not tonight." He waved the man off, managing a smile for Amabel and Finnian.

That smile froze the moment he heard it—the first scream. The sound was sharp. Ripping the joy from the air like claws through silk.

The moment shattered as panic sliced through it; screams tore through cheers like a blade. Arrion's muscles tensed; experience honed from conflict caused him to spring into action. He pushed Amabel behind him protectively before urging Finnian toward safety; his voice urgent but controlled.

"Finnian, go! Stay with your mother. Hide!"

Finnian stumbled, caught between panic and obedience, but Amabel grabbed his arm and pulled him back toward the castle entrance. She looked over her shoulder once, catching a glimpse of the man she'd adored all these years.

Arrion wanted to run with them. But he saw what tore through the crowd: a cloaked figure, massive, with wild magic writhing around him like smoke. The look in his eyes wasn't rage; it was grief sharpened into a weapon.

Amabel and Finnian vanished into the castle's shadows while outside Arrion faced down chaos manifesting before him. Finnian rushed with his mother into a room off the main hallway. "It'll be ok, mother," Finnian said softly.

Arrion pulled his sword, watching as the people he had worked so hard to protect ran for their lives. He could no longer stand idly, and as he was about to step into the melee, the cloaked figure stepped even closer.

"King Arrion!" the male bellowed. "You drove my people and many others deeper into the woods of the Wildlands! You preach safety and security, but what of the safety and security of those you banished? For their deaths, you must pay!"

Arrion's eyes widened. Although he could not see what kind of creature this man was, he had no doubt he was one of many that had been pushed out of the Fae Realm in Arrion's efforts to protect his people. Instinct tightened Arrion's grip on his sword, senses alert for any movement as he readied himself for what may come next.

The cloaked male laughed bitterly. "Oh no, my King," he said, "I don't want you. I want you to hear the screams of those you love most, the way I did when you drove my family to their deaths!"

Arrion's blood ran cold. "Amabel... Finnian..." he whispered. Arrion's resolve faltered briefly; a crack in the armor of a king. As his royal guards surrounded the unknown man, Arrion felt as if the world narrowed, and against his better judgment, he dropped his stance. He ran into the castle, seeking out his beloved wife and son, all while the cloaked man's laughter echoed behind him until the sounds of swords slicing cut it short.

With his heart thrumming against his ribs like frantic drumbeats, Arrion abandoned defense for a frantic search within the walls of the castle.

Stone walls blurred as he raced through the castle's corridors, feet pounding, breaths shallow. Magic prickled in the air, something scorched and chaotic. He felt the agony before a crippling smell overtook him: burning silk and blood.

"Amabel!"

He burst into the side chamber, just in time to fall to his knees.

There it was, the tableau of loss that broke empires. In a silence punctuated only by the muffled sobs and labored breaths of Finnian lay Queen Amabel; a scene etched with remnants of elemental fury and echoing with an unspeakable void where once love had been whole. In that moment, his soul began to shatter, for Amabel was his bonded mate, and with her death came the agonizing fracturing of the core of his being.

Finnian looked up, eyes wide, mouth moving, but Arrion couldn't hear him. Not over the roaring in his ears. Not over the sound of his soul tearing itself in two.

"No," he whispered.

She had saved their son, had spent the last of her magic doing it.

He reached for her, but something inside him, something ancient and sacred, snapped. The bond. The mate bond. Gone.

And the scream he released shook the walls.

Arrion barely registered the burn marks on the floor or the faint lilac flames still clinging to Amabel's fingertips as she lay lifeless. He hardly breathed as the agonizing pain of having his bond severed tore through his body.

Amidst echoes of grief and tendrils of magic still pooling from fingertips that would weave no more enchantments, Arrion stood transformed by sorrow's cruel alchemy; his eyes a storm of emotions.

"I'll kill them all! No matter where they hide! No matter who they are! Only the pure blood Fae of this realm will survive! I will hunt them to the ends of the continent and beyond!" Arrion screamed, and Finnian flinched, feeling the guilt of his mother's death settle over him.

The king who had once ruled with kindness, the man who had loved with such reverence, was gone. In his place stood a storm wearing a crown with eyes like violet fire, and vengeance rising like a tide that would not recede.

Finnian watched helplessly as rage overtook reason. A chasm opened wide that swallowed fatherhood whole, and before him stood not a king but an entity forged from torment. His father morphed into an avatar of retribution named for turmoil itself: King Arrion the Terrible.

1
KENNA
PRESENT DAY

In the early morning, as sunlight danced through the leaves of the trees in the In-Between Forest, I found myself once again hauling my cart of concoctions and botanicals into town. I often made mid-week trips to avoid the crowds on market days at the coven. As a well-respected herbal healer in Cauldera, I spent most of my time making salves and other healing tinctures, ointments, and growing herbs and other medicinal plants to sell at the market the Witches' Coven held each weekend.

The trip would likely have been faster by horse, but I did not possess such an animal and, instead, had to drag a cart down the poorly-maintained path to the east I had created to get my supplies, furniture, and other needs to the cottage.

If I headed north of the woods, I would find myself in the Wildlands. To the east was Miridia, which housed the coven lands in Cauldera. North of that was Amaradia, where non-magical humans dwelled, and then Antharel, where less pleasant beings carved out a life. To the other side of the In-Between was the Fae Realm. To the north of that, Enactel, and to the south, Citri.

The In-Between didn't welcome travelers—it barely tolerated them. Most Witches wouldn't dare cross the border unless they had no other choice. Magic hung thick in the air here, ancient and unpredictable, the kind that didn't come from spells or scrolls. It pulsed in the roots, whispered through the leaves, watched from the shadows with glowing eyes that vanished if you stared too long. The forest itself formed a living wall between worlds—Fae on one side, where magic came as easily as breath, and coven lands on the other, where it had to be earned, studied, tamed.

Sunlight barely made it through the canopy. Vines twisted like they had opinions. Branches gnarled and bent overhead, forming an almost skeletal cage of bark and shadow. Most days, the forest kept to itself and left my property alone—an unspoken agreement, I liked to think. But on market days, when I hitched up my cart and dragged it toward the coven, the forest seemed to watch my struggle.

My mind wandered as I walked. The trek was slow and arduous, and often left me time to recall the difficult childhood at the coven I was headed toward and the upbringing that drove me to live in a wood most considered haunted, or at least cursed.

Often, thoughts of the other coven Witches belittling me for my mixed magic, or even going so far as to draw energy from me, came to mind. I shivered as I thought of the night I had woken in the old Headmistress, Mrs. Lancaster's, office after the other earth magic Witches had gone too far.

The coven in Cauldera housed elemental Witches from across Miridia. Most humans could learn basic magic, parlor tricks, really, but the coven prized true affinity: the kind tied to the elements themselves. Earth, fire, water, air, lunar, solar… and then the rarer ones, like ice or shadow. Each Witch had a pull toward something. If left untrained, that magic would just fizzle out, wasted.

I'd been pulled into the earth dormitory almost the moment I arrived. Mrs. Lancaster saw to that after my mother left me in her care.

Being half-Fae meant magic didn't whisper, it roared. Earth responded first, always. Water came second, trailing behind like a curious sibling. I'd grown good with healing, too. I wasn't born into some gilded bloodline, but whatever ran through my veins was old enough to make people uncomfortable. And they felt it. Oh, they knew.

I still remembered the first time they used me. I was barely ten, still unsure of the way the sigils moved under my fingers, still getting headaches from reading too long by candlelight. One of the older girls, Maris, I think, had coaxed me over.

"Here, just stand still," she said, guiding me toward the ritual circle. "You don't have to do anything. Just... exist."

I blinked. "What kind of spell is it?"

"A charging spell. We need more power to anchor it. You're perfect."

I hesitated. "I—I don't know if I should."

Her smile was sweet and false. "Of course you should. You want to help the coven, don't you?"

I'd said yes. Of course I had.

By the time the chanting started, I could feel the tug in my chest, like a thread pulling loose, unraveling. My knees nearly buckled. Afterward, while I gasped and clutched at my ribs, Maris just laughed.

"Stars above, you really are a conduit," she said to the others. "No wonder they keep her."

Later, I'd woken up in Mrs. Lancaster's office, palms scraped, heart pounding.

"They used me," I said, standing slowly from the bench I'd been lying on. "They drained my magic without asking."

Mrs. Lancaster didn't look up from her ledgers. "And did the spell work?"

"Yes, but—"

"Then you were useful." She finally glanced up, her eyes cold and

sharp as iron. "Better to be useful than forgotten, child. You want them to fear you? Or pity you? Because pity doesn't keep you safe."

"I didn't ask for this," I whispered.

"No. But the world rarely asks us what we want. You need to learn to be strong, Kenna. This world is an unforgiving place, and I cannot protect you forever."

That night, I knelt in the garden behind the keep, hands sunk deep into the soil, fingers pressing against the roots like they could hold me together. I didn't speak aloud. I just thought her name—the Mother Goddess. Earth mother. Maker of all. The one who gave everything—her limbs for the mountains, her blood for the rivers, her skin for the forests. The only Goddess that had actual depictions of her presenting herself outright to followers. She had to understand my pain, right?

"If you're listening," I murmured, "I don't want to be just useful. I want to be whole. I want to feel loved."

The dirt didn't answer, but I felt it shift—just slightly—under my knees.

I heard the sounds of the market up ahead and shook my head, trying to clear the memories. Looking up, I saw the edge of the In-Between before the path to the center of Cauldera began. I looked around me and called into the woods. "Thank you for letting me pass through! I will bring you something on my return!"

I was never sure if the shadow creatures in the woods could understand me, but I always made sure to show them respect and bring them small tokens of appreciation, often food, for not immediately killing me upon entering their territory. It seemed to work well, and sometimes I even found small items I assumed were from the shadow creatures themselves, such as stones or flowers gracing the path outside my gate.

Upon finally reaching the coven gates, I greeted the guards, gave the older guard a salve he had asked for, and made my way through the market outside the keep. It was already stirring, banners snapping above the stalls like they had opinions of their own. I pulled my cart over the uneven stone path, the wooden wheels groaning with every dip and rise as fluttering glyphs shimmered above me—symbols inked in magic that danced faintly in the morning light.

Each banner marked its territory in bold strokes: fire's burnt crimson blazed overhead, lunar's soft silver trailed like fog, and water's deep sapphire rippled like a current through the wind. The air was thick with the scent of dried herbs, sulfur, and freshly turned soil. I caught the metallic tang of spellcraft on my tongue, a taste I'd grown used to over the years, like iron dust and old secrets.

At the far end of the square, I passed two narrow shops, both closed as usual. One marked for shadow, the other for ice. No one loitered there. No laughter spilled from their doors. Too rare. Too dangerous. Even magic had its pariahs.

The wind and fire stalls were impossible to ignore. Wind chimes screamed over whipping gusts, flags flapped like they were in a storm, and fire-slingers sent up sparks just to show off. I weaved around a puff of smoke that rolled past, thankful when the chaos finally gave way to something steadier.

Earth and water always sat near the center; solid, dependable, unmoving. Crates overflowed with dried roots and enchanted stones. Jars of sacred spring water lined up neatly beside mud-charms still soft with thumbprints. This was the calm in the storm, the part of the market that made sense to me.

At the front, where sunlight hit just right, and everyone had to pass through, stood the solar and lunar shops. Regal, like they knew they were important. Gold and silver foil framed their doors, and from the lunar window, I heard a priestess chanting, a whispering tone that floated through the air like incense.

Off to the side, behind a low magical barrier that shimmered faintly with containment spells, sat the Amaradian section. The human vendors. Their stalls weren't made of stone like ours. They were temporary, wooden structures patched together with nails and faith. Canvas roofs flapped in the breeze, making them look like they were shivering. The smell of baked apples and leather oil drifted from their booths, and I caught myself smiling despite the weight of the cart.

At the far edge of the square, past even the Amaradian stalls, was a place no one talked about anymore. Once, the Blood Drinkers of Antharel had occupied that stretch. Their tents had been velvet and smoke, dark incense coiling into the air like warning signals. That ended when one of them got too hungry. All that remained now was a low stone wall, half-covered in moss and silence.

Farther beyond, just past the eye's comfort, stood the scorched stone of the Fae pavilion. I'd never seen it in use, but we all knew the stories. Drawings in old coven books showed silken canopies and trees that bloomed overnight from seeds soaked in magic. Music that came from nowhere, laughter that made the wind sing. All of it ended the day the Fae King shattered.

When the Queen died, they said grief broke him. The western spire of Cauldera still bears the scars from the day he lost control. After, the Witches' council banned all Fae from our lands. None returned. Or if they did, they knew better than to be seen.

I rolled the cart toward my assigned shop, the one with the green-brown sigil of earth magic etched deep into the stone above the door. Unlike the makeshift stalls of the humans, our buildings were meant to last. Thick stone walls. Carvings twined around the entryway like real vines frozen in bloom. My fingers brushed the familiar oak-leaf pattern as I reached the threshold and pushed open the door.

Inside, shelves lined every wall from floor to ceiling, each crammed with jars, powders, enchanted seed pouches, and carefully labeled bundles. The carved shop counters weren't just beautiful—they were enchanted, protected, grounded by the elemental magic they represented. Earth magic was practical like that. We didn't have to pack up at the end of each day or worry about thieves. We simply locked the door, and the magic kept everything right where it belonged.

Hazel, one of the few earth magic Witches that hadn't been wretched to me, was sitting casually behind the counter, reading a book.

"Hello, Kenna!" She beamed.

"Good morning, Hazel." I smiled back. "I have some new items to sell."

Hazel stood to presumably help me put my items on the single shelf I was allotted, but was interrupted by a sharp voice calling from the back of the shop. "Hazel? Who is that? We shouldn't have any visitors today!" Mrs. Lancaster's irritated voice carried out into the shop.

"It's Miss Kenna, ma'am," Hazel replied solemnly, fidgeting as she stood in front of me.

"Kenna? Kenna McCairn?" Mrs. Lancaster called as she strode into the main shop space. "You do not have permission to be here today, Kenna. Only the weekends. The other Witches are always so distraught when you show up unannounced. You know half breeds are viewed as about as useless as humans."

I could see Hazel becoming infinitely more uncomfortable as the headmistress chastised me. Internally, I rolled my eyes but chose not to show the miserable old crone who had raised me a reaction. I didn't want to challenge her, or I would likely no longer be able to come mid-week if she found out this was a regular occurrence.

"Yes, Mrs. Lancaster," I said dryly. "However, I'm here, so can I put these things away, and then I'll leave?"

She studied me for a moment before looking at Hazel. "Hazel, make yourself useful and help Kenna. The faster her things are put away, the less people will see her here," she said tightly, although there was a hint of something else that danced through her old eyes. Was that sadness? Sometimes I wondered if she cared more than she let on. Now and then, I saw glimmers of something that allowed me to convince myself she truly cared. Inevitably, though, she would shatter it with a shrewd remark or a judgment.

After putting my items on the shelf and the small plants on the windowsill, I walked back through the market. I stopped at my usual vendors within the human section. They were the only people who never judged me.

"Miss Kenna, nice to see you," the old baker said from behind his display table.

"Hello, John. Any old bread you'd like to be rid of?" I asked with a smile.

"I'll never understand what you do with it, or why you would want it, but it's one less thing to take home tonight," he said with a shake of his head. John stood from his stool and brought me a small box of crusty bread. I smiled and put it in my cart, thanking him.

I waved goodbye to him as I headed toward the gates again, stopping a couple more times to pick up some old fruit and day-old, dried meat the vendor couldn't seem to sell. The response from all the humans was essentially the same. I took what they didn't want, and they were nothing but cordial with me.

I made my way back out through the gates, again waving to the guards, and headed back up the path through the In-Between. I pulled out the wooden crate containing the items I had gotten from the vendors and set it on the side of the path about halfway through the forest.

"I brought you some snacks! I hope you like them! Thank you again for not eating me!" I called into the woods. No matter how many times I had done this, it never ceased to surprise me when I started walking again and heard soft shuffling and a low growl. If I turned around quickly enough, sometimes I could see glowing blue eyes where the crate had been as they disappeared back into the woods.

AFTER ARRIVING BACK at my cottage around midday, I stood in my garden, surrounded by luscious plants and vines growing in intricate patterns around my work table. Before me was a potted plant in a sad state, which I had rescued from the market on my way through. As I concentrated, a warm current surged through me, rooting me deeper into the earth as a cascade of tingles danced along my fingertips. The plant, which had been brown and wilting, shuddered with the sudden reviving energy. The brown began to green; the leaves began to straighten and plump; and, with just seconds to spare, the shrill voice of Mrs. Lancaster shattered my intense concentration. Had she followed me back?

"Kenna McCairn!" The local coven leader's voice pierced the air like steel scraping on stone, making my skin crawl and my nose scrunch. Her voice alone could kill half of my beautifully sculpted garden.

To my dismay, the plant I had just infused with so much energy wilted back to its former state.

"Well, shit," I breathed with defeat. I would try again later.

"Kenna! Watch your mouth, young lady!" The shrill voice of Mrs. Lancaster was suddenly in my ear.

I felt my muscles tense as I met the sharp, scrutinizing gaze of the headmistress. "Mrs. Lancaster, I'll speak however I like."

"I would expect better from a coven Witch. However, your unbecoming language can't be blamed on you, with that blasted Fae blood your father had to dilute our coven line with by lying with your mother," she muttered. "I tried to warn your mother, I really did. But she insisted on coming out here to this cursed wood to gather ingredients and herbs to help with her visions. Look where it got her! Dead! All because your blasted Fae father couldn't stay away. I had to banish them both from coven lands before you could be born and tarnish our reputation. I had to protect the Witches. There was no way to know what kind of trickery your Fae half would bring about. We Witches stay away from the Fae for safety! It's even worse now that the old king has gone mad. You're lucky I had a soft spot for your mother," Mrs. Lancaster hissed.

From what I gathered, my mother and father had tried to carve out a life for themselves in the dense, shadowy forest that lay between their realms. My father hailed from a strictly traditional Fae family, who cast him out the moment they discovered I existed. I knew nothing about him—not his name, not his face. It was uncertain whether he was still alive, though it seemed unlikely. The magical world was unforgiving when it came to crossbreeding, seeing it as a stain on their purity.

At one point during my childhood, a member of the coven had recounted the tale of how my mother had fled from the relentless Fae warriors who pursued her. It was a night of torrential rain, the skies a swirling mass of dark clouds, when she clutched me, a mere three-month-old, close to her chest. She stumbled through the mud and tangled underbrush to reach the sanctuary of the coven's home. Desperation guided her steps as she implored Mrs. Lancaster to both nurture and teach me. My mother possessed the rare gift of foresight, unlike me, and she likely foresaw her grim fate. Mrs. Lancaster, perhaps touched by a flicker of compassion, accepted the plea and took me in, raising me within the coven's protective walls. I was told my mother perished that very night, but the details were lost to me, and truth be told, I felt no inclination to uncover them.

"Why are you here, Mrs. Lancaster?" I asked dryly. I chose not to react to her rude comments about my lineage.

"I want you to come back to the coven, Kenna," she stated flatly.

"And why on Earth do you think I would agree to that?" I looked into her eyes with determination. "You and the coven have done nothing but drive me away. I'm happy here." I gestured to my cottage and garden. "And here is exactly where I will stay." I turned to walk away, but remembered my sad potted plant and quickly scooped it up before starting toward my tiny home.

Fury raced through my veins. I had no interest in being anywhere near the coven. I had always been treated more like a charge source for the coven rather than a person. I left as soon as I turned eighteen and never looked back. At thirty-two now, I had enjoyed the years away from the drama of the coven.

Leaving meant I was considered exiled, but I honestly didn't mind. I was left alone with my tiny cottage and gardens, and spent time practicing my magic my way. I was always more intuitive than the coven Witches and was certainly not interested in being their supernatural power pack anymore.

"The Hunters are back." Mrs. Lancaster's words sent a chill down my spine. "You may not be my daughter, and I know the coven does not welcome you with open arms, but I will not see you harmed by the dark beings hunting in these woods simply because you are too stubborn to accept help."

The balance between light and dark had always been fragile—stories whispered through covens and passed between firelit circles warned as much. Magic wasn't one thing. It pulsed in different shades, different intentions. Witches like me—those who worked with earth and water, healing and light—were seen as white magic users. We mended. We nurtured. But others twisted the same forces into darker things. Shadows answered them. Pain fueled their spells. They didn't create—they consumed.

And then there were the ones who didn't need magic to be dangerous.

Hunters.

They stood at the far edge of humanity—not quite magical, but not entirely mundane either. They didn't conjure flames or bend the wind. They didn't have to. What they lacked in spells, they made up for in precision and blood.

Despite some ability to teleport using a small carved spell talisman, their forte was in combat. Every movement was calculated. Every weapon they carried had a purpose, and none of them were for show. Daggers etched with runes, arrows designed to pierce enchanted skin, poisons that didn't discriminate between Fae and Witch—they knew how to kill us, because that was their only craft.

Old stories spoke of wolves that followed them. Not pets. Not familiars. Spirits, bound by some twisted bond of soul and vengeance. They said if you saw the wolf before the Hunter, you were already dead.

No one really knew where the Hunters came from. Some claimed they were born from grief, others said they were made—rituals and iron and something just a little wrong. What mattered was their mission: they hunted those of us born with magic. Witches, Fae, anyone who glowed too brightly.

Sometimes they were hired by jealous lords or frightened priests, who couldn't stand anything that didn't fit their narrow view of what magic should be.

Other times... they didn't need a reason.

"Kenna, you are half-Fae, too. A magical delicacy. They will come for you. Just like they did your mother..." Her voice was quiet as it trailed off. She looked down at the cobblestone path we were standing on, leading up to my cottage.

"My mother?" I asked incredulously. My mouth gaped. No one had told me the Hunters took my mother.

"I never wanted you to know," she said faintly. "We found a Hunter's talisman near her body."

"Yet another reason not to come back. The lies are ridiculous. You all are ridiculous. I am half-Fae, that is true, and I'm much stronger than all of you." The wisteria vines growing around my property fence began to shudder. I felt the Fae magic pouring through me and knew my usually green eyes would be shifting to the light lilac color of the Fae if they hadn't already. "Leave. Now." As she stepped back, I saw something akin to fear spark in her widening eyes.

"Kenna, please. I want you to be safe." She put her hands up in a surrendering gesture. The vines began to tug the hem of her long black dress and pull her back. She looked at her predicament and then back to me. "Kenna May McCairn! Stop this now!" Although she was attempting to be stern, her voice wavered. A hint of something else washed across her eyes, but I couldn't identify it.

"Leave," I said once again. "Now." The vines gave her another tug.

"Fine. When you're dead, don't bother haunting me." And with that, she turned to go. I was as unimportant to her as I had thought. I suspected she only needed me as the coven's magical boost. Had she indeed been concerned, she would have put up much more of a fight.

Forgetting the wisteria was still clinging to her hem, she stumbled, but attempted to maintain her composure. I stifled a giggle, which came out as a snort as she stomped off my property and through my gate. With a flick of my fingers, the wisteria tangled in the gate, making it impossible for her to re-enter should she try again.

I turned and began my steady walk along a winding, leaf-strewn path back to my cottage—a quaint abode I'd been told was built by my father as a loving haven for my mother soon after my birth. Tucked deep in the forest where the whispered legends of the Fae land merged with the mystique of the coven, the small, two-bedroom home boasted delicate, hand-carved trim tracing the edges of its roof. Much like me, it dwelled in a liminal space, betwixt two worlds in the In-Between.

When I announced I was leaving the coven, a friend of my mother—a discreet, wise Witch—had pulled me aside in hushed tones, pressing a worn map into my hands and detailing the way to find the cottage. No one had set foot there since my parents' time, and the wild had slowly reclaimed it. Once I uncovered its hidden clearing, Mrs. Lancaster had agreed that it should remain mine as the coven still believed in transferring possessions and land by bloodline.

The In-Between stretched out as a dense, shadowy strip of woods, shrouded in an eerie silence that no one dared to disrupt. It was a cursed, forsaken territory, lying uneasily between the vibrant coven lands on one side and the enchanting realm of the Fae on the other. Twisted branches crisscrossed the narrow path, and a thick carpet of leaves muffled every footstep. It was a place of whispered legends and ominous tales, making it the ideal sanctuary for my solitude, where no one else ventured.

The first time I set eyes on the cottage, it was a scene of sorrow and neglect. The once-loved gardens, planted with care by my mother, had been swallowed by rampant weeds and tangled foliage. The building itself wore a tired face: peeling layers of paint hinted at happier times, while shards of the broken, once-vibrant stained-glass windows clung desperately to their rusted frames. Inside, layers of dust blanketed every surface, and faint shafts of sunlight shone over abandoned, creaking floors. Despite its sorry state, the home called to me, a refuge echoing with memories of the parents I had never truly known.

Rolling up my sleeves, I had committed myself to breathing new life into the place. With each stroke of white paint on the cottage's walls, I could almost see the building smiling in renewed hope. I refreshed the intricate trim with a delicate light blue hue, reminiscent of clear summer skies, and transformed the small garden shed by painting it a bold, barn-red. I restored the windows in careful detail to honor their original style and filled the rooms with thoughtfully chosen furniture, arranging each piece with both care and quiet wonder.

The local humans, devoid of even a trace of magic, arrived with their parcels, exchanging furtive glances as they deposited their items by the door before scurrying away. Their knowing eyes and silent judgments spoke volumes; clearly, they suspected I was "something else," but I gave them no indication of what. They could fear me if it meant they left me alone. I was finally happy.

Contentment settled over me as the transformation unfolded. Drawing upon my natural magic, I began reshaping the overgrown gardens: unruly vines twisted into intricate patterns, weaving themselves into a living wall on one side while forming a gentle fence that cradled the entire property. I planted rows of medicinal herbs alongside a vegetable garden, a tangible symbol of my deep connection with the land and its nurturing rhythm. In the garden's vibrant embrace, surrounded by the scent of fresh herbs and the soft rustle of leaves, I spent countless hours in harmony with the wild, until the delicate balance of my enchanted sanctuary was interrupted by the world beyond.

I reached to unlatch my back door but remembered I still had the sickly potted calendula plant in my arms.

"I suppose I should help you first," I murmured as I trudged back to my garden table. I had made a business selling plants, spices, and natural remedies to the humans and other Witches who frequented the coven's market. I needed this particular plant for some of my recipes.

Once again, I focused on channeling the natural energy through my hands, and I smiled as the plant started to perk up. I continued pulsing magic through it until no brown was visible, and it no longer flopped about when I moved the pot.

"Ah. That's better, isn't it?" I smiled at the plant, which now sported a small pink bud. I knew it would bloom within a day or two, and I could harvest the flower for my salve recipe.

"Why, thank you." Gently caressing the velvety surface of a leaf, I felt an exchange—a silent promise between nature and me that whispered in rustling leaves. I learned long ago that as a gifted natural magic user, nature would be good to me if I was good to nature. By caring for sick plants, the Mother Goddess often rewarded me by providing exactly what I needed for whatever project I was working on. I understood and revered her pension for mutual respect, and I chose to focus on her love only, despite the coven's insistence on worshiping all the various deities. I often thought of her as a guardian and hoped that, someday, I would see her in person as the deserving did in her legends.

"Very impressive. The healing part. Not the talking to plants part," a smooth baritone voice said from somewhere in my apple tree. Either I was losing my mind, or a man was hiding in my garden.

"Who's there?" I called, whirling around and peering up at the tree to try to see my intruder. Instead of seeing a man, I startled back a few steps as a silver arrow shot in my direction. "What the —?" Another arrow whizzing by my head cut off my sentence. I ducked low and rolled behind my garden bench. "For the love of the Goddess, why the fuck are you shooting at me? Who are you?" I yelled. A twig snapped and scrambled to my knees. I used my magic to bend a branch before me, stopping an arrow before it struck between my eyes.

"Are you a Fae, love? I've never seen a Witch do that." I saw the most beautiful silvery grey eyes peering over the branch at me, another arrow ready and waiting. "Your eyes aren't purple, though..." He dropped one hand from the bow, releasing the tension and showing off the smooth movements of his muscles. He scratched his chin, perplexed. "Ah, well. Doesn't matter, I suppose." After a brief contemplative pause, he shrugged and pulled the arrow back once again.

I pushed my long red curls out of my face and blinked incredulously during his little monologue. What the hell was happening? Before he could let another arrow fly, I snapped out of my stupor and flicked my fingers. A wisteria vine snatched the arrow from his grasp and the remaining three out of his quiver.

He looked at me dejectedly. "Now, that wasn't very nice, was it?" With reflexes like a cat, he sprang forward, presumably to grab me. I flicked my fingers again, silently praying to the Mother Goddess for help.

The branch I used to block his arrow swung at the man. I expected it to make an impact and send him flying, but instead, it seemed to pass through him as he faded and reappeared in a mere second. Oh shit. He could teleport.

"You know I've never seen someone use a pretty little flower as a weapon. You're quite fascinating," he murmured.

"You're a Hunter," I breathed, my eyes wide and my heart hammering.

"Oh yes, love. One of the best." His gaze locked on mine like a predator watching its prey. "My name is Killian Cambell. Not that it matters. You'll be dead soon, so there's really no reason to tell you. Although you are quite lovely...what a shame..." He trailed off again, in his own little world. This man was very odd. He was clearly a trained killer, but he had the focus of a fish. I used this to my advantage and wiggled a few fingers, sending vines flying his way. They wrapped around his wrists and ankles. He looked at me with shock and something else. Was it respect?

"You've got balls. I'll give you that." He smirked as his eyes lightened and turned lilac. Oh, shit. "But two can play that game."

2
KENNA

The vines lashed out, retreating from Killian and curling back toward me. I thrust my hands forward, willing them to halt their movements as I dug my heels into the earth. Killian's smile held a mischievous glint as he moved his arms in a languid circle, weaving the vines into a thick, sinuous column that hurtled toward me like a living battering ram.

"Oh, for the love of the Goddess," I muttered, reaching up as the apple branches bent enticingly to offer their grip. They sprang upward in a sudden burst, hoisting me high above my garden—a move that, in retrospect, was not my finest idea. Although the vine battering ram missed me, I now found myself plummeting down, crashing through a canopy of trembling branches. Bracing for impact, I instinctively flung a scatter of vines and branches beneath me, hoping to slow my descent. Instead, I landed in solid, unexpected arms and looked up into the smoldering lilac eyes of the man who pursued me.

"Fancy meeting you here," he purred with a cheeky grin that sent a shock of forbidden electricity along my skin. Up close, every detail of his face revealed a potent blend of danger and allure. His jawline was chiseled and defined, framed by dusty blonde hair that flirted with his eyes—eyes that danced between lilac and that silvery gray I'd first noticed. A slight crook in his nose hinted at past fights, and his perfectly white teeth shone even in the chaos of our encounter. To be honest, he wasn't merely handsome—he was disarmingly seductive.

I felt the strength of his muscles where our bodies pressed together, each taut contour suggesting restraint and raw intensity. For a split second, my fingers ached to trace the lines of muscle hidden beneath his snug leather jacket and tunic, marveling at the sculpted form beneath. That dangerous, intimate proximity ignited an unexpected, tantalizing desire that made my heart race more for the thrill of his touch than for fear.

Snapping myself out of the heady moment, I tried to thrash free from his arms. Instead, my struggle only seemed to entice him further into a tighter embrace.

"Such a shame to have to rid the world of such a pretty little thing like you," he murmured in his smooth baritone, voice dipping into a seductive timbre that made my pulse quicken. The sound only added to his dangerous allure—hot, deadly, and impossibly tempting. Was he flirting? The question danced between us, stirring an unexpected blend of adrenaline and arousal. My mind spun with mischief as I offered a coy smile, my hand trailing seductively along the front of his shirt.

"You could let me go," I whispered, a secretive spark gleaming in my eyes, "let it be our little secret."

"Oh, I'd love to," he replied with a wink. "But if word got out that I let a little Witch charm me..." His voice trailed off, leaving the unspoken promise hanging provocatively in the air.

"Ah, so I am charming you?" I cooed, fully embracing the seductive Witch persona and continuing to run my finger along the edge of his jacket teasingly.

"Love, if you weren't a Witch, this would be going entirely differently," he teased, his grin and suggestive expression nearly melting me right then. For a moment, his nearness and the charged intimacy blurred the lines between danger and desire. Then reality crashed back in.

"Where are you taking me?" I demanded, twisting and squirming to break free of his embrace. Every ounce of strength surged as I thumped against his rock-hard chest.

"I'd really rather tie you up under different circumstances. Don't make me shatter that fantasy by tying you down now to stop your squirming. Be good and stay still," he grunted, holding me tight as if savoring the feel of my body against his. Ignoring his sultry innuendos, I continued to struggle.

"Tell me where you're taking me." Anger flared, mingling with a hint of that inexplicable, forbidden desire. Despite initially trying to hide my Fae eyes, I no longer cared. After all, this Hunter must have been part Fae, too. What was the point of hiding it?

He shook his head lightly. "You'll see."

As frustration surged, I closed my eyes and felt the familiar Fae magic rippling through my body. When I reopened them, I fixed my gaze on Killian.

"Put me down. Now," I growled, my words tight with defiance and a flicker of unanticipated longing. His eyes widened at my demand, nearly causing him to drop me.

"You..." he whispered, astonishment softening into a blend of desire and curiosity. "You're a half breed." His grip slackened ever so slightly, and seizing the moment, I mustered all my strength and shoved against his chest. I tumbled free, landing square on my backside. Ignoring the sharp pain radiating along my tailbone, I scrambled to my feet and ran. Glancing back only once, I captured the mixture of shock and a lingering, almost hungry regret in his eyes as I sped toward my cottage. I needed a ward, a spell, a barrier—anything to protect myself from a threat that had somehow become as dangerously seductive as it was deadly.

3
KILLIAN

As she bolted away from me, my hand instinctively reached for the poison-tipped dagger nestled in its sheath. I prepared to launch it—a flawless arc aimed for her spine—but the moment I did, an overwhelming, nauseating pain surged through me, forcing the dagger to slip from my grasp and clatter into the tall grass. The pain receded as suddenly as it had invaded me, leaving only a heaving breath and a racing heart.

"What the fuck?" I muttered, incredulous. How could this be?

I had taken this contract with no more than a location and the grim order to eliminate the target, a woman pursued by Fae King Arrion. In a world where even my own kind spurned half-breeds like me, beings were conveniently cast aside if they weren't of pure blood.

Unlike the rest of my kind, killing wasn't my first choice of employment, but at this point, I wasn't picky about what contract I took. Being an exiled Hunter meant I only ate when I had the money from completing a job, and currently, I was famished.

I knew I should chase her down and complete the job, but something inside of me balked. The thought of hauling her lifeless body to the Fae King was unbearable. Here was a woman who, in some inexplicable way, mirrored my own inner turmoil. Even as duty and desperation warred within me, I couldn't ignore the stirring desire that pulled me toward her, a lustful curiosity I'd never experienced before.

Her vibrant red curls and the hypnotic curve of her body ignited a forbidden fascination that made the idea of "disposing of her" seem like a cruel waste. Arrion, with all his harsh decrees, might have had no pity for what he deemed expendable, but I found myself rebelling against the order. After countless cold kills, still a part of me recoiled at the thought of ending her life—a thought that now mingled dangerously with an unexpected, raw longing.

In that brief, surreal moment, a realization hit me: I yearned to touch her, to explore the contours of her body instead of snuffing out her flame. It felt as if my mind were on the verge of unraveling; never before had I desired a woman's intimacy so profoundly, so outrageously, out of the blue. Shaking my head in disbelief, I forced myself to rationalize it—it had to be magic, a bewitching spell that defied logic.

Yet, no amount of mental acrobatics could expel the image of her pretty face and tantalizing form from my thoughts. Running my fingers through my disheveled hair, I let out a frustrated groan and turned to walk toward her cottage. If nothing else, I wanted my arrows back.

When I approached her cottage, I noted the fuzzy gleam around her property. "Great. A ward," I muttered as I walked along the edge of it, looking for a weak spot.

"You can't get in. It's warded." I heard her voice before I saw her. Those bright green eyes were back. They contrasted perfectly with her deep red curls. Her lilac eyes were pretty, but the green made her look like a forest queen. I scoffed at myself and tried to stop staring at her.

"I see that. Again, you impress me. Can I have my arrows, please, love?" I made a pouting face as best I could, mimicking her earlier attempt at acting to get her way.

"Stop calling me love," she answered frigidly. She turned on her heels and stomped into her cottage. It was a cute place. I could feel her love for it radiating off the property. The plants adored her. My Fae blood allowed me to trace the path of her nature-based magic, and it was clear this was her passion. I wondered why she didn't use more traditional witchcraft. Judging by this ward, she was a hell of a spell crafter.

I looked up, realizing she had left me standing outside the ward. I'm not sure why I expected anything else. I leaned on a nearby tree and slid down, trying to sit comfortably on the forest floor. I was Goddess-awfully tired; this was the first time I had sat still in what felt like a week. Pretty quickly, I drifted off to sleep.

WHEN I AWOKE, I felt her magic. I cracked open one eye and saw vines wrapped around me with a fiery redhead glaring at me from her perch on a bent branch. She must have shaped it into the perfect little seat. I could have sworn that branch hadn't been there before.

"If you wanted to tie me up, love, you could have just asked," I teased with a roguish smile that hinted at mischief as much as desire.

"You're disgusting," she quipped. "What do you want? Why are you trying to kill me? And don't even try to break the vines. They're infused with spells this time." She didn't break eye contact or move from her perch. She was like an angry little red bird. My hand involuntarily tried to reach out to brush a red curl away from her face, but was met with tightening wisteria when I tried to move. I let out a groan as the vines squeezed me. This little spitfire would be the death of me if the Fae King didn't kill me first for ignoring his order. I didn't have much time left, and she was whittling it down.

"I was hired to kill you…or at the very least, bring you in…" I breathed out, realizing it was pointless to lie. My hands were so tight; there was no way I could control the vines, even if they weren't infused with spells. She looked like I had slapped her. Gradually, her face changed from shock to absolute rage.

"I'm sorry, you what?" Her voice went up in pitch and volume, and the leaves in the tree above me began to shake. I could see the lilac leaching into her pretty green eyes and realized I was doomed if I didn't convince her I wouldn't follow through. I couldn't even if I wanted to now, and I didn't want to.

"Love, stop. I'm not going to hurt you. You saw my eyes. I'm like you. I wouldn't hurt you, not now I know that we're alike." I tried to keep my voice calm.

"I told you to stop calling me that." Her voice was eerily calm. "Why would I believe you anyway?" She had a point.

"You're right. You have no reason to trust me. Hell, I was trying to kill you. But understand, lo-" I cleared my throat, swallowing the weight of the word that followed. I glanced down at the magical vines that bound me tight. "You have to understand that I roam the realms of this continent on dangerous contracts, and I've never met another half-breed. I honestly thought I was the last of my kind. It's been a lonely road until now…" I said, surrendering to a coy smile that flickered from beneath long lashes, the admission hanging between us like a forbidden promise.

For a moment, I caught myself—what was I doing? Flirting with her while my life dangled by a thread? I'd always been a flirt, but never when death was nipping at my heels. Surely, if she deemed it necessary, she would end me without a second thought.

"Are you seriously still flirting with me?" She narrowed her eyes as if I had lost my wits. "I could kill you, and you're flirting. Which head are you thinking with?" She laughed to herself. It was a soft noise that sent a tingling sensation down my spine. If the vines weren't tight enough before, they were now.

"Sorry," I breathed. "I can't help it." I tried to smile at her. She walked toward me and brought her face down close to mine. If I could have moved, I would have been tempted to kiss her.

"Your kind hunts my kind. Why would you think I would find that attractive?" She smelled like lavender and honey. I hadn't noticed that when carrying her, but now it was all I could focus on.

"No. Fae don't kill Fae," I whispered back, voice husky with both defiance and longing.

Her pupils dilated at my words, and her lilac eyes receded to green. Good, she was calming down. By now, even in the short time I had spent with her, it was clear the lilac was only present with intense emotions, like anger or fear. She took a tentative step forwards and reached her small hand toward my face. Her eyes were more inquisitive now, rather than fiery.

"You're Fae...?" she murmured, the question itself cloaked in desire as her fingertips caressed my cheek. My eyes fluttered shut as I leaned into the intimacy of her touch—a surrender I hadn't planned, but one that felt perilously right. Unfortunately, this seemed to shock her into moving away. She jumped and started to pull her hand away, but her face remained a few inches from mine, her head cocked to one side and her eyes shifting around my face, studying me.

My mind was reeling. Why was this woman having this impact on me? I was supposed to be killing her, not lusting after her. I shook my head, trying to clear what felt like a buzz or a mess of cobwebs. When I looked back up at her, a slight curiosity replaced the awe in her eyes with a tinge of fear as she peered at me.

4
KENNA

Being this close to him was intoxicating. I had intended to torture him, but was torturing myself instead. I started to back away as his words sank in. He had called us both Fae. Not a Witch, not a Hunter, just Fae.

My focus must have weakened, and for the love of the Goddess, his arms were free. I froze in place, not sure what he would do. The fear that he would try to hurt me again had set in, and I readied my magic to strike. Instead of lashing out or running away, though, he reached out and brushed a curl behind my ear.

"We are both more Fae than they know," he whispered. His gaze dipped to my lips, and I jerked back from his touch. I swatted his hand away and stepped back even further. I tightened the vines still around his waist and legs, knowing he could remove them with a flick of his hands if he wanted, now that my spells had weakened.

"What do you mean?" I asked cautiously, eyeing him from a few feet away.

"You could use witchcraft, and yet, it's not your first choice of magic. The ward you crafted was incredibly strong and, obviously, the spells infusing these vines were ironclad a moment ago, so don't tell me it's not your forte. You chose Fae magic." He paused, presumably waiting for my reaction. I schooled my features into nonchalance as best I could while he continued. "I'm much the same. I don't have the same taste for killing as other Hunters despite my lineage, and I can't use all the same powers as a Hunter. I can teleport and use their poison in limited capacity; otherwise, I use Fae magic. I *chose* Fae magic." He looked at me as if waiting for me to absorb what he had just told me. He was right, and I hated that. Despite being advanced in my witchcraft studies, I felt much more comfortable with my Fae magic.

"Why are you telling me this?" I asked, squinting at him as if he were hiding something.

"Because I'm not going to kill you, and I want these vines off. I figured being honest was best, rather than ripping them off myself." He grinned again.

Despite not inheriting my mother's gift of foresight, I was very good at reading energy. I could often tell when people were lying by how their auras shifted, which caused the natural world around them to react. Killian's remained the same, and the wisteria clinging to him didn't move, which meant he wasn't lying.

"I believe you. I don't know why you're doing this, but you're not lying." I looked at him point-blank as I walked closer. "If you try anything, though, I will become the all-powerful Witch everyone seems to think I should be, and I won't hesitate to kill you." I stabbed a finger into his chest to accentuate my point. He grabbed my hand, pulling me close to his face again.

"I'm glad you believe me. I would never lie to such a beautiful woman." He released my hand. "Especially one as dangerous as you, love. The Mother Goddess must favor you." I hadn't pulled back from him. Our faces were a mere inch apart again.

"She appreciates my care of her creations and my devotion to her through my work. And I would also appreciate less flirting."

But as I said this, I licked my lips and knew it wasn't true. He was the epitome of danger, a Hunter. Yet, I couldn't pull myself away. There was also something niggling in the back of my mind. He was the only other half breed I'd met and somehow, some part of me felt like maybe it was fate.

I noticed his hand approaching my face again and abruptly pulled away from him. "Get your arrows and go away," I said as I returned to my cottage. I released the vines, which went back to their fence posts. Killian apparently decided his arrows could wait, as I found him scrambling after me instead.

"You really are impressive," he breathed. He had to have been close to me. I could feel the warmth of his body radiating onto my back. I felt his hand brush along the edge of my long curls as he reached for my shoulder, attempting to stop me and turn me toward him. I looked up at him, realizing he must be a good foot taller than I. That had to make him 6'5".

"What now, Killian? Do you want to die? Please, go away." I was tired and frustrated and unsure why I was letting this dangerous being go instead of killing him or turning him over to the coven.

"I don't want to impose…" He looked like a small child peering sheepishly down at the grass.

"Alright. So, don't." I walked away from him once again.

"Wait!" He caught my arm and turned me toward him. "Can I set up my camp here? Just for a night. Maybe two? I won't bother you, but it's getting late, and some things come out at night in the In-Between even I don't mess with…" He trailed off, looking at me through long dark lashes. I wanted to smack myself as my heart went into overdrive. Why did one look at this man make me feel so much desire? I smiled softly at him before I could stop myself. I felt like my body was no longer my own.

"You can stay if you tell me why you call me 'love'. But you have to set up outside my garden. I won't have you killing any plants."

He smiled and let out a little chuckle at that. He leaned his face closer to mine, causing my heart to speed up again. "It's a term of endearment. I learned it from my mum before they killed her. Plus, I don't know your first name, only your last." He smelled like pine and earth, and being this close to him was melting me from the inside out. I felt my eyes start to flutter closed as my mind went into overdrive with varying half-baked fantasies for a second or two. Then my eyes shot wide open.

"*They*? Who are they?" Realizing I was being horribly insensitive, I added, "I'm sorry about your mother. My parents are dead, too."

"*They* are the Fae," he said solemnly. "They killed her after my father gave up her location. Or at least, I blame them for her death… My father was Fae, too, but not so close-minded. They tortured him before he gave in. I can't fault him. My mum was a Hunter. Pretty taboo stuff…." He trailed off, looking distant. "She was a foreigner, but we briefly lived in the Fae capital, Eiradia, where my father was from, after being shunned from her homeland in Enactel when I was born. She took me to her homeland again once the Fae found out, but we weren't exactly welcomed there either. Some of her sayings rubbed off on me, though." He smiled then, a sweet smile, like he was remembering his mother quite fondly.

"Losing a parent is never easy." Pity and understanding filled my body. Our stories weren't that different. "My mother was from another territory in the west called Stérline, but she came to study at the coven here in Cauldera. I guess her family is originally from near the coven. She met my father while she was studying at the coven, but she was killed in these woods. I assume my father is dead as well. Although the coven leader said something about Hunters…"

"I know," he said in a low tone. "I guess that's another reason it's easy for me to stick it to the Fae King. He has a habit of hiring Hunters to do his dirty work, whether it be tracking or killing, and they often take the fall for his horrific choices. I have no desire to help that bastard, but when you only eat when you have money, you do whatever job comes your way." He looked sad while he said this. Realizing he had to work for the man who undoubtedly had his mother and father, as well as my own, killed, a sorrow washed over me.

"I'm sorry." He smiled slightly, but it looked forced.

I knew letting him stay was a risk, but I decided I would ward the house. "As I said, outside the garden, and don't even think about coming into the house..." I glared at him, but it felt fake. I wasn't really afraid of him anymore. I felt more of an odd sense of kindred understanding rather than the rage I should have. This strange draw toward him was becoming infuriating.

"So... where should I go? I mean, your garden would be preferred, but I'd rather you didn't kill me..." Killian wandered in a circle, musing to himself again. I swear he must have had more fun talking to himself than he did to anyone else. "I suppose I could make it work over by those trees... What do you think? I don't want to be in your way," he asked.

"Whatever, Killian. Don't kill any plants," I said as I turned and walked away toward my house, leaving Killian still talking to himself in my yard. I still hadn't decided if he was crazy or if I was.

5
KILLIAN

This woman made me nervous. It was absolutely infuriating. I rambled like a child around her and made myself look like a fool. I stood in her yard, continuing my ridiculous rambling, and watched her walk away. Not a bad view. I smiled to myself and set out to find a spot to set up my tent that wouldn't send the little Witch into a murderous rage again.

I found a fairly flat spot in the middle of a bunch of pine trees. The scent of the woods was calming and what I was used to. I could still see the cottage from here, but it wasn't in her precious garden. I rolled my eyes as I unrolled my pack from my bag and set up my tent. The old canvas tent had been my home for the last two years, and although it was small, I was comfortable in it. Traipsing around the continent bounty hunting didn't allow for many luxuries.

I lay down inside, admiring the view of the trees and the world around me. Much like Miss McCairn, nature was my comfort. I suppose that was my Fae blood.

Snapped out of my reverie, I heard small footsteps approaching. I sat up and looked out my tent window to see none other than the Witch herself walking toward me with something. Was that a sandwich?

"I thought maybe... maybe you would like something to eat," she said as she approached the tent entrance. She handed me the sandwich. "It's herbed bread. I made it... and there is ham and cheese from the market, lettuce, tomatoes from my garden, and some mustard I made last fall. Sorry, it's not much..." She trailed off. Was she crazy? Half of this sandwich was homemade or from her garden, yet she called it 'not much.'

"It's perfect. Thank you. An impressive array of local ingredients, too." I quirked an eyebrow at her and smiled. She beamed at me, obviously happy I was pleased with her offering.

"Okay... well... I'll let you rest." She straightened and walked away from my tent. I smiled as I watched her go. But if I was honest, I knew I wouldn't sleep much, not with that woman a mere fifty feet away from me.

Deciding to enjoy the sandwich, I dug in and had to admit I was surprised at how flavorful the simple sandwich was. My eyes rolled back in my head as I took another bite. Yes, the way to my heart was definitely through my stomach, and that woman would not have any trouble with that.

After I had finished the food she brought, I laid down to sleep. Thoughts of the little Witch, her pretty red curls, bright green eyes, and curvy body, flashed in my mind. Yeah, there was no way I was going to sleep well tonight.

As I slept, memories of my mother filled my dreams. Images of her teaching me the Hunter's legends, as well as our magic, filled my mind.

"When the world was born, there were many beings. All of which had to fight for survival. The Hunters soon learned that our lack of magic made us a target to all the magical beings the deities had favored. So, we chose to befriend the wolves. The wolves became our guides, our protectors, our spirit animals. One day, during battle, an enemy tried to kill the alpha wolf aiding the Hunter's clan. But in an act of self-sacri-

fice, the leader of our clan lay on the wolf to save it. Despite both being run through, they survived. Their blood fused and from then on, the Hunters were given the gift of the spirit of the wolf." My mother's melodic voice bounced in my mind.

"What's that mean, Mum?"

"It means that when needed, the wolves will protect a worthy Hunter. They will not need to rely on poisons, our limited ability to teleport, or the broken spells we have learned over centuries. The wolf will guide the worthy warrior into victory!" She beamed at me as we walked, unaware of the creature behind her.

"Mum!" I screamed, but it was too late. The goblin-like creature's claws had already grazed her chest.

I woke with a start, my heart pounding and sweat beading along my forehead. The nightmare often plagued me, but no matter how many times I saw the scene from my childhood, I always woke in a panic and often took hours to fall back asleep, if at all.

I MUST HAVE FALLEN ASLEEP AGAIN at some point throughout the night, and the next morning, I awoke stiff and sore. The forest floor was not forgiving, the nightmare hadn't helped, and my sleep mat was worn out. I heard movement in the direction of the garden and, after dressing, peeked out of my tent.

The little woman was flitting about in the garden, humming and talking to her plants. She worked her way around, weaving her magic into the sick ones and thanking the ones she was cutting back. She looked so damn happy in that garden, like it was her safe place.

I rolled up my sleep mat and tent and stuffed them back into my pack. After all, she probably wouldn't want me to stay here another night. I would have to figure out where to go next. Being so close to the Fae Realm within these woods meant it wasn't exactly safe for me here, especially when the Fae King realized I wouldn't deliver the fiery redhead on a platter. Not that the In-Between Forest was much better.

Wandering through the maze of a garden, I took in the expansive number of plants, herbs, and vegetables she grew here. This woman would survive the end of days if there ever were one. Entirely self-sufficient.

"Morning, love."

She jumped when she heard my voice, but turned toward me and glared at me before attempting to stifle a small yawn. Had she not slept well either? I had spent the first half of the night trying to tamp down the thoughts of her, but had no idea what her excuse was.

"You're interrupting my routine." With that, she returned to her plants and began humming again while trimming some rose hips off a bush. No doubt for some tea or concoction. I stepped toward her while she was mumbling her thanks to the rose bush.

"I'll be leaving today, I suppose. You clearly don't want me here. I'm not sure where I'm going, but it's not safe for me in the Fae Realm once they figure out that I've let you go, and the In-Between certainly isn't a friendly place either. I'll have to find somewhere else to hide. You might consider doing the same since they'll likely give the contract to another. So... I guess I'm coming to tell you goodbye." The word goodbye dug into my soul like a blade. Why did it hurt me so badly to tell her I was leaving? Wasn't this what we both wanted? One look at her face as she turned toward me told me she felt the same stabbing pain. The sadness in her pretty green eyes broke my heart the rest of the way.

"Oh..." She looked down at the garden path. "But you haven't eaten yet. I could make you something. You shouldn't be out in the woods hungry." Before I could object, she shoved the rose hips into her apron pocket and turned toward her cottage. "I'll be right back. Don't go anywhere," she said musically, smiling over her shoulder.

"Alright." I smiled back at her. I wasn't sure where this was going, but I would take any excuse to stay. Despite our initial meeting, I only knew that my soul wanted to be close to her.

I wandered around her garden, acutely aware of her threads of magic. This tiny, angry woman was full of love, and these plants received most of it. Her flowers flourished, her herbs were fragrant, and her vegetables looked like something from a high-class kitchen. She was amazing; this entire space was amazing.

Of course, I couldn't ignore the massive wisteria draping and twisting through her fences. I still wasn't entirely sure what her fascination with that was. Perhaps it reminded her of someone or something, and that was why she grew so much of it.

I meandered back to where I had been standing before and waited for her in a patch of sun. Within this small space, I felt safe for the first time in a very long time. I was finally comfortable, despite knowing the little Witch was entirely capable of killing me. I was also acutely aware she had removed the wards. Did she feel safe with me, too?

6
KENNA

I went back outside with a small plate, carrying a slice of homemade bread and the option for jam or butter. I couldn't help myself; I didn't want him to go. If you asked me why, I would probably give you the flimsy response that I wanted to keep an eye on him or I didn't trust him. The truth was that the thought of him leaving was physically painful. My soul ached at the idea of him no longer being nearby. What was wrong with me?

I presented Killian with the plate and a smile. "Here you go."

"Thank you." He smiled back at me and took the bread, breaking off small pieces and scooping up both jam and butter before shoving them in his mouth. How quaint...

After Killian inhaled his bread, he sat in the grass and looked up at me. "Do you mind if I stay until later? Traveling at night is better for avoiding the Fae guards, although I'll likely have other creatures to contend with out there in the woods..." He trailed off, looking a bit conflicted, and part of me wondered if he felt the same pull that I did.

"I guess... just don't get in my way," I murmured, trying very hard to sound disinterested. He beamed up at me with a megawatt smile. He had to feel this, too.

The rest of the day was uneventful, and I even enjoyed Killian's company and occasional questions about what I was doing or making, to my own surprise. He reminded me that I enjoyed teaching others the healing arts, and he found my witchcraft just as interesting as my Fae craft.

Killian trudged back to his makeshift camp as the sun set. Currently, it was just his bag, quiver, bow, and arrows leaning up against a tree. He wandered over to me as I watered the last of my plants.

"I guess this is it. It would be nice to have one more night to think about where I could go…" The unspoken words hung in the air as he started looking around. No doubt, he was lost in his own world again. There was a hint of a question in his words, and part of me was itching to see what he would do if I responded.

Despite my better judgment, I started speaking before I could stop myself. "I have a second bedroom." His head snapped in my direction from the rock he was studying in the garden, and the shock on his face was clear. "But I swear to Goddess, I'll kill you if you come out of that room or try to touch me," I hissed and started walking toward the door to my cottage, the look of shock still evident on his face.

"Are you sure?" he asked incredulously, trailing after me.

"I wouldn't offer it if I wasn't. Of course, it's probably a terrible idea, so feel free to talk me out of it." I offered a cheeky smile.

"Oh no, I'm not passing up a real bed for a tent." He laughed and smiled back.

I showed him around my small cottage, unsure why I was still trusting him, but something inside me told me I could. He inspected my tiny kitchen, noting that most of it was taken over by herbs and spices drying, and a few plants on the counter. He also seemed to find my washroom full of potted plants amusing.

"You really leaned into the natural bit of Fae magic, didn't you?" He chuckled as he said it.

"Yeah, well, it's my job. I make healing products and sell them, as well as spices, to the locals. I also design gardens for people locally, too." I said as I led him through the small living room. "This is my room, and you are not allowed in here." I wagged my finger in his face as I said it.

"I get it. No boys allowed." He chuckled.

"I didn't say that... Just not you." I offered a seductive smile and a wink in return.

"You're killing me, love," he murmured. He tipped his head back and looked up at the ceiling, as if praying to whoever he believed in for sanity or resolve. He then tipped his head back down and followed me a few feet to the room I was letting him sleep in. Both doors were on the same wall on the far side of my living room. Both rooms also shared a wall, and I hoped Killian didn't snore.

"This is where you can sleep. Sorry it's such a tiny bed." I motioned toward the single bed on one side of the room. There was nothing fancy or decorative in the space. It had likely been intended to be my room when my parents lived here, but I never slept in it, opting instead to take what I assumed had been their bedroom.

"Are you kidding? It's a bed. That's amazing!" He laughed as he flopped down onto the bed. "I assume you'll be warding me in?" He quirked an eyebrow at me.

"You assume correctly. You can do... whatever... I'm going to start cooking. Don't break anything," I said as I turned to walk away. I made it one step before turning around to look at Killian lying on the bed with an arm over his eyes, smiling. "Kenna," I offered. "My name is Kenna." The smile on his face grew, but he didn't say anything, so I turned and headed to the kitchen.

Despite trying to make a simple chicken soup, I found myself distracted. I poured too much broth into the measuring cup, not noticing until some spilled over the side, wetting my fingers as it ran into the wash basin. I couldn't help but question myself. Why was I letting him stay here? Why had I taken the wards down? The intense pull I felt to be near him was starting to make me uneasy.

"Shit." I shook my head, dumped the broth into the soup pot, and started moving about the kitchen, looking for spices while it heated over the hearth. Finding most of what I wanted and mixing them in, I set about chopping the carrots, onions, celery, and parsley leaves I had plucked from my garden earlier and adding the mix to the now-boiling pot. Thankfully, it was early enough, and the soup would not take long to cook. I was starving.

Turning to the small trap door in the floor, I pulled it up to reveal the larder my parents had built to store food in. I pulled out leftover chicken from a previous meal that I had preserved and began to shred it. I had marinated the chicken with a lemon and then salted and smoked it, which would add an exciting zing to the soup. Killian would either like or hate it, but I had to admit I hoped he would like it. Stirring in the chicken, I swung the cast-iron arm holding the soup pot further from the fire to avoid burning the contents. Mostly, we just needed to wait for the vegetables to soften. Of course, I could have just magicked everything into a complete state, but there was something more calming about cooking the old-fashioned way.

I was missing the thyme from my soup and started rifling through the cabinets. The soup smelled good, but I loved the earthy flavor the thyme added and wasn't willing to serve something at less than its best. Killian apparently was napping, so I had time to find it.

Unfortunately, it might have been one of the spices I moved up to the top of the cabinet earlier in the week to make room for the plants I brought inside. Huffing, I continued shuffling around the contents of the countertops, hoping I was wrong.

7
KILLIAN

Kenna. Her name was beautiful. The Fae King had told me her last name was McCairn, but hadn't told me anything else about her. Not even why he wanted her dead. Certainly not that she was a spitfire or the living, breathing embodiment of a goddess of old. The woman was smart, beautiful, and incredibly talented magically. Somehow, she also squeezed being sweet into that package. I shook my head, let out a groan, and smacked myself in the face for trying to kill her. It was a good thing she had the heart of a warrior, too.

I smelled whatever she was making, and Goddess, it was heavenly. Slowly, I pulled myself out of the comfort of the small bed I was in and drifted into the kitchen to find her.

"What's that? Smells lovely," I mused as I came up behind her. I was probably closer to her than she would have wanted, but I couldn't help it. Kenna was intoxicating, even more so than that soup she was making, which smelled like it might be the best meal of my life.

"Chicken soup, if I can reach the thyme," she said distractedly, rummaging around the kitchen and very obviously trying to move away from me. She dug through a cabinet, scowled, and sat up on her countertop to reach the jars on top of her cabinets. I approached her petite but curvy frame and noticed her reaching for the "thyme " jar while I admired her body.

Instead of gawking like I wanted to, I came up behind her, placing a hand on her lower back, and reached up to pluck the jar from the shelf she was stretching to reach. Her top had lifted just a touch, and my hand rested partly on her bare skin, sending an unexpected shockwave through my body. She either felt it, too, or I had scared her because we both jumped, yet I chose not to remove my hand. I held the jar out to her, looking slightly up to her face.

"Here, love."

She turned to face me, my hand sliding around her back to her side as she moved. She sat on the counter with her legs dangling toward me.

"Thanks, *dear*," Kenna hissed out the last word. As if I was being burned, I whipped my hand away and backed off, not sure what had possessed me to get so close to the woman to begin with. She was enchanting me; that was the only explanation.

She must have enjoyed my reaction because she slid lazily down the front of the countertop and took a slow, seductive step toward me.

"I appreciate your help." She gave me a coy smile before adding, "But I told you not to touch me." She then swept toward me, planting both her hands on either of my hips, causing me to suck in an involuntary breath, and gave me a good shove backward out of her kitchen. "You're in the way."

As she turned to sprinkle the thyme in her soup, I felt oddly empty. Now that she had touched me like that, I wanted her to touch me again. Before I could stop myself, I walked back into the kitchen and placed my hand on her back again.

"If being in the way means being close to you, I want to be in the way," I whispered in her ear. She stilled, and the soup ladle she held clattered into the pot. She gradually turned and looked into my eyes. I could see the lilac fighting with the green as her eyes ebbed between the colors like paint swirling in water. She didn't look mad... Had I crossed the line? Before I could think about it anymore, she had stepped closer to me and put her hands on my chest.

"You feel it, too. I want to fight it... this is insane... but I can't... What is happening?" She looked confounded as she said it, but I knew what she meant. Something was happening between us. I had heard of Fae bonds before, but had never put much stock in them. I lived with the Hunters, who didn't teach much of the Fae lore and I hadn't expected it to apply to me.

The Fae had a legend for everything; many schools taught them as part of their lessons. Being a Hunter born to a mother on the run, though, meant I had never had the opportunity to attend those lessons and had only learned what my mother taught me. The legend she had taught me about the bond was never one I had paid much attention to, but I could recall most of it.

According to the lore, the Fae believed in something akin to a human or Witch's commitment in marriage, but, more substantially, a spiritual bond that could not be broken, even in death. Any Fae could experience it with another Fae. It was said that your soul reached out to the other Fae's soul, and they became irresistible. Mind you, as a man who lived his life running from one place to the next with no ties, that kind of commitment was mighty frightening to ponder in the current predicament. However, I couldn't deny what was happening, and part of me wondered, was this a bond?

"Yeah, I feel it, too," I said as I looked into her eyes. They flashed lilac again, but I knew she wasn't mad this time, just confused. Join the club, so was I. She reached out to touch my face, running a soft, dainty thumb along my cheekbone.

"Your eyes... they're gray, then lilac, and back. Are you mad?" She wrinkled her brow in concern and pulled her hand away. She tried to step back from me, but I reached out to grasp her waist, my other hand steadying her in front of me.

"I'm not mad, love. Your eyes are doing the same. Tell me... what are you feeling?" I already knew, but I wanted her to say it. The magnetic pull couldn't be one-sided. I wasn't imagining this, was I?

"It's... lust... and confusion..." Kenna paused and looked down, clearly feeling awkward. "Why am I so drawn to you? You tried to kill me, but all I want to do is kiss you, even though I should be throwing you to the shadow creatures." As she said this, a bright pink blush spread across her cheeks. It only highlighted her freckles and made me want to move even closer. She had a slightly glassy look in her eyes as well. If I didn't know better, I would think she had been drinking. I wondered if my eyes looked the same and assumed that was likely.

"So do it," I challenged, knowing I wanted the same thing. Her eyes flashed to lilac and stayed that way this time. Hesitantly, she closed the distance between us and slid her slender arms around my neck. Her face was less than an inch from mine, and it took every ounce of my strength to avoid closing the distance between our lips.

"Your eyes..." she purred. A slight smile crept onto her beautiful, full lips. "They're lilac now." She smiled softly, brushing her nose against mine. When I moved slightly to try to meet her lips with mine, she moved away just a touch, so I couldn't capture the kiss. The little minx was teasing me.

"Kenna, please. You're going to kill me," I whispered. We were so close she must have felt my breath on her lips.

"You said my name." A smile quirked up on one side of her mouth in an adorable smirk. This woman would be the literal death of me, either by teasing or by magic; I wasn't sure yet. "I want to make you say it again—" she brushed her nose against mine again "—and again—" and brought her lips so close to mine I was sure she would kiss me "—and again—" before she pulled back ever so slightly and shook her head like she was rethinking every move she had just made.

A low groan escaped my lips. Yeah, this woman was going to kill me. She was either seriously messing with me, or this was some bond thing. She looked drunk, and I was having a hell of a time maintaining my ability to think straight. Before I could think about it too much, her expression softened again, and her thin fingers tangled in the hair at the nape of my neck and pulled my lips to hers.

I felt the initial shockwave rock through my body as her soft lips pressed to mine. Like a lightning bolt running through my spine, its energy expanded out through my extremities. That shockwave was followed by a wave of desire that I struggled to control. She tensed slightly as if shocked but didn't pull away. I imagined she was experiencing something just as intense. Holy hell, what was this woman made of? I had never felt this before, but I wanted more.

My arm snaked around her waist, pulling her close to me, and I felt her tongue test the seam of my lips. I allowed her access, and a small, irresistibly sexy moan escaped her mouth despite the stiffness I still felt in her body. She tightened her grip on my hair, and I slid my other arm around her, holding her tight. Her hourglass shape was unmistakable while she was pressed against me, tight in my arms. The large chest she was hiding under her loose tunic also caught my attention. After a moment, I felt her body melting into mine, which made it all the harder for me to control myself.

"What. Is. Happening. To. Us?" She whispered each word between kisses. Despite the breathy nature of the words, they still held a hint of fear.

"I. Have. A. Guess," I whispered against her impossibly soft lips. She tasted like sweet plums. I loved plums. She broke the kiss to look at me. Her eyes were a bright shade of violet, more vivid than the lilac I had seen before. Based on how she studied me, I assumed mine mirrored hers.

"Tell me." She was breathless, and it was incredibly sexy. Deciding to give her swollen lips the smallest of breaks, I trailed kisses down her neck. She initially stiffened as if uncomfortable with the interaction, but then melted into my touch and lolled her head to one side, allowing me to reach all of the soft skin leading down to her collarbone. Between soft kisses and gentle nips, I tried to explain, but she was so damn distracting, I was having a hell of a time.

"The Fae bond. I think..." I trailed off to nibble at her ear. This woman was either poison, an antidote, or both. She tensed in my arms but didn't pull away or make me stop. As I continued my trail of tender kisses, she began to speak.

"I read about that during lessons at the coven. The life bond... But I'm only half-Fae." She used her grip on my hair to make me look her in the eyes again. "Do you really think? Seriously? You tried to kill me less than twenty-four hours ago!" She looked a bit panicked but wasn't actively trying to get away from me.

"I have no other explanation for this, Kenna. I have never felt this way around anyone. We're both half-Fae, but we chose our Fae side. It makes sense that those instincts would take over. And I already apologized for trying to kill you." My mouth turned up in a grin at her before touching my forehead to hers. "Do you want to stop? I won't make you do anything; I promise. I may be a Hunter, but I'm not a savage."

Kenna's eyes flashed green, and I worried she would tell me to stop, but then the bright violet came back, and I heard things falling behind her. I looked over her shoulder to see her house plants being bent and manipulated into sliding everything down the countertop, making a bit of room. She wasn't even using her hands, which remained tangled in my hair, to direct the plants. I looked back at her, and the seductive darkness in her eyes was unmistakable.

"No," she purred, and I knew she had somehow accepted what I thought was happening despite our initial introduction and the obvious hesitancy just a moment ago. She wasn't fighting it anymore, so I wouldn't either.

I easily lifted the little woman onto the countertop. Her hips were now level with mine, and she allowed me to step between her thighs, wrap my arms around her waist, and press her close to me again. She moaned as my lips touched hers again. Her hands began to roam down my neck and onto my back, eliciting a groan from me. No other woman had touched me in a way that made me feel the things this woman did.

"Kenna..." I breathed into her lips. I heard some shuffling beside us and, out of the corner of my eye, caught a small vine from a plant tentatively pushing the arm holding the soup pot over the hearth farther from the fire. I smiled against her lips. She didn't want to burn the soup and expected this to last long enough to do so.

Her hands moved to my shoulders in an attempt to push my leather jacket off. Halting her movement, I unwound one arm from around her waist and broke the kiss to tilt her face up to mine, forcing her to look into my eyes.

"Are you sure? If you start this, I'm not sure I can stop. I don't know what you're doing to me, but I'm losing my senses."

"That's the point, Killian." Kenna looked at me through long, dark lashes and smiled. Oh damn, I was done for. A low rumble escaped my chest, some sort of primal growl. If this were to be my end, so be it.

I grabbed her hips and picked her up off the counter as I pressed my lips to hers once again. Trusting my instincts not to run into or trip over anything, I methodically moved us toward the small room she was letting me stay in. I reached the door frame of the guest room after somehow managing to maneuver around the archway from the kitchen and avoid the padded bench and table stacked with books in front of the second fireplace. She let go of my neck and stuck both her hands out in a defiant display, grabbing the door frame and stopping us both. My heart skipped a beat. Had I gone too far? I thought she wanted this.

"No. My room. The bed here is ridiculous," she breathed into my mouth between kisses. Thank the Goddess she wasn't making me stop, but holy hell. When she had given me the tour, her door was closed. I had no idea where I was going and remained frozen in the door frame. She must have noticed because she broke the kiss, and her small body slid down the front of me until she was standing. It was a good thing we still had pants on, or this would have gone entirely differently.

Kenna smiled smugly at me—she had obviously felt my predicament on her way down—and grabbed my hand, dragging me behind her. To say I was in shock was an understatement. This angry little woman who would have strangled me with a wisteria vine was now dragging me to bed. What was her obsession with wisteria? My brain started trailing off. I had a bad habit of getting distracted, and this was the worst time possible. I was snapped back to attention when her small hand left mine, leaving an empty feeling. She unlocked her door and pushed it open.

The walls were light cream, with lace curtains and purple and blue gauzy fabrics hanging from the canopy above her rather large bed. I wondered how she had gotten such a big bed into such a tiny house while I stood at the door, taking in the space before me. She had a big closet full of clothes, a dresser, and a vanity table that matched her bed. Her bed had what looked like very soft purple bedding and several pillows you could sink into. On the floor was a large lilac rug with a leaf pattern woven into it. That didn't surprise me one bit and even made me smile. Kenna reached for my hand and pulled me into her space.

"A better setup than that other room," she cooed while standing on her toes and wrapping her arms around my neck.

She still had that glassy, drunk look, but she was absolutely adorable.

"Very cozy," I said softly before placing a gentle kiss on her lips.

Kenna released her hold on my neck and grabbed my wrists, pulling me toward the bed.

"Oh yes, the bed is the best part." She smiled seductively before pulling me into the blankets with her.

8
KENNA

I pulled Killian into my soft bed with me. He caught himself on his elbows but still pressed his body into mine. I had no idea what was happening to me or why I was so willing to accept it. I was never like this, but something inside my soul urged me, despite the fear that still lingered in the back of my mind. I knew he was right; I had read enough accounts of the Fae bond to know that what I was feeling was what he had described. I also knew the only way to stop feeling so drunk was to charm his pants off.

Not that I minded. This man was gorgeous, and if I was going to be bonded, it might as well be with someone pretty. Of course, if you asked a Fae, they would say anyone with Fae blood was inherently attractive, but either way, I supposed I was alright with my bonded one being Killian. Maybe, just maybe, I would finally feel like someone cared. At least if we bonded, he would be physically incapable of killing me.

I also couldn't lie to myself. I wanted this. Everything in my body was screaming for his touch. I didn't think I could have resisted even if I had tried. So, I stopped trying.

I wound my arms around Killian's neck and pulled him closer

to me still. The press of his chest against my breasts wasn't enough. I started reaching up for Killian's shoulders to push the leather jacket off him. I was too warm, despite it being a cool summer night, and there were too many layers between us.

Killian sat up, getting the hint, and shrugged off the jacket before pulling his shirt over his head and tossing it to the floor. Without thinking, my hands reached out to run my fingertips over his firm, muscular stomach and chest. He let out a soft breath before he leaned forward and looked me in the eyes.

"Like what you see, love?" he teased with a wink. I nodded and scooted back further up on the bed so my head was on the pillows. When Killian crawled up between my legs to meet me, I hooked one leg around his knee and used my hips to push him to the side and over, rolling us so I was on top. His eyes went wide, and a huge grin spread across his face. "You want to be in charge? Have your way, then." He folded his hands above his head, no longer touching me. A bold thought ran through my mind and using a basic binding spell, I secured his wrists above his head with a rope made of natural fiber.

I leaned down to kiss Killian, my red curls falling forward. I parted his lips with my tongue. He pressed forward, deepening the kiss, struggling to keep his hands off me, pulling against his magical bond. I gave him a coy look and ran my hands up his arms to his hands, twining my fingers in his. Releasing the magical hold on his wrists, the rope fell away, and I pulled his hands forward, willing myself to be bold. I broke the kiss and sat back as I continued to guide his hands directly to my breasts.

I thought Killian might pass out when I pressed his hands to my chest. I knew what I wanted and liked, and I somehow knew he could give it to me. After a few seconds, the shock must have worn off because his fingers began kneading into my soft flesh. I allowed a soft moan to escape me and closed my eyes, leaning back a little more. My core was centered above his bulge, so I knew that this movement was teasing him as much as it was me.

I still had too many layers on. I slid my hands up my waist, over his hands, and began to untie the top of the light green tunic I had on. Killian's hands stilled then, and his fingers brushed mine.

"Let me." His voice was husky and full of desire. I looked into his eyes, which were still that gorgeous bright shade of violet from our first kiss.

Killian made quick work of my top and tossed it to the floor. His eyes slid over my top half, taking in my breasts that threatened to spill from my almost too-small undergarment, and down my abdomen. His fingertips ran from my shoulders to the tops of my breasts and down my stomach. He stopped when he reached the magical mark I had given myself of a wisteria vine that ran across my hip and up my right side.

"You have a thing for wisteria," he mused while he massaged my side. "And you're absolutely beautiful." Killian sat up with me still straddling him, and kissed me with a passion I hadn't tasted yet. His tongue pressed into my mouth and danced with mine before he bit my bottom lip. "You have too many clothes on, though," he said as I felt the tie of my breast band release on my back. Kissing Killian was so intense that I hadn't noticed him undoing it.

I allowed him to slide the straps down my shoulders and toss the damn thing to the floor. He took a second to take me in before saying, "Good Goddess, Kenna. You're built like the Goddess herself." His hands slid up my sides to cup my breasts and pinch one nipple, then the other. I let out a moan, signaling my desperation for his touch to continue. He dipped his head and took one nipple into his mouth, sucking gently before nipping at it. I sucked in an involuntary breath. Good Goddess, he was amazing.

Killian continued to suckle and nip at each peak until I was moaning so loudly, I was thankful I didn't have neighbors. At some point, I had started to move my hips to grind my core against his very hard bulge. I pulled his face back up to mine, grinning at the suction sound as he released the nipple he had in his mouth. Kissing him fiercely, I slid my hips back. Killian groaned and reached for my waist to pull me back before he realized I was reaching for his belt. The heavy silver tribal knot at the front of the leather strap gave me significant trouble. Killian stilled my frustrated fingers as he broke the kiss.

"Not yet," he said with a devilish smirk. Using the same maneuver I had earlier, Killian flipped me on my back so that he was positioned over me and between my thighs. He reached a hand down and rubbed his thumb over my core, sending electric tingles through my entire body. I moaned into his mouth as Killian captured my lips with a kiss. "I'd like to keep making you moan like that, I think," he said with hooded eyes full of desire.

Killian began to kiss down my neck again, causing me to shudder with anticipation. His fingertips traced over my breasts and pinched my nipples, earning him a whimper from my mouth. He continued his onslaught of pleasure-filled touches, kisses, and licks before pulling back and beginning to slide my leggings down my hips.

After making quick work of my bottoms, Killian groaned with pleasure as he took in the sight of my body, covered only by thin summer underpants. His eyes traveled down to the apex of my thighs as I leaned back into the pillows, and his gaze settled where I could feel wet warmth pooling.

His thumb brushed my most sensitive spot once again, and I whimpered.

"Killian... please..." I whined. His eyes locked on mine.

"Say my name again." His breath quickened, and his fingers were hooked on the edge of my underpants, slowly pulling them down. I thanked the Goddess and whimpered as the torturous maneuver stoked the fire in my body...

Breathlessly, I whispered his name. "Killian..."

I heard the rip before I realized he had torn the garment right off and tossed it to the floor. I should have cared, but I didn't. Not when his warm, wet tongue met my sensitive bud, and every nerve ending in my body went haywire.

My fingers wound through his hair, and my back arched. He continued to lick and suck at the point of absolute pleasure, knowing I was losing my wits. A loud moan slipped from my lips.

"Yes... please... yes..." I was incapable of forming complete sentences.

From between my legs, I heard his husky voice. "Look at me, Kenna." I looked down at his violet eyes peering up between my thighs. There was so much desire and longing in those eyes, it was a miracle I didn't come right then and there. "Say my name, Kenna. Say my name and tell me what you want."

"Killian... make me come..." His tongue shifted into my folds, and I felt his warm heat inside me. I threw my head back and let out a long, loud moan. "Oh, Goddess, yes!" His fingers entered as soon as his tongue left, and he continued his onslaught on my sensitive bud. My whole body tensed, and I felt my walls clench around his fingers. Sweet release followed as I reached my peak. "Yes! Killian! Yes!"

Breathless but tingling with the best orgasm I had ever had, a smiling Killian lifted his head from between my legs and licked his lips. He pulled his fingers from inside me, leaving me feeling empty, and made eye contact while licking my juices off the two fingers that had just pushed me over the edge. Good Goddess, this man was unfairly talented. Killian slid up my body, stopping just before kissing me.

"Do you want to taste yourself, love? You're delicious," he said with a smile fit for a demon. I nodded my head, and he leaned down to kiss me. I tasted his usual spicy flavor mixed with my own sweet juices. Something I never expected to enjoy sent heat straight through me.

I started working at his belt again, freeing it easily. This time, he allowed me to unbutton his leathers and slide them down his hips. I didn't expect the lack of drawers or undergarments. His hard length sprang out as his leathers slid down, and he kicked them off.

I couldn't help but stare. When I had initially said Killian was built well as he carried me toward the woods, I wasn't expecting this. Killian reached for me and began kissing my neck. He hadn't realized I was gawking yet, thankfully, so I slid my hands down his waist and took his length in my hand. His breath hitched, and he nipped at my neck.

He was of average length, but my fingers barely made it around his girth, and I considered that I might not be able to accommodate his thickness. I purred at the thought of him filling me completely as I slid my hand up and down his length. He moaned into my neck and nuzzled into me.

"Goddess, Kenna. If your hand feels this good…" he breathed. I released my hold before he could finish his thought and pushed him back. Although he looked a bit bewildered, he allowed me to press him down into the blankets on his back so that I, once again, was on top.

Instead of straddling him, I stayed kneeling by his side and kissed him deeply while I resumed stroking his length. He groaned into my mouth, and I broke the kiss to start trailing kisses down his neck and chest and across his stomach. The lower I kissed, the more erratic his breathing became.

When I reached the V-shaped dip that started at either hip and trailed down toward his member, I looked up at him with a smirk, making eye contact before sliding my tongue lazily around the tip of his hardness. His eyes rolled back into his head, and he fell completely back into the blankets.

Taking this as an invitation to continue, I pressed my lips to the tip of his hard length and slid him into my mouth, slightly stretching my lips to accommodate the girth. This earned me a long, low moan from him, and his fingers began to tangle in my curls. One of my hands followed my mouth to make sure his entire length received attention.

His fingers, now thoroughly tangled in my hair, guided my pace. He allowed me to stop when I chose and lick the tip of his length and then suck him back into my mouth. He continued guiding me up and down, moaning and breathing heavily. I could feel him tensing and assumed he was close. Before I could speed up, he pulled my face up, causing a soft *pop* noise when the suction from my lips left the head of his member. He smiled dreamily at me.

"Kenna... you are amazing..." he whispered between gasps for air.

I pouted at him. "Why did you make me stop then?"

"Because I'm not done pleasing you yet, you reckless Witch." He sat up to kiss me and pulled me into his arms. I slid one leg over his legs, straddling him with his warm hardness pressed against my belly.

I slid my body up against his and used one hand to position him at the entrance to my core. Before I could slide down on his length, he gripped my hips and stopped me.

"Do we need...?" He trailed off, looking suddenly nervous.

I looked at him and tilted my head, feigning disbelief. "I'm a medicinal healer and a Witch. No." I let out a small laugh and leaned down to kiss him.

He wrapped his arms around me and deepened the kiss, only breaking it to say, "Just making sure," before kissing me hard and pushing my hips down in one swift motion. His length slid into me easily with the wetness between my thighs, but stretched my walls further than ever before, causing a surprised gasp of pleasure to escape my lips. I had never felt so complete.

Despite his easy entrance, my body took a minute to adjust to his girth before I leaned back and began to rock my hips, moving up and down. Killian let out a low groan. "Kenna..." His head rolled to the side. I picked up my pace, and he squeezed his eyes shut tight. "Kenna…" he moaned. The sound of my name leaving his lips in that sensual tone immediately spread heat through my body, and I had to slow down, or I was going to come again before accomplishing my goal.

I began to leisurely lift off his length and slide back down with a significant amount of control. I wanted to speed up and find my own release, but I was enjoying hearing this once-fierce warrior sound so helpless to my touch and moan my name for what must have been the tenth time.

His hands gripped my hips as he began to speed up my pace. He opened his eyes and looked into mine. The violet color of his eyes was so vibrant that they looked as if they were glowing. Now that he was controlling my hips, I reached to play with my nipples, never breaking eye contact.

What I didn't expect was for him to sit up, push my fingers away with his nose, and bite my nipple. What I would have expected to hurt sent so much pleasure to my core that I had to control myself not to fall over the edge too fast. He continued to control my up-and-down motion while assaulting my nipples with his teeth and tongue. I had never felt this way in my life. Every nerve ending in my body felt on fire, and I loved it.

With one of my nipples between his teeth, Killian still managed to moan out my name. Good Goddess. He began to slam me down on his length, forcing me to take all of him in, and the feeling was sensational. Between the rough thrusts and his teeth scraping my nipples, I was so close.

"Lose control, Kenna. Let me make you come." His breath was cool over my skin as he breathed out the words.

A few more thrusts was all it took. Those words started a massive orgasm ripping through my body. As my tunnel clenched around him, he bit down on my nipple, sending me over the edge yet again. I continued to shake and shudder with each wave of pleasure he managed to coax out of me until his own release soon followed, and he moaned my name one last time. I felt his thick heat fill me, and with a small smile, let out a satisfied sigh.

Killian and I both fell back into my bed, still tangled together, with his length still throbbing inside me. As I lay on his chest, I felt him shift his weight, pulling out of my core.

"No. I like this." I squeezed his arm with my hand. He adjusted the position of the arm that wasn't around me to prop his head up and look at me.

"Alright," he whispered. I sighed, feeling him against and inside me and enjoying the warmth I felt slipping out of me.

"I feel whole like this. Just stay," I said.

"Oh, I am for now, love, but we're an absolute sweaty mess, and well…" He trailed off.

"Yes, I know." I groaned, knowing he was referring to the heat leaking out between my legs. "But that was amazing. Honestly, the best orgasm I've ever felt." I beamed up at him.

"Orgasms," he corrected. "I must have made you come four times, love." He grinned playfully.

"Yes, well… I'm looking forward to five through infinity," I cooed before leisurely extracting myself from him and sauntering toward the washroom, ignoring the evidence of Killian's extensive climax running down the inside of my thighs.

I moved the hand pump that brought water into the washroom attached to my bedroom. There was a small hearth built into the floor, which doubled as heat for the washroom in the winter and warmed the water in the tub. It would take a few moments for the tub to heat, but it would be worth it. I smiled to myself at how amazing it had been with Killian. Messy… but incredible.

Thinking about it, however, just started another spark of heat in my core. I was surprised at myself for wanting more after that performance. Somehow, though, I did, and my body hummed with desire. I could hear him walking toward the washroom and couldn't help but bend over to tease him while I checked the water temperature. I was going to have fun with this, even if it killed me.

9
KILLIAN

Despite being incredibly proud of the four orgasms I had coaxed out of her, I still wanted more. I had filled her with my essence, yet here I was, hard enough for another round.

Kenna had just stood up and walked slowly, with a deliberate sway to the washroom. She was undeniably attractive, and knowing I was the one who had satisfied her just made me even harder.

I got up and hastily followed her toward the washroom, where she had started filling the basin. She bent over the tub, running her hands through the water as steam curled around her. I couldn't resist— my palm met her backside in a quick, impulsive strike. She startled and glanced back at me with a coy smile that promised trouble. When she bent forward again, slower this time, it felt deliberate. I wasn't going to refuse that invitation.

I walked up behind her, my erection evident, and ran my fingertips up her spine before positioning myself at her entrance. This woman was incredible. Not only had she felt fantastic the first time and knew how to do some incredible things with her mouth, but she wanted more. I silently thanked the Goddess for this little spitfire as I pressed into her core for the second time that night.

This position worked for me, although I think any position with her would have worked. I was so aroused by her invitation that I hadn't realized how roughly I was pushing into her tight tunnel, and Goddess was she tight. I gave her body a few seconds to adjust before resuming my desired rhythm. When I looked down at the woman positioned in front of me, I noticed her right hand was moving between her legs.

"Yes…" I said, breathing hard. "Touch yourself, Kenna." She let out a low purr when her fingertips met her sensitive bud. I could feel her little fingers swirling around her most sensitive spot while I pressed in and out of her. It did things to my restraint.

"Killian…. faster!" she cried. I noticed her fingers moving faster and realized she was close. Wanting to please her and to find my own release, I sped up. I might have been a bit rough, but she didn't seem to mind.

With my hands on her hips, holding her in place, I slammed in again and again as the washroom filled with more steam and her little fingers worked feverishly to bring her to her peak.

I felt her tunnel clench around my length as she cried out my name. The sound shattered what control I had left. With only two more rough thrusts, I filled her for a second time with my essence.

Panting, I leaned over her back and wrapped my arms around her waist. I kissed her shoulder before gently nipping her skin.

"I don't think I can say this enough, love: you are amazing," I whispered in her ear.

"Thank you," she said, still breathing hard. "You're pretty amazing yourself." Her small chuckle sent a bit of pressure down to her core, reminding us both that we needed to clean up.

"It's never been this intense before. Not that this—" she motioned between us "—is a regular thing for me. Maybe it's the bond?" She looked at me quizzically to see if I knew the answer.

It made sense; the bond was designed to lock two Fae into eternal love, which, of course, led to producing offspring.

Wait. Eternal love... Was this going to make me love her? Did I love her? The final part of the bond was "making love," as the legend put it, and we had just done that. Twice. Hadn't we? Shit. I barely knew her. How was I supposed to love her?

She must have sensed my panic because she released her hold on me and stepped back, looking dejected. She nibbled her finger while she asked, "You regret it, don't you? I'm sorry. I shouldn't have teased you. This didn't have to mean anything. It's okay. You can go tomorrow... I wouldn't blame you. I—"

I cut her off with a kiss. The hurt in her eyes was killing me. How could she think I regretted that? Was I scared of the implications of a lifelong bond with a spitfire? Yes. Would I rather it be with someone else? Hell no. I knew right then and there that this was definitely the bond, and it had most certainly taken hold of me, if not both of us.

"Kenna. Love, stop," I said, taking her hands. "I don't regret anything. I thank the Goddess I got to experience that with you."

She looked back up at me with a bit of surprise. "Then what is bothering you? And don't lie to me. I can read auras." She looked so determined. I wasn't going to lie to her. I didn't think I could anymore. This bond was going to be complicated. I just wasn't sure how to say it.

"Kenna, this bond is... a lot. I've never belonged anywhere. I don't know how to be what you need. Hell, I don't even know what you need." I sighed, knowing it didn't come close to what I was trying to say, but it wasn't a lie.

"You're scared of love," she said, the surprise leaving her face. "You're scared of the final part of the bond because of what we just did." I could see the gears turning in her head as she put the pieces together. "Killian, for lunch yesterday, you tried to kill me. I don't expect you to love me. I certainly don't love you. And I would really appreciate it if you didn't try to kill me again... not that you can now..." She grinned at me. "We barely know each other, and although that was devastating in the best way, there is much more to both of us. I'm willing to learn about you if you're willing to learn about me. I know I'm difficult, but at least give it a chance. Please?" Now she looked scared that I was going to reject her. I gathered her into my arms and breathed in her earthy lavender smell.

"I am scared, but you are impossible to say no to. Plus, it appears that you're stuck with me now. Unbreakable bond and all." I chuckled into her hair.

"As long as that performance gets an encore for the rest of our eternity shackled together," she whispered into my ear.

"Every single night, love. Every. Single. Night," I whispered back before picking her up and depositing her in the basin. "Right now, we need a bath..." I looked her up and down. She smirked, turned to the shelf next to the tub, and began to pour the soap into her small hands.

As I stepped in behind her, she turned and rubbed the soap across my chest, massaging it into my skin. Expecting it to be lavender-scented, I was surprised when it appeared to be a more pine-like scent. She smiled at me and continued to create tiny bubbles on my body as she rubbed the slick liquid all over me, even in my damp hair. Her touch cost me what little restraint I had regained.

What surprised me more was when her hands glided down to my hardened member again and slid bubbles along my length. She cupped me carefully in her hands as well and cleaned all our earlier escapades away. Seeing this gentle side of her was both arousing and comforting. She casually slid around me, pushed me to the side so she could scoop up hot water in a pitcher, poured it over me, and allowed the bubbles to rinse free.

When I opened my eyes, she picked up a different bottle. As she tipped the bottle to pour the soap into her hands, I caught the smell of lavender and knew it was her own personal blend I had smelled on her skin earlier. I reached for the bottle.

"Let me return the favor, love," I said and smiled at her before kissing her forehead.

I poured the liquid into my hands and rubbed them together to create a lather. Running my hands along her shoulders, I started to coat her in bubbles. Paying particular attention to her chest, I noted what made her breath hitch as I coaxed a soft moan from her. Moving my hands lower and across her stomach, I carefully lowered my body to allow myself access to reach her legs and inner thighs. Kenna looked at me with violet eyes while I smoothed the lather down her legs and back up. She was enjoying this, and I was quite pleased she was.

I switched places so I could fill the pitcher with warm water to rinse the soap away and then wash her hair with a honey-based concoction. That was where that beautiful combination of smells I associated with her came from.

Before she could get out, I wrapped my arms around her and pulled her close. Good Goddess, I wanted her again, but this was different. Right now, I just wanted to hold her, to feel her skin touching mine, to take in her smell, to feel her heartbeat against my chest. That damn bond was taking over my body, but I honestly didn't mind. She felt so right in my arms. So, I held her, kissing her lips, her forehead, and the crown of her head before finally giving in and allowing her to step out and offer me a soft towel.

AFTER WE DRESSED, I followed Kenna into the kitchen. Judging by the light outside, it wasn't as late as I had thought.

She turned to me with a smile. "Want some soup? I can heat

it." She handed me a bowl to hold while she ladled the cold soup into it.

"I want you... but the soup will do," I said. A slight shudder ran through her body, knowing she wanted me just as much, but she resisted and instead stuck her pointer finger in the soup at the edge of my bowl. "Why is your finger in my soup, Kenna?" I chuckled.

"Shush and be patient," she said, concentrating. She was apparently using magic to heat the soup, as evidenced by the steam that began to rise from the bowl. "There. Go eat it." She turned me around and pushed me toward her small kitchen table.

I sat down and watched her do the same with her bowl before she came to sit with me. The first spoonful was full of so much flavor my eyes widened, and I almost forgot to swallow before saying, "Kenna, this is really good!" I shoveled more into my mouth. I was starving, especially after our earlier rendezvous.

Kenna giggled at me and continued sipping her soup. "I'm glad you like it. I'm sorry it's so simple." She looked down at the bowl before her.

"Love, you don't need to make fancy things for me. I'm used to scraps. Plus, if you can make a simple soup taste this good, anything fancy would kill me." I smiled at her as I said it. "Is there more?" I held up my empty bowl to her.

Her eyes widened in surprise. "Are you sure you tasted it?" She giggled before taking the bowl from me and filling it again.

10
KENNA

*A*fter I had given Killian his third bowl of soup, I pulled him down onto the small, padded bench with me. I had a stack of books on the side table, and he began poking through them while I picked up the novel I had been reading the last few nights. As I sank into the pages before me, Killian smiled and wrapped his arm around my shoulders. I snuggled into him before really realizing what I was doing.

I stiffened as part of me chastised myself for easily falling into this. I reminded myself, yet again, that just a day ago, he had tried to kill me. Somehow, this bond was stronger than what I knew to be true. I was comfortable with him, and despite our poor meeting, I felt safe tucked under his arm.

Killian settled in next to me and began flipping through a book of maps and cultures that I thought must have been my father's. I had not read it yet, but he seemed interested in the content. I studied his face, noting he looked relaxed and wasn't on edge like when I had first met him. Although if I were being honest, I suppose our initial meeting wasn't meant to be pleasant.

"What are you looking at?" Killian's voice brought me back to reality. His brow was creased, and he looked a bit concerned.

"Do I have something on my face?" He rubbed his face with his free hand while balancing the book on his lap, trying to rid himself of the nonexistent offensive thing he thought I had spotted. I just giggled, which made him stop. He pulled me in tighter, and I snuggled into his chest, curling my legs up under me.

"There's nothing on your face. You look so relaxed. This whole thing doesn't bother you?" I asked quietly, burying my face into the fabric of his shirt, not wanting to see his reaction, because even though I felt safe, I was still grappling with the abrupt change. He leaned back from me to try to see my face, but I wouldn't let him, which resulted in him tickling me instead. "No. Stop. Please!" I wheezed out between giggles.

"Stop worrying, Kenna." He smiled at me.

Still catching my breath, I replied, "I can't help it...you're stuck with me and..." I trailed off and looked down again. Killian shifted so he could look at me.

"Look, for almost the entirety of my thirty-four years, I've been used to being free of ties and free of other people, so yes, the idea of being 'stuck' with a woman I don't really know for the rest of my life is a wee bit frightening, but, Kenna, I don't feel 'stuck' with you. I feel good sitting here with you. You have almost nothing to entertain me, the smallest house I've ever seen, and you care more about plants than people–" He had a point. "–but for some reason, my Fae blood chose you, and I'm happy it did. I'm happy just sitting here with you. So stop worrying and let me get to know the true, fiery you, not the insecure you that has suddenly replaced the little spitfire that tied me up in the garden and threatened my life." He grinned and settled back beside me before turning his head, brows creased again. "Speaking of age... you are...?" He trailed off, looking very concerned.

"Oh, Goddess." I laughed, realizing he was worried I was too young for him. "I'm thirty-two. And please tell me that being tied up in the garden isn't one of your fantasies." A half-smile quirked on my lips.

"Oh, thank the Goddess…" Killian let out a relieved sigh. "And what if it is?" He grinned mischievously at me and quirked an eyebrow.

Instead of answering him, I kissed his lips and settled next to him. He didn't seem to mind and slid his arm back around me, squeezing me tightly to his side. I felt my body relax despite being pressed into his hard, muscular frame. It was dark out now, and I was starting to tire, but I couldn't bring myself to move away from him.

WHEN I WOKE, Killian had laid me on my bed and pulled my soft blanket over me.

"You fell asleep," he whispered. I turned to look out the window and guessed based on the lack of light outside, it had gotten quite late. I normally enjoyed going to bed much earlier, so I wasn't surprised I had fallen asleep on him. After he was satisfied I was tucked in, he stood and started toward the door.

"Wait. Where are you going?" I asked him with a touch of panic. I didn't understand why he was leaving me there.

"To the room you told me to sleep in, Kenna." He gave a mischievous smile.

"Stay. Stay here. Please." My entire being felt hollow without his touch. I wanted him near me, and even in another room in the same house, he seemed too far away.

"Are you sure?" He wasn't being cheeky for once and seemed genuinely interested in my response. "I don't want you to feel like you have to do something just because of this bond," he added.

"Shut up and get in bed," I murmured sleepily, rolling onto my side. Killian didn't need to be told twice. He slid under the soft blankets next to me, pulling my back to his chest when he wrapped an arm around my waist. Killian kissed my shoulder, and I felt him relax behind me.

Despite the comfort of his presence and my recent nap, I found myself struggling to recapture sleep. I rolled over and faced Killian. In the moonlight, his dusty blond hair fell over his forehead and just brushed the tops of his eyelids. His eyes were closed, and he looked peaceful, although I could tell by his breathing that he wasn't asleep yet.

I tentatively reached my fingers out to carefully brush the hair from his eyes and watched it lightly fall back onto his forehead. He, indeed, was gorgeous. A small smile spread on his lips, and without opening his eyes, he pulled me in closer and kissed my cheek.

"You're sweet, but you need to sleep, love," he said, nuzzling into my neck. I giggled and kissed his cheek.

"Hard to sleep with you here," I murmured.

He started to move away. "Okay. I'll go then," he teased before I grabbed his arms and pulled him back into bed.

"Don't you dare."

Killian smiled and pulled me against his chest. I lay my head on his shoulder and put my hand on his chest, noting the steady beat of his heart. He was nothing like the Hunters I had been warned about, the ones I had read about in class at the coven. This man was sweet, attentive, and a Goddess-awful tease. I felt the insecurity start rising, and the worry that he was manipulating me like Hunters sometimes did began to rear its head again. He must have noted the tension in my body because he squeezed me tighter to him, wrapping both arms around me.

"Stop it, Kenna. I'm not going anywhere." He opened one eye to look at me when I didn't respond because I honestly didn't know what to say. Upon seeing me chewing my finger, he opened both eyes and tilted my head toward him. "Tell me what it is." His tone was calm, but there was a hint of a demanding undercurrent.

"I'm worried you're using me or manipulating me... This all happened way too fast..." I said quietly, still chewing on the end of my finger.

"Kenna, I really can't say anything to prove it to you," he sighed, "but whatever this bond did to me makes it impossible for me to be away from you... or lie to you. I feel empty without your touch. Seeing you worried physically hurts me. I don't think I'm capable of using you, but I'll try to prove it to you every day if I have to." A small smile spread across my lips. What he said did make me feel better. Being so insecure was strange to me. I usually didn't care what others thought, hence why leaving the coven had been so easy for me.

"I'm not normally like this..." My words died in the air. I wasn't sure why I felt the need to defend myself.

"I know, Kenna. I'm well aware that you're a fiery, sneaky little Witch. I think you're just as scared as I am, even if you're better at hiding it," he mused.

"Well, clearly I'm not." I chuckled. Killian laughed and kissed the top of my head. I felt his fingers twirl in my curls, and I let out a soft sigh. No one had bothered to play with my hair before, and this was lovely.

"Sleep," Killian breathed. He continued to play with my curls until the darkness of sleep overtook me.

11

KILLIAN

Sleeping with Kenna lying delicately in my arms was the best sleep I had had in years, and it even seemed to quell the nightmares I frequently had. Waking up to her small frame pressed against my body was even better. Part of me hoped this would never end, and the Fae King would simply forget about her. I hoped that maybe, just maybe, I was given this small slice of the heavens and would be allowed to keep it for once.

I smiled to myself as I realized she was still asleep despite the sunlight pouring into her room. She was curled against my body with her head on my chest, an arm across my torso, and one leg tossed haphazardly over mine. I couldn't move, even if I wanted to; luckily, I didn't want to.

I brushed her curls back from her sleeping face and looked at the beautiful, relaxed woman lying on me. Her head was tilted up just a bit, so I could see parts of her face and her small smile.

"You awake, love?" I asked faintly, unsure if she was smiling in her sleep or actually awake. A small groan escaped from her.

"If I say no, can we stay here?" she cooed in a sleepy voice.

"I will stay in bed with you all day if you want, but one of us is going to get hungry at some point." I chuckled.

"Hmm, I can think of something you can eat," she said under her breath. A low groan escaped from my lips. My mind wandered to last night. "Get your mind out of the gutter, Killian. I have muffins in the kitchen." I caught her cheeky grin, though, and knew she had gotten the exact reaction she was looking for.

Kenna released her grip on me and rolled out of bed. Her curls stuck up in funny places, and she still looked half-asleep, but she was beautiful. After pulling off her clothes from the night before, she slipped on a shirt after haphazardly wriggling back into her undergarments and half stumbled into a pair of leggings. Her bent-over posture while pulling them up gave me a fantastic view of her backside. Trying not to get too distracted, I hastily pulled my shirt over my head and slipped back into my leathers.

I followed her to the bedroom door, catching her around the waist before she left the room. Pulling her back into my chest, I kissed her neck. She melted in my arms, and I tightened my grip, afraid she might crumple to the floor.

"Killian... do you want breakfast or not?" Her voice was breathy, and she let out a small sigh as I kissed her shoulder.

"I do, but you're looking very tasty right now," I murmured into the crook of her neck.

"Uh, yeah, I'm sure my morning breath is very appealing." She chuckled and peeled my hands off her hips before heading toward the kitchen. I let out a frustrated groan and followed her.

When I trudged into the kitchen, Kenna pulled a muffin from a breadbox on the counter. She dropped the muffin onto the countertop with a thud. Her face turned into a frustrated scowl, and she turned to me.

"So, we have rock-hard muffins, or I can get some vegetables from the garden and make omelets." She looked so annoyed, and her hair was still all over; it was cute.

"You look adorable right now," I said, taking a step toward her, "but I think I would prefer the omelets." I took another step, hoping to pull her into my arms, but I was instead met with a rock-hard muffin being thrown at my chest. "Hey!"

"I'll go get the vegetables. You can come with me if you want." She looked at me with a hopeful expression. Did she want me to go with her?

"Alright, but only if you kiss me first." I quirked a smile at her. She glared back at me before grabbing the neck of my shirt and pulling me down so she could kiss my cheek.

"Come on then," she said and turned toward the door.

I started for the door before looking at the offending muffin in my hand, intending to toss it into the woods for the wildlife to enjoy.

Following Kenna into the bright morning sun was like waking from a fog. Watching her tender, intentional movements, I noticed the details and the magic in everything she had chosen to surround herself with. She was so joyous simply picking vegetables and plucking herbs. I marveled at its simplicity.

After fighting for far too many years to survive, the idea of having something this calm and comforting was so foreign yet so alluring. I only hoped that we could have this forever.

Kenna turned to look at me, and the bright green of her eyes was lit by the sunrise cascading over the walls of the garden fence. She smiled at me and lifted an eyebrow in question.

"Please tell me you aren't going to eat that." She pointed a dainty finger at the fossilized muffin I carried. Looking down at my hand, I chuckled and tightened my grip in preparation to toss the breakfast abomination into the surrounding field, but Kenna stopped me. "Wait," she said softly, gesturing for me to follow her. I thought she might just be leading me to a compost pile, but instead, I was met with two tiny fuzzy red faces poking out from under a log along the edge of the forest just outside her property.

"Foxes?" I asked a bit incredulously.

"Yes." She smiled. "These two are Violet and Poppy." She gestured to their little noses poking out. "They're probably nervous because you're new, but I rescued them from a couple of snares out there—" she pointed vaguely into the In-Between "—and they followed me to the edge of the woods. So, now they live here. It's a lot smaller than the cave they came from, but they don't seem to mind." She beamed with pride.

I raised an eyebrow. "Love, are you sure their tastes aren't too refined for a petrified muffin?" I said in jest. "Is there a raccoon around here I could pawn this off on instead? I wouldn't want to offend these little beauties if they're your friends." I gave her a cheeky grin. Kenna grabbed the muffin, but I was faster and whipped it out of her reach. She must not have expected me to move and stumbled forward a bit, off balance. She stopped a few inches before me, and my arm instinctively went around her waist. "Just couldn't stay away, could you?" I murmured.

12
KENNA

Killian quirked up one corner of his mouth in a haughty smile as he pulled me closer. My chest pressed into his, and I could feel his heartbeat quicken. I smiled back and pressed my lips to his. He sighed with satisfaction and leaned into the kiss. Unfortunately for him, the kiss distracted him while I snatched the muffin from his relaxed fingers.

He pulled out of the kiss abruptly and smirked at me. "Well, that was awfully foxy of you," he said coyly with a wink. I gave him a look that deterred further innuendos and began crumbling what I could off the muffin.

The two young foxes gingerly exited their little den and sniffed around the crumbs. Poppy, always the braver of the two, gobbled up the bits first. Violet daintily followed her example. Killian let out a small laugh before wrapping his arms around me. He reached forward and broke apart the muffin with me, his hands covering mine.

"You are really quite amazing," he cooed in my ear. I craned my head to the side to look at him.

"And you must have very low standards if feeding a muffin to foxes is so amazing," I teased.

"No, love, you truly are. You just thrive in nature, and it's incredible to watch. I can use nature with my Fae magic too, but nothing even remotely close to this," he said, waving his hand in an arc from the foxes to my garden with a hint of awe. I blushed, not entirely sure what to say. The mate bond did not come with a manual for handling the surprisingly sweet things that came out of Killian's mouth.

To avoid further embarrassment, I tossed the remaining muffin chunk to the little foxes, who happily chirped and grunted their approval. Dragging Killian behind me, I took him back to the garden.

"We should pick out what veggies you want," I said, trying to calm the heat in my face. I again questioned how we had gone from trying to kill each other to awkwardly flirting in a matter of days, which simply made my face heat back up.

Killian must have noticed and chuckled before pulling me back into his arms and whispering, "I think I changed my mind. Can I add you back to the menu?"

I pushed away from him and gave him a withering look as I began to pick some of the green peppers and pulled up an onion. "You'll get whatever I pick then, if you're so distracted," I retorted.

"Fine with me," he said with a grin. "I trust you if that soup indicates your cooking skills."

After choosing several more vegetables for the omelets and fielding Killian's attempts to get handsy whenever I bent over, I ushered him back into my tiny kitchen. I set a cast-iron rack over the hearth and lit a small fire. I placed the pan on top of it to heat it while I prepped the ingredients. Turning toward Killian, I pointed my spatula in his direction and instructed him to chop the vegetables. He obliged and stood next to me in comfortable silence while he worked.

I cracked the eggs over a bowl and mixed them until the yolks and whites became one. Killian watched me as if this were the most interesting event he had ever witnessed.

"What?" I asked, unsure why he was so fascinated with eggs.

"Nothing," he said quickly before adding, "It's just so new to me to be doing these normal, everyday things. I'm not used to having a hearth to cook on or even having eggs from a known source."

"A known source?" I queried. He smiled wistfully before replying.

"When I travel, I don't carry much. The backpack, basic cooking supplies, a tent, and my bow and quiver." He gestured to the pile of his belongings leaning up against the wall next to the cottage door. "It's faster to travel without a bunch of extra weight and excess stuff. Quieter, too."

I motioned for him to put some of the vegetable mixture he had been working on in the solidifying eggs in the pan. As he did, he continued his reply to my question. "It was fairly often that I had to scrounge around wherever I was to eat whatever I could find. Sometimes, if I got lucky, I would find a nest of eggs to cook on the fire. If I wasn't so lucky, I didn't eat. At the beginning of my hunting career, there were so many days when I went without food out of fear that I'd eat something that would kill me, either because it was toxic, or because its friends would find me and I'd become the food." He loosed a breath before looking me in the eyes. "Desperation will either bring out your bravery or defeat. Luckily for me, desperation was the push I needed to eat things I had never seen before. Also, luckily, those things didn't kill me, or I'd have missed out on this." He smiled as he bumped my shoulder with his.

I wasn't entirely sure how I felt about his answer. For some reason, what Killian must have gone through to survive had never really crossed my mind. Part of me recognized he had had a difficult life, but it was hard to reconcile that with the cocky, skilled, beautiful man standing next to me. We shared an inner fire that kept us fighting for survival when most would not.

"Will you tell me about it? Your travels, I mean," I asked, unsure how to respond to the pain etched on his face. After a second pause, he looked up at me through his lashes.

"Yeah, but maybe some other time. Right now, though, I'd really like to eat our creations before they get cold." He motioned to the omelets I had slid onto plates. I smiled at him, although it felt forced. I knew he was recalling something painful. That was evident in his furrowed brows and the darkness clouding his typically clear eyes, but I didn't know what to say to begin to heal that wound. I had no idea what the wound even was.

In fact, at that moment, I realized I genuinely didn't know much about the handsome man in front of me. We had been thrust into this bond almost immediately after our meeting and had not had the opportunity to learn about each other. The thought brought about a small cloud of sadness that lingered over me as we ate. Despite Killian's exclamation that these were, in fact, the most amazing omelets he had ever had, I still couldn't shake the feeling. I did my best to hide the frown that kept attempting to inch onto my face, but I was sure Killian was aware, courtesy of our supernatural tether.

After eating, Killian helped me wash the plates in the small water basin by the window and put them to dry on the small wooden rack next to the hearth. Leaning back against the edge of my counter, he let out a contented sigh and smiled at me. "So, what's in store for the rest of the day, love?"

I pondered my response and tried to clear my head of the fog that had descended in my mind. "I need to take some of my remedies and smaller plants to town. I should replenish my booth in the apothecary. Especially now that it's a 'designated day' for me to go," I mused while turning to the countertop and starting a list of things that would need to be packed and carted down the bumpy dirt path to the town of Cauldera.

"Isn't that the town with that big old coven school?" Killian asked.

"Yes, I used to live there…" I trailed off before sadly adding, "But things got bad, so I left." Killian looked confused and slightly concerned, but didn't press me too hard to explain.

"Will you tell me about it?" he said with a little smile, tinged with a hint of knowing.

"Maybe some other time." I grinned back, feeling lighter. "But right now, we have some packing to do."

13

KILLIAN

I followed Kenna and carried what she would let me as she flitted between the small cottage, the garden shed, and her small traveling cart, which she had yanked from behind the shed. The number of items she intended to bring into town was enormous. I had no idea how such a small woman could drag the hulking mass behind her.

"Kenna, are you sure we need to bring all of this?" I said, peering down the road in the direction she had pointed earlier. "Is it even going to make it there in one piece?"

"You can stay behind if you can't keep up," she teased.

"Where's the fun in that?" I winked.

"It would certainly be quieter," she quipped while her gaze traveled up and back down my form.

"If you wanted me out of my clothes, love, you could have just asked. No need to undress me with those beautiful green eyes of yours." I grinned.

Eyeing me appraisingly, she shook her head. "Oh, for Goddess's sake, Killian. Not everything is about that!" she scolded, putting her little hands on those gorgeous, curvy hips. "You have to change into something less conspicuous so the coven members don't see you and suspect you're a Hunter. They'll kill us both if they do," she said flatly. "The coven leader, Mrs. Lancaster, has absolutely no tolerance for Hunters or those who harbor them." Her eyes dipped, and she dropped her hands to her sides, looking sheepish after her small outburst. I took a few steps closer to her, put my hands on her hips, and pulled her closer to me.

"If you need me to stay here for your safety, I will," I murmured into her hair before kissing her temple. "I will never willingly or knowingly put your life in danger."

She sighed and turned her head, kissing me lightly on the cheek. "I know, but you don't know that woman like I do. She barely tolerated me, so I doubt she would have even a shred of decency toward you," she said softly.

"What do you mean she barely tolerated you? You're a Witch," I said as I pulled away from her, holding her at arm's length so I could see her face. It made very little sense to me that the coven leader would treat one of her own poorly. Those beautiful kelly green eyes darkened to match the forest surrounding her home.

"That's a story for another time," she said through gritted teeth. She shook her head, and her eyes lightened again. Looking up to my face, she asked, "Do you have anything with less leather and..." She trailed off, placing her hand on my jacket to examine what had once been a rather painful entry point for a puncture wound. "Something with fewer holes and, uh, old blood?" She picked at the edge of my jacket, which was indeed stained a dark brown.

I smiled. "Aye, I do. Will you help me?" I quirked an eyebrow as the corner of my lips turned up.

"Good Goddess, you're ridiculous," she sighed in exasperation. "Come on then," she said, motioning for me to follow her with a flick of her hand.

I followed behind Kenna, enjoying the view of her hips

swaying as we returned to the cottage. If I kept this up, I would pitch a tent instead of changing my clothes.

Once inside her cottage, she upended my bag on the kitchen floor and began rummaging through its contents.

"Hey!" I exclaimed. "There are valuables in there, you know."

She at least had the decency to look embarrassed before holding up a plain brown tunic top and darker linen pants. "Sorry. This will work, I think," she said abashedly, lowering her eyes.

"I know you're nervous, and I've got nothing to hide from you, but if you're going to paw through my bag, just be gentle." I sighed. While avoiding eye contact, Kenna began to fold and carefully place my things back in the bag. Midway through, while putting my undergarments back in the largest compartment, her movements stilled.

At first, I thought she realized she was holding my drawers, but then she looked up at me with those emerald eyes and exclaimed, "Why am I putting things back in this bag?"

"Because you dumped them out," I said with a confused chuckle.

"No, yes, I know that; I mean, why aren't you unpacking? Are you still planning to leave?" Her face scrunched in a way I noticed happened when something was bothering her.

"No, we just hadn't talked about it, and I wasn't going to assume." I smiled. "If you want me to unpack, just tell me where to put my things." She motioned behind her, still holding my drawers, toward the opening that led to her bedroom. I couldn't help it; I just had to laugh.

"Kenna, can you put my drawers down? I can't take anything you say seriously while you're waving my unmentionables about in your kitchen." I let out another chuckle. Her face turned from pink to fuchsia and then as red as the tomatoes she grew in her garden as she looked down at her hand.

"Oh!" she yelped, tossing the offending items into the bag

quickly. Then she giggled before looking up at me from beneath her lashes. "Sorry." She giggled again, and some of the redness from her face began to recede.

"If you want to play with my underthings, might I suggest you do that when I'm actually wearing them?" I cocked an eyebrow at her as one side of my mouth quirked up.

"Good Goddess…" Kenna mumbled, standing up. She reached for the handle of my pack, but I took it first. She resorted to grabbing the few small items that had escaped her frantic repacking and led me toward her room. "My dresser is full, but you could pull the one from the guest room in here." She motioned to a spot on the other side of the bed with reasonable space.

I smiled at her. "As much as I love this, shouldn't we be going now? I don't really want to be trudging back up here in the dark," I said. She turned and looked out the window, no doubt looking to see where the sun was to determine the time.

"Yes, we should. But you still have to change. And to avoid any other disruptions, I'll wait outside for you," she said as she began walking past me.

"Oh no, you don't," I said with a grin as I pulled her to me and pressed my lips to hers, requesting entrance with my tongue. She exhaled, and I felt her melt into my arms. She allowed me to taste her mouth, and my tongue met hers. I felt her little hands start to run along the lines of my leather jacket before fisting into the fabric at the front of my shirt. Good Goddess, she was irresistible.

"Killian, we don't have time for this," she whined.

Breaking the kiss only long enough to whisper into her lips, "We will always have time for this," my hands slid down her back and grasped her backside. Kenna was curvy enough to fill my hands, and her leggings were leaving very little to my imagination.

I effortlessly picked her up, and she wrapped her legs around my waist. I began to walk her back to the bed, but she pulled her mouth from mine, and I let out an annoyed growl as she shook her head.

"We seriously don't have time," she said with a hint of disappointment.

"Do you trust me?" I said smugly. She nodded her head a little hesitantly.

"You know I do, but that isn't going to fix the timing issue," she said with a sigh.

"I don't need long. I just need to taste you," I whispered into her ear. Her back stiffened as the words sank in, and she leaned back just enough to look me in the eyes. "Yes or no, love? We don't have all day," I said softly with a grin.

The only response from Kenna was a slight grin of her own before she brought her lips back to mine. I laid her down on the bed and began stripping her clothes off, running my fingertips across her soft skin and admiring the gift the Goddess had laid before me. I was a man starved, and she was my salvation.

"Might as well kill two birds with one stone." Kenna smiled as I pulled her top over her head, and she began pulling my clothes off my body. Hurriedly, we stripped each other of any layers between us. I kissed her mouth once more before moving my lips down her cheek, jaw, and neck. Nipping at the point where her graceful neck met her lightly freckled shoulders brought out a small moan from Kenna.

"Ah, you like that, aye?" I murmured into her neck before nipping at her shoulder and making my way to her breasts. Lathing my tongue over her nipple then sucking, I remembered I didn't have as much time to worship every inch of her as thoroughly as I'd truly like. She let out a moan, indicating once again this was a location she enjoyed attention. Tucking that thought away for another time, I worked my way down her stomach to her hips. Nipping at the skin by her hip bone, I furthered my explorations. Despite having made love to her before, it felt like I was discovering a new treasure every time I touched her this way.

Moving my tongue closer to her apex, I blew cool air over the places my tongue had already traced. Kenna's hands tangled in her blankets as she let loose a moan that made me painfully hard. Yet again, reminding myself I did not have all the time I wanted, I also tucked that tidbit away for later.

Just before I reached her apex, Kenna placed her hands on either side of my head, pulling me toward her face.

"I'm not done with you yet," I breathed before she kissed me deeply.

"No, you're absolutely not. But I don't plan on neglecting you either," she said as she wound her thin fingers around my shaft, pumping once, twice. My eyes just about rolled into the back of my skull as my desire for her soared.

Kenna pushed on my chest, and I leaned back on my knees, watching her as she scooted farther up the bed.

"Lie down," she demanded. I did as she asked, and she smiled at me smugly before kissing the tip of my member and then sucking it into her warm, wet mouth.

"Kenna," I groaned and felt her mouth vibrate with the victorious little chuckle she let out. Fighting the urge to surrender, I twisted my upper half to grasp her hips and lifted her over me so that her dripping mound was positioned over my face. She let out a little squeak of surprise but didn't try to move away.

Grasping her hips with my hands, I breathed in her heady scent. She smelled musky but floral, and my mouth began to water. I pulled her opening closer to my mouth, and she let out a soft moan around my shaft as I licked her most sensitive spot and then drove my tongue inside her wet heat. She tasted sweet and earthy, and the flavor only made me more famished for her.

Kenna let out a whimper and began pulling me deeper into her mouth until I felt the tip of my cock press into her throat momentarily, before she started sliding me back out between her lips again.

I was desperate to hold my focus and not pour my seed into her mouth yet. Redoubling my efforts, I began sucking at the most sensitive little nub at the top of her opening. She let out a loud moan, which almost sent me careening over the edge of my climax, but I refused to leave her unsatisfied.

Maneuvering my hand, I found the right angle to plunge a finger and then two into her wet opening. I began moving my fingers in and out with a little curl of my fingertips at the end, just before pulling them loose. I felt her walls tense around my fingers, and her movements became slower and more erratic.

The swipe of her tongue and even the slow, unhurried movements of her mouth around my shaft felt incredible. Trying my best to savor the feeling while also making sure she was satisfied, I began pumping my fingers into her heat faster, harder, and continued licking and sucking her pleasure bud. The combination of her scent and taste, mixed with the warmth and wetness dripping down my chin, threatened to send me over the edge once again.

When I thought I couldn't hold back any longer, Kenna let out a deep groan as she tensed around my fingers, and my mouth flooded with her flavor. Seconds later, I followed her over the edge and into bliss.

I felt her throat tighten around my member as I spilled my seed into her. Swallowing, she moaned again as my member throbbed its release in her mouth and down her throat. *Holy fuck.* I moaned as the last of my release poured onto Kenna's waiting tongue. She licked up my member, causing a tremor to rock through my body.

Pulling my fingers from Kenna's core, I heard her sigh before I shifted my tongue to where my fingers had been and tasted her once more. Her knees on either side of my head began to shake, and I smiled to myself before giving her one last flick of my tongue and lifted her off my face. I licked my lips before running a hand over my chin, clearing the remnants of her pleasure from my stubbled face.

"Goddess, you taste so good," I breathed. Kenna looked down at me with glossy, pleasure-filled eyes as I lay in a mess of tangled, sweaty sheets. She leaned forward to kiss me, and our tongues tangled again. As she pulled away from the kiss and stood, presumably to redress, I noted the musky, slightly salty flavor of myself on her tongue.

Kenna licked her lips before she bent over to pick up her fallen, discarded clothing, giving me a full view of her still-glistening core. She looked over her shoulder at me with hooded eyes and a wink as she shimmed back into her clothing. "We both do."

14
KENNA

After pulling myself somewhat together and dressing, I dragged myself outside and waited for Killian to follow. My body still tingled from Killian's ministrations, and I desperately tried to refocus on the task at hand. I looked to the sky. Much to my displeasure, Killian was correct in that he had not needed long, and our little escapade only appeared to have cost us half an hour.

Killian stumbled out of the cottage door after me, with a boot half laced and his shirt only pulled halfway down. Despite his scruff, it was evident his face was still flushed. He smiled at me before rubbing the back of his neck and looking a bit flustered. Trying to hide my smile, I turned back toward the handle of the four-wheeled cart and motioned for him to follow me as I started dragging the cart behind me out of the shade of the trees and onto the small dirt road. Killian didn't let me get far before grasping my hand, stopping my labored movements.

"If you'd just give me a moment to tie my boot, I'll pull it for you."

"It's fine, Killian. I do this every week."

"Well, now you have help. Let me help you." He looked at me with pleading eyes. I huffed and let him take the handle from me.

"Why can't you just teleport us closer to the market? That would really help," I mused, half-teasing. I didn't actually expect him to, but I was also curious why it wasn't something he offered.

"I'm only half Hunter, Kenna; I can only teleport myself. My Fae blood is stronger," he said dejectedly. I could see the anticipation of disappointment in his eyes, and it broke my heart. How many times had he been told he wasn't enough simply because he was only half Hunter?

"I was teasing, Killian. I didn't actually expect you to teleport us. Not with all this stuff." I gestured to the cart behind him and smiled. He smiled weakly back and began to pull the cart along, motioning for me to lead the way.

"Plus, if I teleported us, I'd miss out on the view of your ass bouncing along in front of me." He winked and let out a chuckle. I smacked his arm and gave him a look that could have curdled milk. "What? It's a nice ass!"

"This ass is leaving you here if you don't get yours in gear," I chided. Dutifully, Killian pulled the cart behind us easily, making me feel rather pathetic. Thank the Goddess he hadn't seen me try to pull the menagerie of items in the rainy spring. I'd gotten the cart stuck four different times and spent countless hours trying to pull it back onto the more solid road. I'd arrived home well past dark that night and was the most terrified I'd ever been of the In-Between as eyes that glowed various colors had watched me. Off in the distance, I'd heard the bellowing of beasts that even the strongest Hunter avoided.

A LONG WHILE LATER, after listening to Killian either complain or make varied sexual innuendos, we arrived at the outer walls of the small market. The market was warded and sectioned off with thick stone walls because it was on the border of the coven's keep. The coven took security very seriously, and the market drew people from all over Miridia, Amaradia, and sometimes even farther away realms and territories, although Hunters and the Blood Drinkers of Antharel were banned. All had to enter through two openings in the wards for inspection, which were heavily guarded.

As we waited in line to pass through the market gates with the other merchants, I overheard two women in front of us chattering about various gossip. For the most part, I tuned them out, focusing more on Killian. However, one bit of gossip did catch my attention.

"You know, I heard the Fae King is planning to take over Cauldera and then move on to the other territories," the older of the two women whispered.

"Mother, that's ridiculous. The Fae King is hundreds of years old with no heir. Why in the Goddess's name would he bother taking over Cauldera when his own kingdom will perish when he finally leaves the realm of the living?"

"Maybe he found another woman to bear his children," the older woman quipped.

"You know the Fae only get one bonded, and he was lucky he even found his to begin with. I highly doubt he's moved on."

The younger woman wasn't wrong. The Fae King was old, even by Fae standards. As far as I knew, he never had another heir after the prince went missing, or if he did, the heir would be too young to rule, or illegitimate, neither of which he would stand for. The idea that he wanted to take over the coven lands caught my attention, though. I'd never heard mention of him trying to take over other territories before, although that didn't necessarily mean he wasn't capable of it.

I snapped out of my thoughts when the line of merchants began moving forward again. Turning to Killian, I grabbed a cloak off the cart and pulled it over his head before kissing him and whispering in his ear, "Please try to blend in. If anyone becomes suspicious, we'll be killed." He clasped my hand in his and squeezed.

"I'll be your shadow, love. You tell me where to go and what to do." For the first time, his eyes were serious.

"Thank you." I dropped his hand and started toward the market gate.

"Ah, Miss Kenna. Nice to see you back. Did you remember my salve?" asked the older guard I'd learned was called Sal.

"You think I could forget you?" I pulled a salve out of my pocket and handed it to him. "Only use that twice a day. Potent stuff." I smiled at him.

"Thank you." He pocketed the salve as the younger guard cocked his head to the side to study Killian.

"Who's that?" the younger man pointed directly at him. "And who wears a cloak in the summer?"

"This is my friend. He's visiting. He's very... pale... so he needs to protect himself from the sun," I said hesitantly.

"Good on you, boy. Don't want to end up an old shriveled bag like me!" joked Sal from his post. "Go ahead, Kenna. Don't linger too long. I don't like you being in those woods at night." I smiled at him and nodded my head once in acquiescence.

Nodding at the younger guard still staring at Killian, I began leading the way into the market, toward one of the permanent stone structures where my items were sold as part of the apothecary the Earth Magic Shop contained.

Killian kept his head low as we walked through the opening. He continued to pull the cart forward and said nothing until we reached the wooden door leading into the Earth Magic Shop.

Hazel, who was staffing the shop once again, smiled at me as she opened the door. "Kenna!" she exclaimed. "I'm just going out for lunch, but you can go on in and set up. Lock the door behind you so you don't have to worry about patrons, and make sure it's locked if you happen to leave before I return. I've got my key."

"Thank you, Hazel." I returned her smile as she stepped out of the way. She openly gawked at Killian as his muscles flexed beneath his shirt while he lifted a large crate from the cart.

Holding her hand to her mouth as if she could keep Killian from hearing her, she leaned closer to whisper in my ear, "Where do I get me one of those?"

My insides clenched, and I had to fight back the short blast of possessiveness I felt at her comment. "You don't," I said with as natural a smile as possible. "He's one of a kind."

Hazel laughed and started toward the human end of the market, filled with food from various vendors and territories. "Don't have too much fun!" She beamed. As she turned the corner into the less permanent structures housing various other goods, I let out a breath I didn't realize I was holding.

"She was nice," Killian said, eyeing me. He evidently noticed my reaction.

"She's very... personable..." I said tightly.

"You mean she's extra friendly with men?" he asked, obviously trying to find a polite way to say it.

"She's a sweet girl, but yes, she's a bit overzealous." I sighed. "She was one of the only Witches who never judged me, though, so I try not to judge her."

"Can you blame her?" Killian stood flexing behind me. "I mean, look at me."

"Okay, then." I rolled my eyes. "Can you quit doing whatever you're doing?" I said, waving my hand up and down at him. "Help me put these bottles on those shelves. I can't reach without the ladder."

"Of course." Killian smiled and took the first bottle from my hand, giving me a quick kiss before turning and placing it on the top shelf where my concoctions always seemed to end up.

Despite Mrs. Lancaster's attempts to deter customers from buying my products by shelving my things out of reach, I had a reputation she couldn't squelch. I had long since given up on requesting my things be displayed differently and trusted that people would find them, whether she liked it or not.

Killian and I worked surprisingly efficiently together, putting most items away rather quickly. He stood watching me in the window as I placed each small plant I had brought with care into the sill. The plants were the only thing the crotchety old coven leader didn't sequester out of sight.

As I placed the smallest mint plant on the windowsill, I heard the door rattle, indicating someone was unlocking it. I initially assumed it was Hazel, but froze when I saw through the glass of the door Mrs. Lancaster herself fighting with the old lock, which thankfully seemed to be stuck.

"Killian! You have to hide!" I hissed.

"And where do you think I'm going to do that, Kenna? I'm not exactly small!" he gritted back.

"I don't know!"

"I need you to trust me," he whispered as he stepped closer.

"With what?"

"Just trust me." His hands wound into my curls and pulled my face to his. He kissed me right there in the middle of the store as Mrs. Lancaster finally pushed through the door. My knees began to wobble, whether from the intensity of his kiss or the fear of the coven leader seeing me like this—I wasn't sure.

Mrs. Lancaster cleared her throat loudly. "Kenna McCairn! I expect better of you!" she seethed. Pulling away from Killian, who smartly kept his head lowered and did not look at her, I peeked over his shoulder as I felt my cheeks burn.

"I'm sorry!" I squeaked. "My things are all set up for the week! We'll get out of your way!" I dragged Killian behind me by his hand. He tipped his head to her enough to show respect, but at an angle that didn't give her an unobscured view of his face. He had embarrassed the hell out of me, but he was a genius. The prudish Mrs. Lancaster would be too flustered to follow; somehow, he had anticipated that.

We scurried out into the open part of the market where the humans set up their tents, dragging the cart behind us. Killian burst out laughing as soon as we turned a corner. The merchant there, selling rugs, looked at him with concern, whether for himself or Killian was debatable. Smacking his arm, I got his attention.

"What was that?" I hissed, the embarrassment still flooding my veins.

"What?" he chuckled. "I just saved us!"

"That was the headmistress of the coven!" I spat. "And now she thinks—who knows what she thinks, but it can't be good!"

"Why does it matter?" he asked, honest curiosity coloring his tone.

"Because I've spent the entirety of my life trying to prove to that wretched woman that I'm not the dirt beneath her shoes!" Understanding dawned on his face as he pulled me to his chest.

"I'll, um, let you have a moment," the rug merchant murmured awkwardly as he stepped to the other side of his booth.

"Kenna, her opinion of you, although obviously important to you, doesn't dictate how incredible you are. I wish you could see yourself as I do. It's her loss if she can't see who you truly are," he whispered into my ear as he stroked my hair. I pressed my forehead into his shoulder and breathed in his scent, a mix of sweat from the heat and the aura of pine that never seemed to leave his skin.

I pulled back from him and squared my shoulders, looking into his eyes. I knew he understood on some level, and although his words were comforting, they were not enough to heal that wound.

"We should go. I don't want to be in the woods at night," I said, taking his hand and leading him behind me. Sparing a glance behind me, I saw the rug merchant give a weak smile and wave as we exited the side of his booth and headed back toward the opening in the ward around the market.

"You don't want to look around? There's nothing here that you want?" Killian asked, apparently surprised we were leaving already.

"It's not that I don't like the market..." I started.

"But you can't risk me being seen," he said with understanding. "That's fine for now, but someday we'll come back here, and I don't give a rat's ass who sees us." He smiled, and I let out a soft laugh.

"You must have high hopes for the views on half breeds and Hunters to change then," I mused.

"I have high hopes for *us*," Killian clarified with a genuine smile as we began walking again.

15
KILLIAN

As we approached the opening in the ward, I could see the younger guard from earlier peering at me again. There was something different about him, but I couldn't quite pinpoint what it was. He was young, but somehow felt much older. I supposed being a military guard member would do that to you, but something felt off about him.

Making sure my hood cast enough shadow over my face to obscure any identifying details, I trailed behind Kenna, pulling the cart and doing my damnedest to blend in. Kenna, to her credit, seemed less nervous this time around and smiled at the older guard once again.

"Aye, Kenna," he called to her. "I tried that salve on my knee when I took a break, and it has already helped. Your talents are unmatched."

"I'm glad it's working for you." She smiled. "Now that we know it works, you can buy more at the apothecary." She motioned back toward the stone structure.

"Oh, can't you spare a few more jars of it for this old bag of bones?"

She breathed out a small laugh. "Sal, I can't just give out all my products for free. How am I supposed to make a living?"

The older guard gave her a toothy grin. "Alright, then, little lady. Go on home, then. Just know I'll probably single-handedly fill your pockets with how much I'll be purchasing!" He chuckled. Kenna gave him a small mock salute and began walking forward again, motioning for me to follow.

"Yes, best be on your way, friends." The younger guard's voice slithered like a snake along my spine. "I wouldn't want you to fall prey to any monsters in those woods." He made eye contact with me and sneered as I passed, his intense stare raising my hackles. I felt the threat in his words, and my body responded, preparing to protect Kenna. Not that she needed much protection if she could fight me off like she did.

Recalling that I was supposed to blend in, I willed my muscles to relax and tipped my head before looking forward.

"Your friend's an odd one, Miss McCairn," said Sal as I passed. "Doesn't talk?"

"No, he doesn't." Kenna feigned sadness and looked back at me.

"Shame." Sal shook his head. "Be safe."

He motioned us through the ward gate, and we began the trek back toward the cottage. Risking a glance behind me, I saw the younger guard still staring in our direction despite Sal moving on to the following individual entering through the same gate we had just left. Again, I felt the intensity of his stare, but I was falling behind Kenna and pulled the cart along to catch up.

As we walked, Kenna pointed out the various plants along the sides of the path. Her memory was incredible, and I marveled at everything she recalled with ease. She knew the medicinal use of almost every plant we walked by. If it had no medicinal use, she knew whether it could be eaten or whether it could be used for more nefarious purposes. Her interest in poisons was fascinating yet terrifying and, oddly enough, a bit of a turn-on.

As the sun began to set, I heard the noises in the forest around us change. Kenna noticed the shift in my demeanor and looked out into the forest. She quickly pulled a couple of plums from her pocket and tossed them in the tree line.

"They've never bothered me, so I don't bother them. I guess it's somewhat of an understanding. I give them something every time I use the path in thanks for not eating me."

"What are they exactly?" I queried.

"I'm not sure, honestly. I haven't ever seen them fully. I see their eyes in the tree line sometimes. I've seen the shadow of a thing resembling a mountain more than a man, but I've never seen them fully. Like I said, I don't bother them, and they don't bother me." She shrugged.

"You saw the shadow of a mountain walking through your woods, and that doesn't bother you?" My eyebrows lifted in shock.

"Not my woods," she corrected. "I live in their woods, technically."

Shaking my head, I started walking again to follow her, scanning the surroundings consistently. The feeling of eyes on me intensified, and I was sure I was not interested in meeting a mountain. Considering Kenna's actions, I dug in my pockets and found a few stray nuts that had somehow remained. I set them along the side of the path. "Sorry, it's not much. Please don't eat me," I whispered into the woods before hurrying along behind Kenna.

LATER THAT EVENING, after returning to Kenna's cottage, we sat nestled on her bench together. I was perusing a book she had had on top of the stack, and she was writing in a small notebook. From what I could see, it appeared to be a collection of data from her trips to the market. When she finished checking off today's delivery, she turned to look at me. I could see the fatigue in her eyes, mixed with a hint of curiosity.

"What is it, love?"

"Will you tell me about the places you've been to? Is that okay to ask? I've just never been outside Cauldera. I mean, except for this part of the In-Between, that is. If you don't want to talk about it, that's fine. I want to know more about you, though," she chattered. I smiled at her. I knew she was worried she would bring up something painful, but I respected her desire to learn about me.

"That's fine, but you'll have to tell me about yourself sometime in exchange." I grinned. She wrinkled her nose but nodded. "What do you want to know?"

"Tell me about the territories you've been to," she said, setting the notebook down on another stack of books. She curled into my side as I draped an arm over her shoulders.

"You'll have to be a bit more specific, Kenna. I've been to all the territories on this continent—some I've seen willingly, and some not so much…" I trailed off, trying to keep myself on track and not get lost in my inner commentary, or in my less-than-pure thoughts about how close my hand was to her chest now.

"Tell me everything." She beamed. "If that's okay, that is," she added, lowering her eyes only to look up at me through her lashes.

Rubbing my free hand across my face, I sighed. "Where do I even start?" I mumbled. "Most of the continent is like Miridia. It's warm most of the year, and crops are grown year-round. There are only a couple of places that have different climates. Amaradia is much like Miridia, but there are only humans there. Although other creatures travel through there. They have a port along the coast, so quite a few travel there to leave this side of the continent."

"Doesn't Antharel have a port, too?"

"They do, but it's not a territory many would want to travel through. It's very rocky, and not much grows there. It's mostly mining, and the people and other beings there tend to be a bit…" My brows knit together as I tried to find the words to describe the occupants. "Well, they're a bit gruff. They don't take kindly to outsiders, so it's usually safer for people to go through the port in Amaradia."

Kenna's brows furrowed as she thought about this. "Why were you there then? Isn't that where the Blood Drinkers are from? It doesn't sound like a nice place."

"Oh, it's not. But I was contracted by a wealthy nobleman to 'remove a problem' in his mines." I sighed, the weight of my past suddenly weighing very heavily on me. Kenna took my hand and smoothed her fingers over my palm.

"You mean you killed him," she said softly.

"Yes," I breathed. "Does that scare you?"

She looked up at me with those bright green eyes. "No," she said assuredly. "Survival means doing things you normally wouldn't. I understand that."

"You're more forgiving of my past than I am." I looked down at her dainty hand in mine. "But I'm glad you feel safe with me."

"Of course. You can't kill me, or it'd kill you, too." She smirked.

Rolling my eyes, I continued to tell her about my travels. "You likely know the In-Between better than I do, so I'm going to skip over that, if you don't mind." She quirked an eyebrow at me but motioned for me to continue before sliding her hand along my thigh. I shivered under her touch and tried to focus, but I felt like I had the brain capacity of a squirrel every time this woman touched me. I cleared my throat and continued. "The Fae Realm is a unique place. It feels as if everything is aware of you there, and the strangest plants and animals are everywhere."

"Like what?"

"Like flowers with blinking eyes, rabbits with antlers, glowing grass, and frogs that talk." My fingers popped up as I counted off the flora and fauna I had encountered. "It's hard even to explain some of the things I've seen." I let out a disbelieving laugh. "That realm is so drenched in magic; anything is possible."

She stared up at me with wide eyes. "I'd love to see that," she breathed.

"I'd love to take you. It's only a day or so through the forest, but the King wants you dead, and as soon as you set foot on his land, he'll know. I can't protect you there," I said sadly. "I might be half-Fae, but he is entirely too powerful for me."

"That's alright." She patted my hand before she started tracing small shapes on my skin, lighting my nerves on fire. "What else is out there?"

"The Wildlands are full of marauders and exiled creatures. I haven't seen it, but there are rumors of a water dragon living in the lake at the base of the mountains."

Her eyes lit up, and she paused her movements. "That sounds incredible!"

"The Wildlands are too dangerous to be incredible, Kenna. It's even more terrifying than these woods. At least here, the things in the woods leave you be. The creatures there hunt humans, Fae, Witches, and even Hunters for sport. It's an aggressive, unrelenting land. Many beings living there take an 'eat or be eaten' approach to outsiders."

She scrunched her face up in disgust. "Alright. No Wildlands, then. Where else have you been?"

I smiled at her easy responses and unquenchable curiosity and felt her fingers start moving along the skin of my forearm again. "By far, the hottest place I have ever been to is the realm of Citri. It's wide open, save for the dunes and mountains along its border. The people there are very exclusive, and it's a very religious region, full of unique magic."

"What religion?"

"They worship the Goddess Leile," I answered.

Her eyes widened. "The Goddess of love and sex?"

"Yes. They call themselves the devoted. My time there was a bit awkward, as they don't wear much clothing, and it is considered sacred to engage in, shall we say, intimate activities—so it wasn't uncommon to be walking down the city streets and witness a couple in the throes of their passions. That's how they manifest their magic." I thought her eyes might pop out of her head, and I couldn't help but chuckle. "Don't worry, love, I only partook in one orgy, and my time with you topped every experience I had there. Leile would be proud."

She blushed and looked away before swinging her head back to look at me. "You took part in an orgy?" Her shocked voice rose in pitch.

"Just one," I teased. "It wasn't really my choice, but it allowed me to get close to the man I'd been hired to, uh, remove. His wife was not from Citri and never acclimated to the very free approach to love the region has."

"Killed. You can just say you killed him. I know what your job is, Killian."

"Out of everything I just told you, you pick up on my choice of words?" I laughed.

Her cheeks pinked, and she looked down at our hands. "I'm not going to ask you about the orgy, if that's what you're looking for."

"Why not? It was harmless and could inspire us," I said as I raised an eyebrow in challenge.

"Just tell me about the rest of the continent, Killian. I don't need to know how many women have had your cock in their various orifices." She grimaced.

"Don't worry. Your orifices are the only ones I want to stick my cock in for the rest of my life," I teased. "Seriously, I only want you."

"Good," she said in a matter-of-fact tone. "Have you been anywhere else?"

"The only other place I've been is the Hunter's Hovel, in the snowy mountains where I was born. Most Hunter families live there, but when the settlement found out my mother was having a half breed child, they exiled her as soon as I was born. She fled to the Fae Realm and then into the Wildlands and survived with me for a few years, but eventually died trying to get me to safer lands, or so I'm told.

"She made it through the In-Between and into Amaradia before she finally died of blood loss and poison from all the wounds the creatures we had encountered gave her. Another Hunter traveling the same path found me wandering as a small child. He raised me until I was a teen and my Fae magic manifested. Then he exiled me the same way my mother had been, and I learned to survive on my own from there on out." I paused, taking a deep breath. I wasn't fond of talking about this.

"I bounced from territory to territory until important people noticed my skills. So, now here I am, a Hunter with no home," I said flatly. I felt the anger boiling in my veins, but refused to show Kenna how much the betrayal of my people hurt me. She touched her fingers to my chin, turning my head toward her.

"Your eyes are lilac," she said, aware of the intensity of my emotions despite my best efforts. "No matter what you've been told or what has been said about you, you do have a home. Here, with me." She looked into my eyes with such care that my breath caught in my throat. Seeing my body tense, she pulled my face to hers and kissed me tenderly. "Thank you for telling me that. I can only imagine how hard that must have been." She placed another kiss on my jaw this time.

"Kenna…" Her name was a breath on my lips as my body

responded to her, and my heart did a funny little leap. Was this what it was like to feel loved?

She shushed me, pressing her fingers to my lips. "Let's go to bed, Killian," she said, dark, sensual heat swirling in her eyes. "Let me take your pain away for now." That was all the invitation I needed to sweep her into my arms and carry her to the bed, kicking the door shut behind me.

16
KILLIAN

The next few weeks flew by in a blur. We spent the mornings collecting herbs or foraging for food items, and the afternoons in Kenna's kitchen, where she taught me some of her more straightforward recipes for healing. Our nights were spent cuddling on the bench with Kenna's endless questions about my travels before eventually ending up in bed, wrapped in each other.

We spent time learning about each other. It wasn't all physical, although a lot of it certainly was. There were times when Kenna lay in my lap as we sat in the sun in her garden, and she read some of her old books to me. Other times, I showed her some of the talismans the Hunters used, and she teased me about it being broken magic.

Our days became a mix of the mundane sprinkled with our own brand of magic; something that teetered on the line of emotions I wasn't quite ready to name.

In these moments, I saw a side of Kenna I was sure she didn't readily share with others. The softer, sweeter, more vulnerable parts, and I, in turn, shared stories and memories with her that I didn't dare tell anyone else. A mutual trust and understanding settled over the start of a relationship I had never expected. I felt seen, wanted, and as if I finally belonged. It was comfortable, easy.

It all felt so normal that I often didn't know what to do with myself. I wasn't used to being present somewhere for so long. My skin crawled with the urge to leave, but my heart and soul cried out for Kenna at once at the thought.

The thought of the Fae King crept into my mind from time to time, and I worried he might appear to finish the job I'd been assigned. I vowed to myself that I would die before anything happened to her. If it meant she was safe, I would burn the world down for her, and in that moment, I began to realize how much she was starting to mean to me. Was this love?

Kenna always brought me back to the present in those moments, though. This tiny sanctuary she had created lulled me into a false sense of safety, one where love and passion flowed easily, and life seemed simpler and less dangerous.

Upon waking naked in bed with an also very naked Kenna draped over my body, I finally came to accept it was okay for me to belong somewhere. I was comfortable here and finally felt like I mattered to someone for reasons other than my ability to end lives. I lay there pondering that thought as Kenna began to stir.

"What time is it?" she croaked as she flipped her unruly red curls out of her face. She looked like she hadn't slept very well, but then again, we had stayed up half the night worshiping each other from head to toe.

"No idea," I said. "Does it matter? Market day is tomorrow, right?"

She nodded and put her head back on my chest, mumbling something in a sleepy voice.

"What was that?"

"I said, I don't think I can walk after our Citri reenactment last night," she groaned, and rolled off of me and onto her back. I chuckled.

"You weren't complaining last night when I bent you over and used that—" I was cut short when her hand smacked over my mouth.

"I told you that you were never allowed to talk about that again," she gritted. She had a slight blush on her cheeks.

"Are you embarrassed?"

"No! I…" She shook her head and looked away. With my thumb and forefinger, I gently tilted her face back to look at me.

"Never be ashamed or embarrassed for what makes you feel good, love. Never."

She smiled at me shyly before giving me a slight nod in acceptance.

Kenna inched her way to her side of the bed and slid out of the sheets. Her ass still had a red mark from the night before, and I could see the small love bite marking her shoulder from where I lay. My cock hardened, thinking of the intensity of the previous night.

"We need to go get vegetables for your omelet," she sighed, looking over her shoulder. Noticing the bruises on her shoulder, she looked at me again. "Get a little carried away?" She arched an eyebrow.

"Oh, no. Not nearly enough." I smirked. Kenna rolled her eyes at me before pulling on the undergarments she dug out of her dresser and dragging a tunic and leggings over them. I didn't move, couldn't move, as I watched her bend over to pull the leggings up. Memories of bending her over her dresser and sliding my cock as deep into her as I could flooded my mind. We had dented the wall with the edge of the dresser. I hadn't realized how hard I was fucking her until I noticed that detail. It was a wonder the small woman could move today.

"Get up, Killian," she demanded, throwing a pair of my discarded pants onto the bed.

"Or you could come back to bed." I raised an eyebrow. Her eyes flashed from their typical bright green to a vivid violet. She was recalling last night as well, based on her expression. She whined before shaking her head and walking toward the bedroom door.

I stood up, looking around the room we had destroyed. Items from her dresser were all over the floor, shoved aside when I had grown too impatient to wait for her to move them. Shaking my head, I pulled on my pants and a tunic, and picked up the trinkets.

After placing them back on her dresser, I worked the room, collecting dirty clothing to toss in the basket she had tucked into a corner. With each piece of clothing I picked up, memories of how they had been discarded ran through my head. I couldn't even count the number of times I had been inside her, tasted her, and felt her over the past couple of weeks.

I was abruptly snapped out of my thoughts when I heard Kenna screaming at the top of her lungs. I took off at a full run out of her bedroom and through the kitchen, and out the entry of the cottage, toward her garden. I didn't make it far before I stopped, wrapping a crying Kenna in my arms.

"Oh, love... I'm so sorry," I whispered. Rubbing her back, trying to console her, I looked over the top of her head toward her garden, where nothing was left standing. Her wisteria vines were smoking and releasing tiny embers into the wind. The garden was nothing but ashes. This had to be intentional, and part of me wondered if it was because I hadn't brought her in.

"It's gone... Everything... It's gone... My mother planted this and now..." She burst into fresh tears in my arms. Understanding washed over me. She was so protective of this space because it was the last thing, besides her cottage, that she had of her mother's. She must have been devastated, and I had no idea how to fix this. I wanted to take her pain away, but how did you fix a burnt garden? So much love had gone into it, like a second home for her.

"I know, love. I'm sorry." I smoothed her hair and squeezed

her tight. "I'm here. I'll find who did this. I'll make sure they suffer." I tightened my hold on her and continued rubbing her back while small sobs escaped her frame. She felt so fragile, so broken. All I wanted to do was put the pieces of her heart back together, but I had no idea where to start.

Scanning the property line, I hoped to catch a glimpse of or a clue about whoever had done this. There was a flash of silver, and then, two Fae warriors stepped out, one of whom looked eerily like the overly curious market guard.

"I see you received our message," one said while gesturing to Kenna's destroyed garden. I felt her tense, and she whirled on them before I could stop her. I knew the Fae and had worked for them before, so I was aware Kenna could not pierce their armor or match their magic, no matter how furious she was.

"Kenna! No!" I yelled, but it was too late. The wind whipped around us, and she began moving her hands in a circular motion. I wasn't sure what she was doing; she had no plants left to control. Suddenly, a dark amber-colored light began to grow in her palms. Oh shit, she was spell-crafting, pulling the embers to her, and was going to do something really stupid.

I tried to take a step toward her, but was met with a barrier that I bounced off. "What the hell? Kenna! Don't! They're stronger than they look!"

"You failed in your mission, Hunter. We knew you would not complete it when this one here—" the other Fae warrior motioned to the guard "—notified us of your interactions at the market. We will take it from here." His voice was cold and sent a chill down my spine. I tried again to push through the barrier they had placed before me. I tried to go around it, too, with absolutely no luck. I began to panic. If Kenna released her magic, they would deflect it back. Oh, Goddess, don't let her die. I need her...

17
KENNA

Anger ripped through me. The sight of Killian thrashing and banging against the warriors' barrier ripped open the dam. All of the pain, loss, and tragedy of not knowing my mother came pouring out. The anger that my father had been taken from me before I had had the chance even to know him surged through my veins. I shook with the rage coursing through me, and my vision began to darken. As my peripherals lost their sharpness, the heat in my hands grew.

Everything that was taken from me, everything I'd lost, everything Killian had said about the Fae King, just clicked. These bastards had killed my mother and father. Maybe not them specifically, but their kind had ordered it. I shuddered—*my* kind.

I felt my skin prickle, and the hairs on my neck stood as the tiny ember I had started began to grow. I allowed myself to pour all my pain and fury into this little ball of energy and nurture it.

This was the darker side of myself Mrs. Lancaster had always been fearful of. I remembered overhearing her tell one of the other coven leaders that my bloodline was dangerous because I could access other magics. I poured all my anger from that into the ember as well.

My hands felt like they were on fire, and I could hear Killian screaming my name, but my ears began to ring, and the wind whipping around me blocked out most of the noise. I felt like I was crawling out of my skin. My insides were churning, and my gut was wrenching. Never before had I felt this much fury.

I looked up at the two warriors before me. Their eyes were sparkling, and they laughed at me.

"Oh, how cute!" The one I thought I'd seen at the market gates nudged the other with his elbow. "She thinks she can take us!"

"Come now, Princess. You can't possibly think you have it in you to take us both out. After all, you are just a *half breed*," the other sneered. Laughing again, they leaned on each other and bent over in a fit.

Laughing. They were fucking laughing. The ember burst into flames in my hands, and I felt the wind increase around me. Ashes and burnt leaves whipped around me in a frenzy. The warriors swatted them away like small bugs.

"Are you quite done with your temper tantrum, little Witch?" the bigger one mused. "Don't forget your little Hunter is still trapped in my ward. I'd hate for something bad to happen to him..." He trailed off with a devilish grin. My eyes narrowed at the threat.

"Excuse me?" I managed to say through clenched teeth. "Did I hear you correctly?" I advanced toward the two bumbling fools, hearing Killian thrash and call my name once more. "You are of the Fae guard, are you not?" I asked, though I needed no answer. One tried to speak, but I interrupted him. "If you are indeed Fae guards, then you must be aware that your Fae King likely hired a hunter and had my mother murdered, among many others who didn't follow his purity decree." I moved closer. "Surely you know I was left to be raised by narrow-minded Witches who cannot see beyond their own noses." Another step forward. "And now, you threaten to take from me the one person who is not utter rubbish in my life?" I advanced again, balancing a ball of flames in one hand while gesturing animatedly. "Yes, I am aware he attempted to kill me, but let's be honest; he stood no chance." The warriors flinched slightly as my hand waved about.

I felt a darkness rising from deep within. "The moment we locked eyes, that bond the Fae so cherish took hold. And now, you wretched creatures have nowhere to hide. I am not certain who exactly killed my parents. I do not care. All I see are two Fae warriors with targets on their chests. It is time to pay for your fellow man's sins."

Something ripped free from me at that moment, and with a banshee cry, I released the ember from my palms. With a blinding light, it rocketed toward the warriors. Their shocked faces were priceless, and I had just enough time to smirk before realizing my ember was about to hit one hell of a reflecting ward.

"Shit." I spun on my heels and tried to run. I felt the scorched earth rumble beneath my feet, and a crack opened. I leaped forward to avoid tripping, but was caught by the ankle mid-air by what was left of one of my wisteria vines. My mother's wisteria vine… I hit the ground hard and felt the breath leave my lungs. When I tried to breathe, the burning sensation felt like my entire soul was on fire.

I had time to look up and see the desperation on Killian's face as he cried out my name. His fists were bloody from hitting the ward, and sweat poured from him.

"Kenna! Please! Run!" he cried. Before I could react, I felt the hot impact of the fire ember I had thrown. It had made its return trip and engulfed my body in a force so strong that whatever breath I had regained left me once again. I felt my bones creak and crack, and my skin felt like it was burning.

I collapsed into the ashes beneath me and looked up at Killian. A single tear escaped my eye and trickled down my cheek as I whispered, "I'm sorry…" and then the blackness consumed me.

Floating in the darkness, I was marginally aware of Killian's voice, but I couldn't see him. I couldn't see anything. My entire body felt like it was melting away, and my lungs burned. Was I dead? No, I couldn't be.

My eyes slowly opened as I felt my weight shift. Someone was picking me up. As my eyes adjusted, a splitting pain erupted from my skull. I was being tossed over the shoulder of one of the assholes who had attacked us. My heart sank. Where was Killian? I tilted my head up and tried to focus my fuzzy vision. In the distance, Killian was still banging on the spherical ward that surrounded him. My vision blurred again, and with the last bit of strength I had, I reached for him, but it was too late.

18

KILLIAN

Screaming her name, I watched the taller warrior toss Kenna over his shoulder like a rag doll. She had to be unconscious. Her hands were blackened where the fire had left her palms, and she looked so weak, so fragile.

I grabbed for the talisman I wore around my neck, preparing to teleport, but was met with pain that rocked through me like electric shocks. The barrier they'd created contained even the old Hunter's spells. Fuck.

With my last bit of strength, I summoned my energy and tried to break the ward surrounding me. Drawing the attention of the shorter warrior, he walked back toward me.

"It's almost too much fun watching your little bond destroy you," he snickered. "I'll sleep much better knowing your soul will tear itself in half with her absence." Ignoring his comment, I continued to slam my bloody fists on the barrier, calling Kenna's name.

"Kenna!" I screamed, my voice starting to break from the constant yelling. I couldn't help it. My heart ached for her.

"That won't help her now. She's out like a light." He grinned. "Not as much of a fighter as she thinks she is, now, is she?"

"Let her go. Take me." I turned to him. If they needed a prisoner to pay my debt, it shouldn't be Kenna. It couldn't be Kenna. I would never let them hurt her, regardless of what they did to me.

"Afraid it doesn't work that way, boy. You failed to complete your mission. The girl is supposed to be dead, and she isn't. So, our grand King Arrion requested we fix this mess you made. Watching you break into pieces while your bond is forcefully disconnected, thread by thread, is just an added gift," he said maliciously as he walked around the barrier trapping me.

I felt the fury inside me build. I refused to lie down and let this happen. Pulling on all the Fae magic I could muster, I made the ground under me begin to shake. I pushed and pulled the energy, trying to warp the ward enough to snap the fibers of the magic. It was no use, though; I was too weak.

I looked back at Kenna, where she lay limp, hanging over the warrior's shoulder. I thought of her words to me before the fireball had hit her. If anyone should have been apologizing, it was me. I couldn't protect her when she needed it most. I finally found someone who made me feel as if I belonged, and I couldn't save her.

"Nice try, half breed, but your magic is pitiful compared to ours. You can't even draw on the full range of your abilities. Too bad your father had low standards... Pathetic," he spat. I glared at him but didn't dignify his words with a response.

Kenna must have regained consciousness for a moment as I saw her lift her head a bit and reach her hand out. My heart broke seeing her so frail. Something snapped inside me, and I began trembling. As I looked up at Kenna, I could see her trembling, too.

"What the fuck?" The shorter warrior started to back away from me. Kenna's eyes snapped open, and she made eye contact with me. There was fear there, but also a deep-seated anger. She was feeling everything I was.

Suddenly, warmth rippled through my body. Looking into Kenna's eyes, I knew what she was doing. She was trying to give me some of her strength.

"No, Kenna! Goddess dammit! Don't waste your strength!"

She almost imperceptibly shook her head, as if she did not think this was a waste.

With a sudden burst of energy, I tried again. The warrior's eyes bulged, and the taller one stopped, looking over his shoulder to see the commotion. Both blanched as they saw the fabric of the ward tearing in two as I pried it open with my hands. I had never been able to do something like that. Kenna was a hell of a lot stronger than I had thought.

As I stepped through the now crumbling ward, I looked at Kenna. She had a tiny grin on her face, which was adorable, but she was slipping into unconsciousness again. I shook my head, snapping myself out of the random thoughts rolling in my head triggered by that cute smile on Kenna's face, and I refocused. Fueled by anger, I stepped toward the shorter warrior. Now, it was my turn.

Despite not having my bow and arrows, I was adept at combat. Whirling on my opponent, I threw out a blast of energy pulled from the ground around me at the shorter warrior, hitting him square in the chest. However, I hadn't accounted for his magical armor, which absorbed the energy.

"You'll have to do better than that, pretty boy," he sneered. My body tensed, and my adrenaline soared.

The taller warrior must have picked up on my change in posture because he unceremoniously dumped a limp Kenna to the ground. I was momentarily distracted, willing her to get up and run away, allowing the shorter one to sweep my feet out from under me.

I scrambled back a few feet before being able to stand again. Realizing I had one warrior on either side of me, I had to think quickly. They both began to advance on me. One had his hand on the hilt of his sword, and the shorter one already had his dagger drawn. I looked at them both, swiveling my head back and forth before giving them a mocking smile.

"Come on, then. I expected a more interesting fight from two of the king's men," I taunted. Any sane person probably wouldn't have done that, but I was losing my mind trying to save Kenna and didn't care what happened to me.

Both warriors sprang forward with agility, much like wild beasts. I used what little strength I had to teleport out of the way a short distance, hearing the Fae men clash and groan. They had expected to hit me and not each other. Grinning slightly, I realized my time was limited.

I shot over to Kenna, lifted her into my arms, my body relaxing at the contact, and started to formulate a plan. Where could we go? Who would help us? Who could heal her? That was a nasty burn...

As my mind raced, I didn't spot the two warriors coming up behind us. Kenna must have, though. Even in her semi-conscious state, her grip on my shirt tightened, and she whispered, "Don't let them take me. I won't survive."

My heart again broke at her words, and I knew all too well that she was right. I had failed my mission, assigned directly by the king, and now he was taking matters into his own hands. He wanted her dead and wasn't going to stop trying to kill her until he was successful.

"Shh, love. I'm here." I couldn't tell her I wouldn't let them hurt her or take her. I had already failed at that... I sure as hell wasn't going down without a fight, though. I squeezed her tightly to me and started to run. I had no idea where I would go, but I had to go somewhere. Unfortunately, I was a touch too late.

The hilt of the taller warrior's sword crashed into the back of my skull. The blow made me hit my knees. Not loosening my grip on Kenna, I tried to stand again. Another blow came, this time to the base of my skull. It would be a miracle if I made it out of this alive. I didn't care, though. I needed to keep Kenna alive.

I hit my knees again. This time, the shorter warrior held a dagger to the side of my neck and ripped the teleportation talisman from my throat. With surprising deftness, he tossed the talisman into the embers that marked what had once been Kenna's garden.

Shit. I wasn't getting up this time unless I wanted Kenna to watch me die, which I didn't. The taller warrior walked around before us and leveled a scrutinizing gaze at me. I didn't flinch.

"This bond of yours is unlike anything I have ever seen. Most would cry and scream as you did before, but she has remained calm and was able to transfer some of her gifts to you. How curious..." He looked at me as if I were an animal to study. I supposed to him, I was. After all, I was just a half breed. "If you're going to be that much trouble, I suppose the king wouldn't mind us gifting you to him as well, especially given your ability to share her gifts. He certainly wouldn't be upset at the idea of killing you himself." A frightening grin spread across his face as he lifted the arm with the dagger in it. Before I had time to react, he brought the pommel of the dagger down on the top of my skull, and the world went black.

19

KENNA

I awoke in a small, cell-like structure that looked as if it had been carved straight into stone. Upon closer inspection, that was precisely what it was. I was in a dungeon of some sort. Perfect. I slumped over. How backward was this place? My hands still felt on fire, and when I glanced down, they looked like I'd finger-painted with soot.

The normally always-present buzz of my magic was missing, and I felt weak. I assumed the drain was a side effect of the stupidly heroic amount of power I'd thrown around trying to keep myself—and Killian—alive. I sat bolt upright.

Killian.

I felt the panic rising within me. I had no idea where he was or if he was safe. I vaguely remembered him trying to save me, but my memory was fuzzy, and truth be told, I still wasn't thinking right. Usually, when I started panicking, my magic would take over and function as a protective mechanism. Now, though, I felt nothing except very, very alone.

The pain of loss in the pit of my stomach swelled. The ache in my body was one thing, but the agony of being away from Killian was a whole new sensation; as if my soul was being torn in half. I tried to summon my magic but felt a burning sensation run through my body instead of the familiar hum; a small, pained cry left my lips.

"Oh, good, you're awake."

I looked up at the sneering guard.

"Where's Killian?" I narrowed my eyes.

"Your bonded is alive, if that's what you're asking. Although I can't be sure for how long..." His words faded as he tapped his chin in contemplation.

"Excuse me? I asked you where he is," I said again.

"Not your concern, little one. You'll both meet your ends soon anyway." Despite his words and tone of voice, something else danced momentarily in his eyes, although I wasn't sure what.

"Tell me where he is!" I hissed. He stepped closer to the bars of the cell, his face colored with something akin to distaste.

"You do not make demands. You are a prisoner. If you keep acting like a self-righteous, important little wench, I won't have any problem adding to your injuries. Don't tempt me." His lips tensed into a straight line.

Charming, I thought sarcastically. Absolutely irresistible. I eyed the wedding band on his hand. "Give my sympathies to your wife. Or husband. Or, honestly, whoever's unlucky enough to deal with this sparkling personality on a daily basis."

He stared at me with an emotionless expression, but I thought just for a moment, I saw the hint of a smirk.

By usual standards, I was sure that many women would find him attractive. He appeared older, maybe middle-aged, but that was difficult to discern in the Fae as they lived such long lives. He had auburn, close-cropped hair and bright, violet eyes. Of course, he was a Fae warrior, genetically incapable of being ugly, but there was nothing particularly appealing about him to me.

"I'll be sure to mention it. She probably agrees with you," he said with a huff that sounded suspiciously like a laugh.

Yet again, despite assuming his insides must have been cold as ice, a flicker of something else passed across his carefully crafted exterior. Was that a concern? No, that couldn't be right. I shook my head slightly, as if I could rattle that thought out of my ear and make space for something more logical to enter my brain.

He looked at me one more time, almost sad, and started walking up the small staircase outside my cell. I felt like I was in solitary confinement. Hell, I probably was.

I huffed and slid down the wall of the cell, noting the glittery composition of the stone. I ran my fingertips along the smooth rock and felt what were probably once ridges and sharp edges that had since been smoothed over, and now appeared polished. I hadn't noticed before, but the stone was filled with veins of quartz. Beautiful. Efficient. Magic-proof. Of course it was.

"Well, shit," I murmured to myself. "Now what?" Knowing there was no way I could break through magically, I felt my usual spitfire attitude leave me, replaced by fear and shame. Why had I felt the need to fight back, even when Killian had told me explicitly not to? Because I was Goddess-awful stubborn and didn't listen to anyone. I glared at the wall as if it could reflect my irritation with myself back toward me. It wouldn't, but I felt better aiming my frustration at something.

I pulled my knees up to my chest and crossed my arms. Resting my head on my arms, I hoped Killian was safe. Horrible thoughts flashed through my mind. I shook my head. No, he would be alright, and I had to be alright. I would know if something awful had happened to him. The bond would be tearing me apart if it had. Then again, I wondered if the quartz blocked that, too.

My chest constricted and my heartbeat sped up. This was not the time to panic. Anxiety was not my norm, but the inability to feel the tether tying me to Killian awakened something fearful within me that I typically kept locked away, something I had learned long ago to hide. I took a deep breath and tried to settle my nerves. Killian and I would need each other to get out of this alive.

I stood up then, a newfound wave of resolve washing over me. I wondered if I could use my Earth-based magic or if the quartz would block that, too. It seemed logical that I should be able to manipulate a natural resource like I would a plant, water, or fire, but I had never tried. I steeled myself and attempted to pull energy from the room around me. Nothing; I felt absolutely nothing.

Before I could rally my resolve a second time and search for some energy thread I could grasp onto, the same guard reappeared.

"The king will see you now," he said. My gut wrenched.

"See me, or kill me?" I muttered, eyeing him warily.

"Depends on his mood, I suppose," he said nonchalantly, examining his fingers. "Now, be a good Witch and put your hands out so I can cuff you." He held out a pair of what looked like silver cuffs with quartz stones laid into the sides and a series of engravings designed to lock in magic. They might be considered a pair of pretty bangle bracelets if they weren't designed to be infuriating, keeping my magic out of reach.

I held my hands out, knowing I had no choice in my current predicament, but kept my eyes glued to his face, watching his every move. He slipped the cuffs on my wrists, and I heard the audible *click click click* of the bracelets as they tightened. At least they weren't linked, so my hands could move freely.

"There's a good little Witch. Follow me," he said, but his eyes held an undercurrent of wariness I couldn't quite place. It made my insides twist with anxiety, and a sense of unease settled over me.

He motioned impatiently for me to come with him. As I walked toward him, he gripped my arm like a vice and dragged me forward at a pace I wasn't prepared for. I stumbled and hit my shoulder on an outcrop on the wall. Pain shot through my arm and into my fingers. I hissed through the sensation, determined not to let the guard know how much that had hurt, not that he seemed to notice anyway.

I wasn't expecting to hear a similar hiss of pain as we walked up the stone steps and out of the underground dungeon.

"What in the bloody hell?" A velvety voice drifted from a darkened cell. Killian.

"Killian!" I called out without a thought. Pulling against the guard, I tried to rush to the cell but was immediately brought to my knees. The guard must have been paying more attention than I had realized. Tears filled my eyes as he dug his bony fingers into my shoulder joint, taking special care to press into the bruise that was no doubt forming. Killian hit his knees as well and let out an agonizing moan as he grabbed for his shoulder.

"What the bloody hell did they do to your shoulder, Kenna?" he said through the pain. I couldn't speak. I was in too much pain and shock to form the words. My body immediately felt the pull of the bond at full force. All I wanted was to be close to Killian.

"Aha," another guard outside Killian's cell said with a grin. "The bond has progressed. How convenient! The king will be intrigued by that." He gave us both a look that made my stomach threaten to empty its contents. Killian crawled closer to the bars of his cell.

"I'm fine. Just stay safe. We'll be alright," he said soothingly. I knew he was trying to help me calm my inner thoughts, but my mind was reeling.

"Killian... what if..."

"No, love. Don't start that. I know you're scared, I can feel it, but no matter what they do to us, we are always together. The bond ensures that. Don't you dare think otherwise." Despite his words, the bond betrayed his fear as well, and I felt it humming beneath my skin.

"I just found you, found someone to care for me as is. No conditions. No desire to change me. And my reward for that is a dungeon cell?" I scoffed to avoid crying as I recalled something Mrs. Lancaster had told me once. *The world rarely asks us what we want. You need to learn to be strong, Kenna. This world is an unforgiving place.* Her words echoed in my skull. The world might challenge me, challenge this bond, but I would never give up on Killian. I would be strong as Mrs. Lancaster had said, for Killian, if not for myself.

Killian looked at me then, the emotions from deep within shining through his beautiful gray eyes. "Don't focus on the things we can't predict. Focus on the love we have and the joy and comfort we get to return to when we're free, because we *will* be free. We'll have that again, love. I promise," he whispered.

"Ah, yes, the king will find this most amusing," the guard from my cell mused. He gripped my arm tightly again, causing a fresh wave of pain to run through my body. I didn't care so much for my own pain at this point; I was more horrified watching Killian's face contort with the effort to hide that he felt it, too.

The guard started to pull me away from the cell, but I struggled against him.

"No! Please! Just let me see him!" I pleaded. I must have been stronger than he thought, or squirmier, because I broke free from his iron grip long enough to reach the cell and touch my fingers to Killian's cheek. Killian leaned into the touch, and a soft calm washed over me. I imagine he felt it, too, as his face relaxed slightly. He slowly turned his head and kissed my fingertips lightly before grasping my hand. That simple touch made my stomach flutter.

"My heart is yours, Kenna. I cannot deny that now. Stay safe, and we will get out of this. Do as they say. I can't have you getting hurt anymore." A small smile played at the corner of his mouth.

I pressed my face through the bars and kissed him without a thought. "I am yours," I promised.

"Enough of that," the guard from my cell said dryly. "No

conjugal visits here." He started to drag me away toward the king. I knew I should be scared. I knew I should be struggling. Instead, I could only focus on the tingling on my lips left by Killian's kiss and the tiny spark of magic I had felt pass between us when we touched. Maybe we weren't doomed after all.

20
KILLIAN

When Kenna's lips touched mine, the pain I felt earlier not only left my body but was replaced with a jolt of something new, aside from the usual tightening of my trousers. She felt it, too, because her eyes lit up as the guard pulled her out of my reach. What I wouldn't give to rip that guard to pieces right now. Knowing Kenna was safe was one thing, but knowing she was on her way to see the king, who had just weeks ago ordered her death, was more than a disturbing thought. She meant so much to me that I couldn't fathom what life without her would be, if I could live at all.

Despite the fear in my heart, I found it challenging to focus on anything besides that spark of magic. It made absolutely no sense. They had trapped me in this cell, where I had no access to the natural resources I typically drew my Fae power from, and they had strapped a damn talisman to my wrist, which essentially rendered my Hunter half powerless to use any spells I could recall. Yet somehow, I could feel just the tiniest spark of magic buzzing through my body.

My mind was alive with questions, and I began to pace in my cell. The guard assigned to me chuckled.

"Oh, don't worry, Hunter. I doubt King Arrion will kill her right away." His chuckle gave way to full-on laughter. Anger pulsed through me, and I instinctively reached for my missing quiver. He laughed harder this time when he saw my movement, doubling over in amusement. I turned to look out the window, trying to ignore the obnoxious guard. It hadn't escaped my attention that he hadn't called me a half breed like the rest. I wondered if he knew.

Before I could ponder that thought too much, a tiny red spark had appeared in my hand where I had touched Kenna's. To my surprise, it snuffed itself out, but in some way, Kenna had potentially transferred her ability to create that spark to me, and with my mini jolt of magic from our kiss and the intensity of my anger, I was able to conjure the tiniest bit of one. Had that been intentional on her part? I had no idea, but it might come in handy if we could figure out how to access that spark more.

Again, my train of thought was broken by the obnoxious guard, who thought he was quite hilarious.

"You won't find any hope hiding over there, boy. No one has left these cells unless it's to die," he sneered before releasing what was probably akin to a giggle but sounded more like a cackle.

"Are you done?" I asked through gritted teeth. I was getting rather irked with his incessant carrying on.

"Why? Am I disturbing you?" he said, still laughing as he approached the cell bars. They might have taken my power, but they hadn't taken my strength or wits. I walked toward him, my eyes locked on his.

"Yes. You're exceedingly annoying." My efforts to egg him on were successful as he began to mock me. Before he could react, I grabbed the edge of his armor and pulled him hard against the bars, smashing his head on one of them. He hadn't thought he needed a helmet, so the impact was enough to knock him unconscious. I would relish the silence, even if it was just for a moment.

Having time to focus, I thought about the spark more. When I tried to conjure it again, nothing happened. I could still feel minor twinges of magic running through my body, but the spark would not form. Slamming my fist into the stone floor, I felt a slight pain in my hand and suddenly realized what I had done. Kenna would feel that, too.

Feeling guilty about my selfishness, I took a deep breath to try and calm my nerves. Kenna didn't need me to hurt her inadvertently; she had enough to deal with. I could only hope the guard was right and that Kenna would be alright.

Regardless, I knew I needed to figure out this spark in case we faced the worst-case scenario. Thinking back to when Kenna had used it and I had accidentally conjured it, I tried to find the common denominator. Suddenly, it dawned on me: anger. Anger fueled the energy needed to create this magical weapon.

Shock suddenly riddled my body as I realized how furious Kenna must have been to create the massive fireball she had when I had only created a spark with my rage. It was a wonder she hadn't burnt the whole forest down. Guilt flooded my system. I hadn't been able to comfort her when she needed me most. That realization was all it took.

Again, rage bloomed within me at the guards who had separated us. The pain of being separated when bonded was enough, but tearing me away from the woman I now loved when she needed me was an entirely different agony.

The tiny spark bloomed once again in my palm. However, before I could focus on it, my thoughts had finally registered. Did I love Kenna? I had told her my heart was hers, and that was true, but I hadn't said I loved her. Somehow, thinking about it made it that much more real. A warmth spread through me, and I knew it was true. I loved that little spitfire of a woman, and there was no going back now, no matter how strange this bond was.

To my surprise, the spark did not extinguish. Instead, it changed from a reddish-orange color to a pastel purple and began to pulse and grow. The more I allowed myself to accept that I loved Kenna, the more the spark grew into a purple, fiery orb of light. I closed my palm, snuffing it out before anyone could see.

The gears in my brain began to turn, and it became clear that love was also a triggering emotion for this new gift. I smiled to myself. Kenna had been furious when she attacked those guards, but had she felt love, too? Could it have been for me? The thought that my love for her might have been returned only served to feed the desire within my heart to get to her; the bond was growing stronger by the minute.

Ripped from the reverie of my thoughts, I abruptly felt a searing pain in my skull. Bringing my hands to my head and pressing into my temples, I let out a cry of pain, willing it to stop. Whatever they were doing to Kenna had her in absolute agony, and I felt every bit of it. Fury raced through my veins.

As quickly as it had come, it stopped, and when I looked down, the orb had reappeared in my hand. I was going to have to be careful. If a guard saw that, there was no limit to the talismans, charms, or other things they would use to stunt mine and Kenna's shared magic, or worse.

21
KENNA

Knowing I had no choice, I allowed the guard to drag me down a corridor toward an enormous, arched wooden doorway. Assuming the king was waiting behind that door, I summoned what courage I had left within myself and gritted my teeth. The guard who had so pleasantly dragged me from my cell gripped my arm tighter as the doors swung open.

"No funny business, little one," he whispered. He was close enough that I could feel his hot breath on my earlobe, and it sent a disgusted shiver down my spine.

"Back off," I spat at him as he pulled me through the door. A sharp pain ran through my hand but rapidly dissipated. I had little time to think about it before an unfamiliar voice drew my attention.

"Ah, my darling child," a large man said. I assumed he must be King Arrion from the large crystal and vine crown adorning his head, but his appearance wasn't quite what I had expected. I had anticipated an old man in white robes with long white hair and a scraggly beard for some reason. The man before me was hardly that.

He stood at 6'5", an average height for a Fae male, with short iridescent gray hair and a matching mustache, both meticulously groomed. His eyes were the same lilac color mine were when I harnessed my full Fae potential, and his skin was a very light creamy white color, lacking any sign of wrinkles or aging.

Instead of old robes, he wore a lilac-colored jacket and trousers, the only thing discerning them as Fae being the royal purple knot embroidery, which was no doubt magical, around the hem of his wrists. The sleeve clasps were also ancient knots and appeared to have gemstones inlaid, which I imagined also had some magical properties. He had a pastel purple dress tunic and a royal purple cravat to match his meticulously coordinated outfit, including polished brown leather shoes. He looked like a meticulously carved statue to match this Goddess-forsaken castle, not a decrepit old king.

At first, I was so surprised by his appearance I didn't say anything. However, my senses quickly returned, and what he had said to me finally registered.

"Darling child?" I asked suspiciously.

"Yes, of course! You are Kenna McCairn, are you not?" His smile was polished. Too polished.

"And if I am?" I narrowed my eyes at him.

"Darling girl, I understand your suspicions. It appears there has been a bit of miscommunication here." He motioned to a chair across from a small table. "Please sit with me so we might talk." With a flick of his wrist, the chair intended for me skittered back before he sat in the other one.

"I'd rather stand," I said coldly.

"Oh, come now, I know that dreadful Hunter told you all sorts of lies about me, but I promise I wouldn't hurt you." He smiled again, but it didn't feel right. His presence made my skin crawl. Suppressing a shiver, I shook my head.

"Killian wouldn't lie to me. He can't," I said resolutely. I knew the bond prevented Killian from telling me anything but the absolute truth.

"Yes, that is true. You're a smart girl. The Fae bond creates absolute honesty between partners. What a shame your soul partnered you with such a... well, an unworthy match." He shuddered. "But he would only know what he is told. If he was misinformed, then he wouldn't know any better. Yet another problem with the inferiors..." He trailed off.

"If you're referring to the fact that he's a half breed, you must have forgotten I'm a half breed, too. Doesn't that make you shudder in disgust? Or is there some other reason you detest him?" I raised an eyebrow at him, standing taller.

"You're an observant little thing, too, like your father. The cheekiness you must get from your mother, but that can be fixed. My gut wrenched as he mentioned my parents. How did he know them? The more he spoke, the more he disgusted me. "No matter. Sit, and let's discuss this like adults." He gestured toward the chair again.

"You didn't answer my question. Why are you so disgusted by Killian but not by me?" I glared at him in a challenge.

"Girl, you will learn to respect your elders soon enough, but I will try my best to be patient. Sit. Down." His previously inviting smile was gone, replaced with a menacing sneer.

"Not until you answer me." I crossed my arms defiantly. King Arrion's face twisted with what I assumed was fury as he raised his right hand toward me.

"You will sit, or I will make you," he growled. I stood still, making no effort to move toward the chair.

"I gave you my terms." As soon as the words left my mouth, a searing pain shot through my head, and I hit my knees. I brought my hands to my temples, trying to press away the pain, but all I managed to do was let out a cry of anguish. Through my blurred vision, I could see Arrion standing over me, his right hand angled in my direction. There was no doubt he was doing this to me. Instantly, the realization hit me that this wasn't just affecting me. I was in absolute agony, which meant Killian was, too. "I'll sit!" I cried out in pain.

As quickly as it came, the searing pain subsided, and my vision cleared. The guard who had brought me to the king came to my side and wrenched my previously damaged arm, forcefully lifting me to the chair.

"I said, no funny business," he growled in my ear. I shot him a glare but said nothing. I turned my attention to Arrion.

"I'm sitting in your damn chair. Will you answer my question now?" I hissed, the pain from my shoulder still throbbing.

"You're very persistent. Fine. The Hunter is created from Fae blood, but his Fae blood was corrupted by a, shall we say, lesser type of being, the Hunters. He is not fit to mix with our kind." He smiled at me again and leaned on the table nonchalantly. "You see, the Fae are superior to other beings, and we simply cannot have these mixed abominations ruining our bloodlines and diluting our gifts," he said while he examined his nails.

"What makes me any less of an abomination?" I asked through gritted teeth. This was something I had heard a multitude of times. Each "pure" bloodline thought they were superior, whether it was Witches, Fae, Hunters, humans, Blood Drinkers, you name it. Everyone was better than everyone else, leaving people like me and Killian at the bottom, just waiting to be stomped because our parents had fallen in love with different people. It infuriated me.

"Oh, now that is an interesting story." He grinned as he looked at me. Something was menacing behind the grin that made me squirm. "You see, my son had a penchant for love affairs, and he had quite a few here in the Fae kingdom. He enjoyed so many women, I think he got bored with the selection here!" He waggled his eyebrows. It was incredibly disturbing, and my stomach churned.

"And what the fuck does your son's whoring have to do with me?" I ground out.

"Oh, my dear, please watch your language! That is no way for a princess to talk."

"A... what?" I looked at him, puzzled.

He resumed examining his nails as he started talking. "You, my child, are the product of my son's 'whoring,' as you put it. You're a Fae princess and, quite frankly, I would expect better manners from my granddaughter." He looked up from his nails and gave a condescending grin. "Welcome home, child. We have much to discuss."

22
KENNA

My jaw slackened at the information presented. Regaining my senses, I shook my head slightly and looked him in the eye.

"I'm not your princess, and I don't care who you say you are to me; I chose my own family," I said through gritted teeth. King Arrion grinned.

"Yes, I expected you to be difficult. From what my warriors said of your mother, she was much the same. I'm still not sure what my son saw in the Witch…." He trailed off again, rubbing his chin in thought.

"You will not speak of my mother!" I yelled, my voice echoing in the large chamber.

"I will speak of whomever I like," he chided. "You can either accept your status and learn to be a well-mannered Fae princess, or I will force the behavior into you. Need I remind you that your beloved Hunter will suffer whatever pain you bring upon yourself…" He raised an eyebrow at me and grinned in challenge. "Although the only reason he is still alive at this point is that it would likely kill you if we killed him. Your bond progressed at a disturbingly fast rate, and now, I fear we're stuck with the parasite. You are far too young to withstand a bond loss." He grimaced, as if speaking about Killian caused him pain.

"If you want me to play your game, I suggest you don't speak about Killian that way," I said as I leaned forward toward him.

"It is not a game, Princess. This is your life now, and I suggest you start thinking about what you say before you say it." He stood from his chair. "Now, are you quite done? I have much to tell you." He gave me a condescending glare. I leaned back in my chair, crossing my arms. "Good girl. Now, I have lived for quite a long time, and I would like to think about stepping back from the day-to-day duties of a king. However, I don't have an heir anymore since your blasted father had to go off and die defending your mother from his men…"

Shocked by his admission, my mind began to reel. No one had been there when my mother had died, so no one had known exactly what had happened. Most assumed my father was dead, but his death, nor the manner in which it happened, was ever truly known. My own grandfather had confirmed both of my parents were killed in a battle against the royal Fae guards, and the part that disturbed me the most was that he seemed to be more upset that my father had cared enough for my mother to protect her rather than the fact that he was dead.

"Anyway, all that silliness aside, there must be an heir to the Fae throne. It can't be just you, of course. You're a half-breed… even if you are from a royal line, and quite powerful. The guards told me about your fireball. Unfortunately, it's not enough." I rolled my eyes and huffed. It was as if having the abilities of two powerful beings somehow made me less than him. "You must marry a full-blood Fae at once and create offspring. Of course, that will surely require some convincing. Who would want to mate with a half breed?" King Arrion let out a loud chuckle before continuing. "That will at least begin to purify the bloodline again. Honestly, I'd rather have my bloodline to rule, even with your tainted blood, than allow some inferior creature to control the realm and ruin Amabel's dreams for this land. Your husband can rule on your behalf, as he will most certainly be easier for the Fae kingdom to follow. That will return things to how they should be. Controlled. Orderly," he ranted as he paced back and forth, flailing his hands about. I wasn't sure who Amabel was, but clearly, someone important to the king. "I'm sorry, my dear, but they just will not follow a lesser being," he said dismissively as he looked at me in what I assumed was his attempt at an apologetic expression. "We'll start the introductions tomorrow and see who might be willing to ensure a purer bloodline going forward. Think of it as a fun match-making event!" He clapped his hands with clear glee as he prattled on.

"I'm sorry. You want me to do what?" I looked up incredulously. "I refuse to just fuck some Fae and make you a great-grandchild so you can pretend to retire!"

"Watch your language, girl!" he said sternly, his voice booming through the chamber. "You *will* do as I say, and you *will* make an effort to smile and look the part!" Even my cell guard looked disturbed by Arrion's demands, but did his best to hide his disgust. Not before I noticed, however.

"No," I said. "I am not your property, and I will choose who has access to my body. This isn't the Old World. Grandfather or not, you don't get to control me," I spat out.

"Oh yes, my dear, I do." The king turned and walked toward me. "And since you are so horridly stubborn, I think I'll leave you in your little cell one more night to see if that changes your mind a bit. You know I do not know what my guards do down there, don't you?" he said with a snide grin. I knew he was trying to scare me, hinting that the guards would take advantage of me, and I would have no one to protect me.

"I'll take my chances, *Grandfather*," I hissed. He raised an eyebrow but said nothing more. He motioned for my guard to come forward.

"Take her back, Laurel. I can't deal with her insolence anymore." He waved a hand dismissively.

"It was lovely to meet you, Grandfather," I said sarcastically as Laurel gripped my arm. It somehow seemed less aggressive this time.

"Don't push him, Princess. He is no longer known for being kind," Laurel chided.

Laurel led me back down the corridor toward the stairs into the dungeons. His grip on my arm loosened a bit.

"So, your name is Laurel?" I asked.

"Yes, like the tree," he said as he led me further down the hall.

"I saw your reaction to his demands. You don't like what he's doing, do you?" I asked in a whisper. If this guard was going to be on my side in any way, I didn't want to get him in trouble.

"I will not speak ill of my King, Princess," he said quietly, but I could hear a hint of sadness in his voice. "Do not worry, though. I will not let anyone hurt you, even if he all but invited them to," he whispered. I stopped suddenly then, whirling toward him in surprise.

"Why?"

"No one deserves that. Especially not our princess," Laurel said. "You are also the only one who stands up to him, and I find it quite amusing. It would be very boring around here again if anything were to happen to you. And my wife would probably be quite cross with me." He smiled.

"I appreciate that," I sighed as we began walking again, feeling a bit more relaxed, knowing that even if he wasn't exactly a friend, he might become an ally.

"Would you like to see him, Princess?" he asked softly.

"Killian?" I whispered. "You would do that? Didn't your friend say 'no conjugal visits' earlier?" I stared at him in surprise.

"I am bonded, Princess. I know how painful it would be to be away from my wife for long. I do not wish that on you."

"Thank you," I said, still surprised. "How do you manage it?"

"Hmm?" Laurel looked at me, confused.

"How do you come here and work and not feel the ache?"

"Oh. I am not trapped inside a quartz cell, Princess. Did you not notice I don't spend time inside the alcove? It is easier on you out here, isn't it? You can feel his soul more easily when outside the barrier, right?" I nodded. "That is the difference. I am free out here and can sense my wife. You are confined, and the bond is strained by the barrier. Without the barrier, being in different places is not uncomfortable," he explained.

"Why are you being nice to me now?" I asked, a bit suspicious. "Before, you dug your fingers right into my injury, and even in Arrion's chambers, you wrenched on my arm…" We had reached the end of the hall, and he stopped at the top of the stairs.

"I am sorry about that. I could not let the other guards see me treat you differently from any other prisoner. I hope that I can prove that is not my normal behavior toward a woman, or anyone for that matter," he said solemnly and turned, guiding me down the stairs. I took in what he had said and realized that even when he had pulled me away from Killian, he had seemed to do this more out of requirement rather than a desire to do so. Yet again, I wondered if Laurel might be an ally I could count on.

23
KILLIAN

The guard I had knocked out earlier was still snoring like a drunken bear on the floor beside my cell when the door to the dungeon area opened again. I moved to the cell door as I heard footsteps, hoping it would be Kenna. I pressed myself to the bars to see if she was all right, and because the sight of her beautiful face simply made me happy.

Kenna and her cell guard came around the corner of the hall, her face instantly lighting up when she saw me, and just like that, my heart stopped doing whatever panicked rhythm it had been in. She was safe. Mostly. And still absolutely stunning, despite the silver cuffs and clear exhaustion.

She smiled, and I felt a wave of relief crash over me. Her guard looked at the one I had knocked unconscious and raised an eyebrow before letting out a quiet chuckle. Kenna looked more surprised than I would have liked.

"What? I'm not useless," I said defensively. She shook her head and walked away from the guard. He didn't move to stop her; instead, he moved between the unconscious guard and my cell door, effectively blocking him should he wake up. I raised an eyebrow.

"What?" she said, mocking me. "He's sort of an ally, I believe," she added. Her guard nodded once, showing his agreement with her statement. I stared at her in shock.

"What exactly happened up there?" I chuckled. A flash of darkness crossed her face, but she did her best to hide it as she slid her small hands through the bars of my cell, taking mine in her grasp.

"Oh, well, you see, my grandfather insisted that I wed some unknown Fae male and produce offspring to preserve the royal lineage, and when I refused, he used magic to cause me rather intense pain... Just usual family nonsense. Nothing important." She looked down at the ground.

"You—he—what? Are you alright?" I was so confused, but I guess that was where the searing pain in my skull had come from. I looked between Kenna and the guard. The guard just shrugged. Kenna let go of my hands and reached for my face.

"I'm fine. Listen to me," she said soothingly. "This changes nothing." She stroked my cheek with her thumb.

"Okay, that's wonderful, and I'm glad nothing between us is changing, but what is 'this'?"

She looked down again. "The king is my grandfather..." She trailed off. I was speechless. Such a simple sentence just derailed every single thing I thought I knew. My Kenna, my sweet, wonderful, earthy Kenna was a princess?

"But he wanted you dead..." I said, narrowing my eyes.

"Yes, he says you were misinformed." Her face twisted in disgust. "But I don't believe a word out of that insufferable man's mouth. Something wasn't right about him," she gritted out. Her guard chuckled. I placed my hands over hers before speaking my next words.

"Kenna, I know what I was told, love. It wasn't by some nobody. He hired me himself." I looked her in the eyes. I knew she was aware I couldn't lie to her, nor would I lie to her, especially about this.

"He... hired you... himself?" she whispered. I could see the gears turning in her head. She was having difficulty processing what I had just told her, but she couldn't deny that our bond meant she could trust me.

"Yes, love. I'm so sorry." I looked down. Slowly, she guided my head level with hers and pressed her face through the bars to kiss me lightly, a spark of magic passing between us. It appeared that would be a thing every time we kissed now, not that I was complaining.

"Don't ever be sorry for telling me the truth. You're the only one I can trust. Something must have changed between now and when he hired you," she said quietly. A small smile pulled at my lips before I kissed her lightly.

"What about your guard?" I teased.

"Laurel? He's nice enough, but I'm bound to you, not him. I'm also assuming his wife likely wouldn't appreciate that." Kenna giggled. I rolled my eyes at her.

"Glad I don't have competition." I brushed her cheek with my fingertips.

"Never," she said, smiling. "Of course, I have to play along and be matched with some Fae, but I promise they won't hold a candle to you."

"What?" I shook my head, still horribly confused by this entire situation. "I still can't fully grasp that you're a princess..." I whispered.

"I know. It's a lot to take in at once. I'm still overwhelmed by it myself..."

"And the matchmaking?" I asked.

"My lovely grandfather has taken the liberty of finding Fae males 'willing to purify the bloodline.'" I was stunned into silence and genuinely had no idea what to say. Kenna could see the distress on my face and reached between the bars, holding my hands tightly. "No one compares to you, Killian. We are bonded, and I fully accept that."

"I know that, Kenna, but you have to understand how utterly insane this is to me. I can't even imagine how you must be feeling, but to find out my bonded is a princess and is to be married off to someone other than me... I... I don't know what to do with that. What am I supposed to say?" I said, my voice tinged with pain and confusion.

"Killian, I promise you, no matter what title they give me, I am still just Kenna. I don't care about status or lineage. I care about living my life the way I want with the man I want," she said softly.

"I know that, love, but you're a princess and I'm a nobody..."

"And we both know that is nonsense. You are not nobody. You are my bonded, whether my ridiculous grandfather likes it or not," she said resolutely. I took in her words and tried my best to compartmentalize the information as I looked into her eyes. I saw nothing but sincerity there, which did ease my fears a bit, but my mind was still a whirlwind of chaotic thoughts and emotions. I had become painfully aware of my attachment to her in the previous days. She was the first person to ever make me feel as if I belonged somewhere, and yet, here I was again, feeling like an interloper.

Behind her, Laurel, the guard, cleared his throat. "I said I would let you see him. I can't let you stay here too long. We need to go, Princess," he said.

"Princess?" I grinned, trying to hide my inner turmoil.

"Yes, Princess Kenna, at your service." She pulled away from me briefly and made a dramatic sweeping motion. I chuckled.

"Well, Princess Kenna, can I tell you something before you go?" I reached through the bars again, cupping her face in my hands.

"Of course." She looked concerned.

"I love you," I said resolutely.

She stilled for a moment before a smile spread across her face. "I love you, too," she said before kissing me.

"Time to go, Princess," Laurel said softly. I got the impression that he did want to help her. He seemed to genuinely care that she had wanted to see me and was surprisingly patient with us. Before she could move away, though, I pulled her close.

"Do you trust him?" I nodded toward Laurel.

"To some degree. His aura seems stable. Why?" Kenna said, cocking her head to the side in question. Deciding now was the best time and probably the only time to ask her, I looked into her bright green eyes.

"Do you feel it when we touch? The energy transfer?" I whispered, not sure who we could trust.

"Yes," she whispered back. "It's magic." Her eyes sparkled as she said it.

"I made a fire orb," I whispered. I sounded like a child, but I was so excited I had to tell her. She looked at me in surprise.

"You did?" she asked.

"Yes, I think it's triggered by anger," I whispered. "And love," I added before I kissed her, slower this time.

"Be careful," she warned after breaking the kiss.

"You too, love," I said as she stepped away from the bars. Watching her walk away was painful, but knowing she had Laurel to keep her safe helped a little. Laurel turned to me before they reached the small steps leading to her solitary cell.

"I'll keep her safe," he said and nodded once before ushering her into her cell. A small smile crept across my face, and I shook my head. Kenna clearly wouldn't have trouble making allies. I turned and sank down the wall of my cell, the smile and the taste of her lingering on my lips. Kenna would be okay for now, but getting out of this place needed to happen sooner rather than later.

Between the sound of the snoring guard next to me and the thoughts racing around my head, I fell into a fitful sleep. Dreams and nightmares collided as the darkness of the dungeon overtook me.

As I awoke and sat up in the damp, cold cell, the flickering torches casting eerie shadows on the walls, I couldn't help but feel a surge of desperation welling up inside me. Kenna was out there navigating this nightmare alone. I was grateful she had Laurel, but felt powerless nonetheless from my cell. I needed to do something.

There had to be a way to get us out of here. Memories of simple moments with Kenna— making dinner, pulling weeds for her, watching her read at night— flashed through my mind. I refused to give up those moments made of pure magic.

Emotions grappled within me. On one hand, there was fear. Fear of losing the only person who didn't judge me, who made me feel safe, a concept I was entirely unfamiliar with. On the other hand, anger that they had taken her from me so soon into the burgeoning relationship we had just established. This could not be our end.

My mind raced as I thought of a plan. The prisoner in the neighboring cell, a man named Callum, was set to be released tomorrow. We had spoken briefly, and I found he was a man of the people, respected by many in the kingdom, and was only in the dungeons after stealing bread to try to feed his family. If I could just convince him to rally support for Kenna, perhaps there was still hope.

"Callum," I called out softly through the wall that separated us. "I need your help."

Callum turned to look at me. He arched an eyebrow, clearly unsure of me. "And what could you possibly want from me, Hunter?"

I crawled to the cell wall we shared and whispered through the gap in the stonework, pouring all my conviction into my words. "Kenna needs your help, Callum. The king seeks to use her to reestablish purity in the Fae bloodline. You know better than most that he is a tyrant with vicious tendencies and black as night morals. He will not hesitate to kill her, especially if she could be the salvation of this realm. She is not like him. She is kind and forgiving, a healer, and someone who could restore peace to the Fae realm. She would bring back safety to your people, your family. She needs the support of the Fae, though. She cannot do this alone. You have the influence, the voice that can sway the hearts of many. Please, you have to do this for her."

Callum studied me for a moment; his expression was unreadable. "And should she fail, we all die."

I pressed myself tightly against the stone, my eyes meeting his with unwavering determination. "We will die if we do nothing."

Callum's gaze shifted to the floor as he considered my words. "I will consider your plea, Killian. But know this; if I choose to help, it is for the sake of the realm and its people, not you, Hunter."

I nodded gratefully, understanding his stance. "That is all I ask, Callum. You have the power to change history. I trust you will choose the right side."

As the torches flickered and cast dancing shadows across the dank dungeon walls, Callum retreated to the corner of his cell. I could only hope that my words had struck a chord within him, that he would see the importance of standing by Kenna in her time of need.

24
KENNA

Despite the king's promise I'd meet the men he had convinced to take on the burden of my impure bloodline, I sat in my cell for three days, utterly bored. Laurel would periodically allow me to visit Killian, but that was rare. There seemed to be more of a guard presence, and I assumed this was why he was not allowing me to see him more often.

The sadness and emptiness that filled my soul were horrific. Each time I was allowed to see Killian, the feeling subsided but returned immediately upon my entrance to the cell. What hurt me most was that I knew Killian must feel the same. The idea of causing him this kind of discomfort was worse than any physical pain I could imagine.

"I'm sorry, Princess. I know this is painful," Laurel whispered through my cell door.

"Laurel, what is going on?"

"News of your unjust imprisonment has spread like wildfire among the common Fae, and they are not pleased with the king's treatment of you. In response, he bolstered the guard presence in the dungeons, a feeble attempt to quell the growing unrest." He shook his head, his voice heavy with sadness.

"What? The common Fae? Why do they care?" The sounds of the common Fae conversing and milling about in the courtyard outside my window began to echo off the cell walls and the dungeon around me.

"Free the princess!" a growing crowd yelled out. I whipped my head around and stared at Laurel in shock.

"There is much more unrest than the King allows the rest of the continent to believe. It is beginning to look increasingly like having you as his figurehead is his last attempt to remain in control of the Fae realm," he said in a hushed tone.

My mind reeled. Why would the common Fae try to get to me, and what could they possibly think I could do for them?

"The night you met with Arrion, a prisoner was released. He had stolen from a local shopkeeper and was only being held temporarily until his family could pay the reparations. Your Hunter makes friends quickly." Laurel smiled at me.

I could barely see out the small, high-set window of my cell. The window was at ground level, confirming that I was technically underground. I could see the feet of what appeared to be a significant number of people stomping in time with the chant. Laurel looked at me and grinned.

"Your people." He gestured with a flourish. I laughed at the absurdity of it all and turned back to Laurel.

"It'd be great if I could see more than their feet. Feet don't do it for me," I sighed tiredly. I felt so helpless in this asinine cell. "What will happen to them? Arrion doesn't strike me as the most understanding ruler. Will he hurt them?"

"I wish I could predict his behaviors, Princess, but he has a mind that makes sense only to himself. I hope he will dispatch guards to dispel the crowd, and there will only be minor injuries." He grimaced. "But I cannot be sure."

Worry settled over me for the people in the courtyard. Despite being thrown into this role with no pretense, I felt responsible for them.

As I thought about how I might try to get the attention of someone outside, a pair of large, dirty, brown leather boots walked into view of the underground window. His voice boomed out loudly above the din of the crowd.

"Go home or be killed!" The sound echoed off the walls of the courtyard as the crowd was silenced.

"Screw you!" someone yelled from a ways away.

"Damnit," Laurel groaned. Before I could respond, the big boots moved surprisingly fast away from the window. I could no longer see them, but I heard the cracking sound, a thud, and a gasp spreading through the crowd. A woman's wailing began to echo around my cell.

"Anyone else?" the man with the dirty boots yelled. "Anyone else like to be made an example of?" The wailing continued, and my head began to throb.

"What is happening, Laurel? He just killed him, didn't he?" I whispered, holding back the sob threatening to break free. I could hear the frantic footfalls of the crowd trying to flee the courtyard. The woman's wailing continued, reverberating inside my skull.

"Yes, Princess, I believe he did," he said sadly. "The captain of the royal guard is not known for being kind or patient, and often does the king's dirty work."

A tear slipped down my cheek. This had happened because of me. That man had died because of me.

"Lives will be lost, Princess. War comes at a cost."

"What war?" I locked my gaze on Laurel's.

"If you think this unrest will not spark a war, you are naive." His face was solemn but not unkind. I nodded, knowing he was right. Wars happened, often for more menial reasons. If war did occur, based on my interactions with the king, it would be warranted on behalf of the common Fae and any other territories he trampled on.

My heart ached for the man who had died and the woman

screaming for him. It was likely he was bonded, and this woman was experiencing the pain of a part of her soul dying with him. I prayed to the Goddess that she would survive.

Heavy footfalls echoed outside the cell. Polished leather shoes confidently strode across my view. Arrion.

"That's enough of that nonsense." His cold voice snaked through my ears. "Jolan. Deal with that drivel." The sound of another snap was heard a second later, and then a subsequent, slightly quieter thud was heard immediately after. "Thank you, Jolan. Now, as for the rest of you. You can leave peacefully, or Jolan will happily dispatch anyone else who feels the need to disturb my peace and quiet," Arrion said dismissively to the crowd.

I gasped. Arrion had used Jolan as a weapon and had just killed the woman because her cries of pain inconvenienced him. The reality of how dangerous this predicament was finally settled in. My eyes widened, and I whipped my head toward the cell door where Laurel stood, looking as shocked as I felt.

I slid down the cell wall and sat on the floor, a hollowness entering my bones. Neither of us said a word; there was nothing to say. Silently, I prayed that the souls of those two bonded Fae would find each other in the afterlife and that their love could carry on in death.

The commotion outside my window subsided, and the dirty boots followed behind Arrion's polished shoes as they strode back into the castle. My stomach churned in disgust. He truly was a nightmare come to life. He possessed so little compassion or understanding that I wondered if he had become more demon than Fae.

I heard Laurel opening the lock to my door, but I made no effort to stand or move. He kneeled before me and looked into my eyes.

"Princess, you cannot give up. Those people need you, and so does that Hunter. You will not be trapped forever; when the time comes, you must be ready to burn the world down. You cannot do that if you extinguish your flame," he said stoically.

"They died because of me," I whispered.

"They died because they wanted something better. Don't let their deaths be in vain."

"How am I supposed to do anything?" I felt the anger that all of this had been placed on my shoulders well within me. "Until a few days ago, I was a half breed healer living in the woods. Tell me how I'm supposed to cure this realm of the disease my grandfather has spread," I spat. "Tell me!"

Laurel did not flinch. He looked into my eyes and calmly said, "I think it was your reputation as a healer that caught his attention. Regardless of being a half breed, you bring something to the realm that might calm the people. Something we haven't had for a very long time." He paused. "Be the spark that lights the flame and sets this wretched place ablaze. The phoenix does not dull its flames to appease others."

As his words sank in, I felt a small buzz in my hands—my magic. I looked down to see a small ember in my palm. It glowed for a few seconds and heard Laurel chuckle before I smothered it and looked at him.

"It appears even those cuffs won't hold you forever."

"I need to see Killian," I said firmly. I needed to feel the strength of the bond. Laurel smiled knowingly.

"Get up then, Princess," he said as he offered me a hand. "Two phoenixes are better than one."

Laurel led me up the stairs and down the hall to Killian's cell. His guard groaned as we came around the corner.

"Laurel, you've gone too soft. They're prisoners. We're supposed to make them suffer," he ground out. Laurel ignored him.

Killian was curled into a ball on the floor, sleeping. His slow breaths came evenly.

"Killian," I whispered. "Killian, wake up."

A small snort left his nose before he stretched and rolled over. "Does this cell come with food delivery? I'm famished." He grinned at his guard. He had not noticed me yet.

"Fuck off," the guard grumbled, crossing his arms across his chest.

"What a wonderful way to wake up," he said sarcastically. I giggled, and he sat up immediately with a grin. "Hello, love. What a lovely surprise."

I smiled at him and stepped up to the bars. Killian got to his feet and came to stand before me.

"Hello," was all I could muster. I was still reeling from the deaths but buzzing from Laurel's speech.

"That's all I get? Hello?" Killian pressed a hand to his chest dramatically as if I had offended him in the worst way possible.

"Sorry, I'm a bit overwhelmed," I said.

"What happened?" His forehead creased with worry.

"I'm fine," I reassured him. "There was just a protest outside my cell, and well..." I trailed off, not knowing how to explain.

"Oh, you saw those two imbeciles get killed, aye?" said the guard. "Most women can't handle death. Too fragile they are." He chuckled to himself.

Ignoring him, Killian grasped my hands and squeezed them. "I'm sorry, love. A protest for what?"

"Me," I said plainly. Killian's guard scoffed, and Laurel gave him an icy look. Killian grinned.

"The cheeky bastard did it!"

"Who did what?" I asked, surprised by his response.

Killian lowered his voice to a whisper before explaining, "There was another man on the other side of that wall when we first arrived. We talked through the gaps. I told him about you. He said he would consider telling the other commoners and maybe collect enough supporters to get the word out that you were trapped in here."

"Killian," I chided.

"What? I'm not useless!" he said defensively.

"You could have gotten yourself killed!" I scolded.

His demeanor went serious as he said, "Kenna, I would die a thousand deaths to keep you safe."

"I'd prefer you don't die at all," I said as I let the gravity of his words sink in.

"Alright, Princess. Time to go," Laurel said quietly. The visits were never long enough. I nodded and gave Killian a soft kiss between the bars.

"I'll see you soon," Killian promised before giving my hands a final squeeze. A small shockwave passed between us, and his eyes lit, signaling he had felt it, too.

I nodded and let Laurel lead me back into my cell, feeling a tiny amount of magic zap through my veins.

25
KENNA

I woke to the sounds of boxes scraping across the stone floor and fabrics being heaped on any available surface. A small woman was pushing things into the tiny cell one by one. Laurel stood looking rather amused behind her.

"I offered to help." He shrugged when he noticed me looking at the chaos. "She's too damn stubborn."

"Laurel! Watch your language around the princess," she chided. Turning to me, she curtsied and said, "I'm Iris. I will be your lady's maid while you prepare for today's events."

"Uh, today's events?" I looked at Laurel for some explanation, but he strategically found something on the wall to study.

"Yes, the dreaded nonsense about finding you a match."

I snapped my eyes to Laurel for confirmation that I had heard correctly.

"My wife doesn't mince words." He smiled.

"No, I don't, but I'll mince you if you don't leave. It's bad enough she has to do this. She doesn't need your snide remarks." She shooed him out of the small and now very cluttered space. "And she doesn't need an audience while she changes, so you and the other guards best keep your eyes to yourselves!"

"Yes, ma'am," he whispered as he kissed her temple and climbed over a box before exiting the space.

"You're Laurel's wife?"

"Yes, child. Keep up. Now, let's get this over with. You'll need a gown, but we can't have you looking too tempting. I want to try to meet the king's standards, but just barely enough to squeak by, not to draw a suitor to you." She beamed. "Green is your color, so let's put you in this drab shade of gray instead." Her eyes sparkled as she plotted away, and I could tell I would adore her.

Sometime later, after my makeup had been applied too thick, my hair was done up in an older fashion that wasn't quite in style anymore, and my body was laced into a gown that washed out my skin tone and clashed with my hair color, I found myself looking into the Fae mirror Iris had dragged into my cell.

"Won't you get in trouble? I don't want anything to happen to you."

"Hush, child, I'm not dull. I've done enough to deter the Fae males you'll be meeting, but not so much that the King will be angry." She smiled brilliantly at me. She was very pretty, as to be expected of a Fae. Her hair was a soft light brown, and she had bright, expressive lilac eyes that showed the intelligence she possessed. She was a lovely match for Laurel, and I wholly enjoyed her banter with him throughout the ordeal.

"Do you know who I'll be meeting?"

"Yes, and they aren't worth my breath," she huffed. "You deserve to be with that Hunter boy you're bonded to, not farmed out to the least desirable high-born males King Arrion could find."

"Could you at least tell me a little about them? So, I can be prepared?"

Iris gave me a look of pity. "I don't think I can do much to prepare you. They're all terrible in their own ways," she sighed. "Jolan is just a big brute. He isn't even high-born, but he is the Captain of the King's royal guard. He thinks quite highly of himself for absolutely no reason. He's not even good-looking. Elicas is nice but quite dull. His father was lovely, but he would be saddened to see the state of the kingdom. I suppose he's the more favorable of the terrible matches. It's a wonder we haven't lost that boy to the kelpies yet... Unless it's all an act. In which case, he should have taken up theater instead of politics."

Laurel laughed before clearing his throat and returning to his position. Iris leveled a glare at him that would freeze over the lagoon in the Isle of Jual on its hottest day. He grinned at her before mock saluting. She rolled her eyes.

"Nexin is someone to keep an eye on, though. He is older; in fact, he is closer to your grandfather's age than yours, and his actions are colored by desperation to remain in your grandfather's good graces. He is poorly behaved regarding women, and you'll want to stay out of his reach. I mean that both literally and figuratively."

"Understood." I scrunched up my face in disgust.

"Baritolo is the last one I'm aware of, and although he is a high-born Fae, he is a drunk. Very disappointing. He could have been so much more," she tutted.

"Lovely." I sighed. "You mentioned the state of the kingdom. What did you mean?"

Iris looked at me with such sadness in her eyes. "King Arrion was once a wonderful and loved king. He doted on his queen, loved his son, and made sure that everyone who dwelled within the Fae Realm was taken care of, not just those in the capital Eiradia or those he considered of pure blood," she said softly before shaking her head. "He even used to offer aid to neighboring territories. Those were better times."

"What happened?" I asked cautiously. I wasn't entirely sure I wanted to know what could turn a man described as 'lovely' into the hateful shell of a man I'd met.

"There was... an incident..." Iris said, closing her eyes for a moment as if uncomfortable. "We don't speak of it. It is forbidden. All I can say is that that day changed Arrion. It was as if his soul fractured, and the rotten bits and pieces were the only parts that survived. He blamed all of the other realms for the loss of his bonded, although no one truly knows what happened. Honestly, you remind me a bit of the late queen."

Laurel scoffed from outside my cell door. "He has no soul. Not even rotten bits. It all died when Queen Amabel did."

I looked at Iris, my eyes wide as a new sense of fear had set in. I knew that losing the bond could drive someone insane if they survived. Often, it was more merciful to die with the bonded one than to survive. If my grandfather had survived the loss of his bonded queen... I shook my head. I didn't want to have any sympathy for that man.

"Don't worry, child," she whispered. "Off you go!" she chirped as she swatted at my behind to exit the cell.

Laurel quietly put the cuffs on my hands, explaining that they were just for show and to appease the king.

"I have no intention of binding you this way for long, Princess. Not that I could even if I did want to," he murmured. "It would do you well to play along for now, though. We have a plan."

I gave him a hesitant nod in understanding, but wondered what exactly he and Iris were talking about. More specifically, I wondered who had made the plan, and if it involved me, why wasn't I included?

When we came up the steps of the cell, Killian was at the bars of his, no doubt aware of my approach through the bond. He looked me up and down with a crooked grin.

"You look fancy," he chuckled.

"I look like a wardrobe vomited on me."

"It's not that bad," he mused. "Just look at one feature at a time. The dress is pretty, if you ignore the shoes."

"Killian," I groaned. "That's not helping."

"Sorry, love, but I can't lie to you. You know that."

I rubbed the bridge of my nose in frustration before Iris swatted my hand.

"Don't be messing up all that work I put into your face, child."

I groaned again but put my hands at my sides. "Killian, this is Iris, Laurel's wife."

Killian smiled at her and nodded politely. "So, what's all this fuss for?" Killian queried.

"Matchmaking, remember?" I rolled my eyes.

"Ah, yes. That…"

"I'll be with her the entire time," Laurel assured him. "She'll be safe, but we must go, or the king will suspect something is amiss." Killian nodded in silent thanks and understanding.

"I love you," I whispered.

Killian's face lit up with joy. "I love you too, *Princess*," he teased before reaching his hands through the bars to hold mine. Leaning in, I kissed him lightly before releasing his hands and returning to Laurel and Iris.

"I'll be fine." I smiled weakly. Killian didn't respond but instead glared at Laurel as if in warning. Laurel raised an eyebrow, and Iris chuckled before Laurel took my arm and led me down the hall toward the king's grand room.

Upon entering the grand space where I had met the king, my grandfather, I noted the four tables with Fae males seated at each. They looked bored, and none of them seemed to have even noticed my entrance. Laurel stepped in front of me as Iris melted into the back of the room, out of sight.

"My King, the princess has arrived."

"Wonderful! Thank you, Laurel. You may take your leave now. I'll handle this." Laurel looked stunned. For that matter, so was I. Laurel had assured me and Killian that he would be by my side throughout the event. He was clearly unaware of the king's plan and was as caught off guard by this revelation as I was.

"Of course, My King. I just thought I might remain present so you will not have to dirty your hands if she becomes unruly."

Arrion eyed Laurel, searching for anything akin to untruth. "I suppose you may stay," Arrion said slowly. Laurel's body loosened just enough for me to notice how tense he must have been. I doubted the others saw, but it made me all the more grateful for his presence of mind. If he had been worried, then I surely was as well.

"Come here, girl. Let me see you." Arrion beckoned to me. I stepped into the sun, shining through the stained-glass cutouts in the dome of the great room. Arrion looked me up and down, motioning for me to twirl. I did so begrudgingly. "Acceptable, I suppose, although not entirely in fashion."

"Thank you," I said. "I quite like the gray of the dress. Don't you think it brings out my eyes?" I smiled demurely at the king, doing my best to play the part of an innocent.

He scrunched up his face and looked away from me dismissively. "I suppose this shouldn't be a surprise, considering your bloodline and upbringing."

"Oh, we never had such nice gowns in the coven." I smiled again and looked at my feet obediently. If I needed to play the submissive, gentle princess to survive, so be it. Laurel's mention of a plan echoed in my head, steadying me as I sank into my role.

"Of course you didn't." Arrion chuckled. "The men and women of Cauldera are inferior in many ways, not just in blood." Dark amusement settled over his face. "Although it appears another night in your cell helped you to recognize your place."

"Yes, I believe it did," I replied, rolling my eyes internally because it had, in fact, been three days. His complete and utter disregard for anything but his own cares was impressive.

"Good. I suppose we should get on with the events at hand. Please, let me introduce you to the brave men willing to bear the burden of purifying the bloodline." My insides twisted with disgust. These men were repulsive, not brave. Any man who believed in such archaic practices was nothing but a coward, afraid he was so undesirable that he would never find true love on his own.

"Of course," I muttered, desperately trying not to show my distaste. Arrion smiled at me, as if he knew I was playing along, but said nothing. He placed his hand on my back and steered me toward the tables, and I struggled to fight the urge not to shrink away from his touch. I felt a shiver skitter down my spine. Iris had been right, and I had been thrown into a den of wolves and one very drunk high Fae.

The big one, I assumed, was Jolan, who sat with his feet propped up on the chair I was supposed to sit in at some point. I realized with disgust that those were the same boots I had seen on the guard who had killed that common Fae couple. He picked his teeth and completely ignored my presence, which was fine. I didn't want to speak to him either.

He wore a plain brown tunic with dark trousers and those dirty leather boots. He evidently was not interested in impressing me and had made what appeared to be zero effort. I noticed his head was shaved, and he had dark violet eyes that never glanced my way. How very unappealing.

Another was staring at the stained glass above us and appeared to be daydreaming. I assumed this was Elicas. He was mumbling something to himself and drawing imaginary lines above his head. I noticed the king gave him a disapproving glare, which he completely missed.

He wore a blue velvet vest over a white tunic and black trousers. He was clean-shaven and looked very well put together. Aside from his wandering mind, he looked like he had put in the most effort.

A man who was likely Nexin sat at the table beside the daydreaming Fae. Despite Iris stating he was older, aside from the gray streaks in his hair, he appeared even younger than the king. His black boots were shiny, and he wore a royal blue tunic with dark brown trousers. He sat back in a lazy pose, with legs splayed in a wholly inappropriate way for the situation, and winked before waggling his eyebrows suggestively when I looked at his face. My insides shriveled, and bile rose in my throat.

The last man, whom I assumed was Baritolo, was dressed in a wrinkled white tunic, which appeared to be from the night before, and brown trousers with a hole in one knee. His reddish hair flopped messily into his face and covered one of his eyes. He hiccupped and slid further down into his seat.

My nose wrinkled at the pungent smell emanating from him. The king rolled his eyes and snapped his fingers. As if he were a puppet on strings, the drunkard sat up straight, suspended by some force of magic, and his hair moved out of his eyes. His gaze remained unfocused, however, and it was clear his upright position was the king's doing.

"Please, darling granddaughter, why don't you start here?" King Arrion placed his hand on my back and angled me toward Jolan, whose boots were still shedding dried mud on the chair meant for me. "This is Jolan, the Captain of my Royal Guard. His bravery is unmatched, and he would do wonders to purify the bloodline. Please, sit." He gave me a shove toward the table. Only then did Jolan move his feet. The mud remained, and I attempted to clear the seat before I sat nonchalantly. "Enjoy your time. I'll return when it's time for you to meet the next gentleman."

Wonderful. I fought the urge to roll my eyes.

"Ye may be a princess, but you're beneath me. I don't care about ya or your story, so be a good girl and keep quiet," the guard grunted without ever making eye contact.

I forced a smile. What was the point of this nightmare if he wouldn't talk to me anyway? Not that I really wanted a conversation with this boar of a man.

"Captain of the Royal Guard sounds prestigious."

"Aye, it is. Not that a half breed like ye would understand." He turned and looked at the king. "Your Highness, if I may," he said, surprisingly politely.

Arrion turned toward him with a smile. "Of course, Jolan."

"I've seen and heard enough," Jolan said brusquely.

Arrion raised an eyebrow but didn't argue. "Come, child, you should meet the other men." He gestured for me to stand. I did so and followed him begrudgingly to the next table. Arrion snapped his fingers in the Fae male's face, and it was as if the man suddenly realized where he was and rapidly came to attention.

"Oh, Your Highness! I do apologize. I was admiring the beautiful dome above us." He smiled at Arrion, who ignored the gesture and motioned for me to sit.

"This is Elicas. He is a high Fae," Arrion said nothing else before striding away.

"Hello, Princess," Elicas said politely.

"Hello." He at least appeared pleasant.

"Are you faring well? This must be quite a shock to you."

I eyed him suspiciously. "It is."

"Please, Princess. Feel free to speak your mind." Elicas leaned over the table to whisper to me. "You will not offend me." A small smile briefly graced his face. I dismissed his statement and sat back in my chair, creating some distance.

"You appeared to be lost in thought when I arrived. I wasn't sure you even noticed."

"I notice a lot of things." He grinned. "Things people don't think I notice." His blueish purple eyes sparkled with mischief. I wondered to myself if he was not as oblivious as he seemed. "I see the men and women who come and go, and the ones who come but never go again. I see bonded couples separated." He leveled a knowing look at me, a dark curl escaping the short ponytail he had his hair tied in, and he brushed it behind his ear before continuing. "I see the darkness in the manufactured light. In that darkness is where the truth is hidden, and you, my dear princess, are the flame that will light the way. Those of us who support you will be there when it counts. Take note of the allies you gain along the way. Some you don't even realize you have, or what they are." He winked. "Don't lose hope, for you are the last little ember of hope we have." He sat back and smiled at me. My mind was whirring with the implications of what he said. Did he disapprove of the king? Why would he be here if he did?

"I'm not sure I understand," I said hesitantly.

"You will." Elicas looked up at the stained glass again. "All in due time." He began tracing shapes in the air. I turned to look behind me and was met with the stare of a fuming King Arrion.

He marched over and mumbled, "May the kelpies take you away, you useless boy," before pulling me up by the elbow and forcing me toward the next table. I glanced over my shoulder to see Elicas grin and subtly nod once in my direction, as if acknowledging my confusion and adding to it simultaneously. I tucked the tidbit about finding allies away to contemplate another time.

"This is Nexin. He is a high Fae and has been a trusted advisor in many conflicts. He has quite a way with words." Arrion smirked at me as he pressed on my shoulders, forcing me to sit.

"Hello, lovely," Nexin purred. My skin crawled, and it took every ounce of concentration not to cringe. "You are a vision of beauty." He held his hand toward me as if to shake it. I reluctantly placed my hand in his, feeling dirtier than Jolan's boots with just one touch from this man.

He grinned and kissed my hand. It was a sloppy, wet kiss that lasted entirely too long to be considered appropriate. Arrion smiled and nodded to Nexin as he walked back to his throne. As I tried to pull my hand away, his grip tightened.

"Ah, ah, ah, Princess. I am not done with you yet." A tight smile was all I could manage. He turned my hand over, studying my palm and tracing the lines of my hand with his fingers. "Have you ever had your palm read, Princess?"

"Does that line usually work for you?" I smiled sweetly.

"Usually." He grinned. "I like a challenge, though, and you seem to be the biggest one yet."

"Get on with it, or give me back my hand," I said calmly. His eyes lit with the challenge.

"See this line here?" Nexin motioned to a line at the top of my palm, near the base of my fingers. "This is your love line." He feigned concentration. "Oh dear, it looks like the line breaks right here." He pressed his finger painfully into my hand. I tried to hide my wince and remain still. "You will suffer a great loss of love but survive it." He released the pressure on my hand, and I breathed. "Do you suppose this has anything to do with that pesky Hunter of yours?" He leaned back in his seat, releasing my hand and studying his sleeve.

I snatched my hand back and began rubbing the sore spot in my lap. "I think you are full of—"

The king cut me off by roughly hauling me up from my seat. "You will not disrespect my guests, girl," he sneered.

Nexin's smile gave me gooseflesh and made the hairs on my neck stand on end. I said nothing.

Arrion dragged me to the final table, where a drunken Baritolo was slumped over with an occasional snore. Arrion, already irritable, had no patience and promptly gestured to Jolan, who rolled his eyes but quickly walked over and kicked the man's chair over.

"Guards! Get this man out of my sight!" Two guards I had never seen emerged from the shadows and dragged a still-unconscious Baritolo out of the great room. Arrion scoffed, and I heard Jolan chuckle from beside the king. Elicas tilted his head and raised an eyebrow, obviously in question, but in the question of what, I couldn't identify.

Turning toward the remaining three men, Arrion spun me to face them and, with a flourish, thanked them for making time for introductions.

"I will speak to each of you in the coming days and decide who is the best fit, assuming you have not found her too repulsive." He looked me up and down in disgust once again. "You are dismissed. Laurel! Get the princess back to her cell immediately." As Laurel approached, I heard Arrion mutter, "What a disappointment," as he returned to his throne.

Laurel took my arm and carefully led me to the back of the throne room, where Iris seemed to materialize out of the shadows. She looked at me with concern but said nothing, likely for fear of her safety as well as Laurel's and mine in the presence of the king.

Before leaving the space, I glanced back at the men and noted the smug looks on Jolan and Nexin's faces. Elicas was the only male showing me a glimmer of concern, quickly masked when the king stared down at them disapprovingly.

26
KILLIAN

I heard the footsteps before I saw Kenna returning down the hall, escorted by Laurel and Iris. Although she had a perplexed look on her face, an immediate sense of relief washed over me. I took in her appearance. She looked unharmed, but I did note the way she chewed on her bottom lip and the way the slightest creases had formed between her eyebrows.

"What is it, love?"

Kenna released her lip from her teeth, and my eyes immediately focused on her mouth. Good Goddess, I missed kissing that mouth. "I had some... interesting interactions with the men the king has chosen." I looked at her, puzzled by her vague statement.

"Good or...?"

"I'm honestly not sure. There was one man...Elicas. He kept saying something about me being the light to lead the people out of the darkness and their only hope. I'm not sure what he meant, though." She whispered and eyed the guard assigned to my cell, who looked to be dozing off. "Don't worry about it." She reached between the cell bars and took my hands in hers. I squeezed her fingers reassuringly before gently tugging her closer to me.

"You're sure you're okay?"

"Yes," she sighed. "Are you well?

"Obviously." I grinned. "Look at these fancy accommodations. A room all to myself and personal wait staff." I gestured toward the guard. "I also have a lovely view of the gallows from this window."

Kenna raised an eyebrow at me, but I could see the smile she was trying to hide. "Better view than I've got, but my walls are shiny."

I chuckled. "And what pretty jewelry they provided you! Much better than those outdated bangles from the other day." Kenna grinned then, the full intensity of her smile beaming at me. "There she is." I removed one hand from her grip and cupped her face. "There's my Kenna."

"I'm sorry," she whispered. "This—" she waved about erratically, "—is a little much all at once."

"I know, love. Just remember I'll always be here for you, up the stairs and to the right." I did my best to appease her apparent nerves. Something was bothering her, and although she had made a valiant attempt, her eyes could not hide her confusion. Kenna smiled demurely at me while Laurel stepped forward.

"It's time to go back to your cell, Princess."

Kenna gripped my hands even tighter as she leaned in to whisper to me. "I don't think we're alone here." I looked into her eyes, a bit puzzled.

"Obviously, love. Laurel, Iris, that ugly bastard—" I waved at my guard "—and who knows who else is down here."

She immediately shushed me, gripped the collar of my now filthy tunic, and pulled me closer. "That's not what I mean." She quirked an eyebrow at me while she waited for that to sink in. Slowly, hope swelled within my chest.

"Allies?"

"Yes," she whispered with a smile. "I'm not sure what they will do or how they will help, but I got the impression that things are not as well put together here as they seem."

"Alright, Princess," my cell guard mocked, apparently awakening, "enough whispering of love and other fluff I don't care to witness."

"Oh, I'm sorry," Kenna said mockingly, "feel free to turn around then." She twirled her finger.

"Listen, you little wretch." He stepped toward her.

Laurel and I bristled immediately, and Iris touched Kenna's forearm.

"The king may think you're the answer to his pleas to the Goddess for power, but you are not my princess, and you'd do best to shut that pretty little mouth before something happens to your pretty little face."

"Enough," commanded Laurel. "You follow the orders of King Arrion, and as such, you will treat the princess with respect."

The ugly guard screwed up his face in disgust before spitting at Kenna's skirts.

The power surge I felt flow from Kenna into my hands was immediate. Her rage was palpable and not just to me. Iris immediately let go of Kenna's arm, as if she had been burned. Laurel even flinched but did not step back. My guard eyed us both suspiciously, and I tried to shift so that our hands were not visible from the side of the cell he sat on. I knew without looking that a small orb of fire had been passed between Kenna and me, and the last thing either of us needed was the Fae King to become more aware of our ability to share power than he likely already was. Something in my gut told me it would be detrimental if he ever knew the full extent.

Laurel stepped forward and placed himself between Kenna and the other guard. "You will pay for that," he gritted. "Either by my hand or the king's. This will not go unpunished."

My guard chuckled. "Oh, Laurel, you think yourself so high and mighty as one of the royal guards. So much better than us regular guards. But we're the real fighters, and you wouldn't stand a chance." Laurel growled before stalking forward and grabbing the other guard's throat. A strangled squeak left the man's mouth before he began to resemble a suffocating fish rather than a man.

"You are nothing but the scum on my shoe. I do not need to prove anything to you. I will, however, protect the princess as I have been ordered to. From my own kind, if necessary. Understood?" The other man's eyes bulged, and he tapped Laurel's hand in defeat. Laurel released him, and he sucked in a sharp breath.

I looked away from Laurel and leaned forward and kissed Kenna lightly through the bars, savoring the brief moment.

"You should go, love."

She nodded. "I love you."

"I love you, too." I smiled. "Up the stairs and around the corner, remember?"

She nodded, and a sad smile replaced the previously sunny one she had graced me with. "Will you be alright?"

"Princess, it's time to go." Laurel took her arm and began to pull her away. Her hand slipped from mine, and I consciously made an effort to hold the fire orb in my hand so that it would not be seen.

"Yes, love. Go get out of that ridiculous dress." I tried to smile despite the rage slithering through my veins. The small orb in my hand pulsed as I watched her dress flutter as she turned the corner.

"She's a pretty girl. It'd be a real shame if the king found out you two can share that fire," he hissed.

The guard's threat lingered in the air, poisoning the atmosphere with malice. I clenched my jaw, feeling the heat of anger rising within me. I tried so hard not to give in to the provocation. I really needed to bide my time playing the long game.

I took a deep breath and forced myself to relax. The orb of fire in my hand flickered but did not falter. With a careful motion, I concealed the hand holding the orb within the folds of my tunic just as the guard turned his attention back to me.

"You think you can intimidate me with your petty threats?" I retorted, my voice cold and steady. "You have no idea what we are capable of."

The guard's eyes widened slightly, a flicker of uncertainty crossing his face before he masked it with a sneer. "Oh, and what will you do? Burn down this entire dungeon with your little flame?"

I met his gaze evenly, a slow sneer curling on my lips. "Maybe not the whole dungeon," I growled. "But I can certainly make you regret your words." With a swift, fluid motion, I extended my hand from under the tunic, the orb of fire burning brightly in my palm.

The guard's bravado faltered as he stepped back, fear glinting in his eyes. He raised his hands defensively, but it was too late. Rage fueling my actions, I hurled the orb from my hand. The flames danced and crackled as they enveloped him in a searing blaze.

He screamed in agony, flailing and trying to beat out the flames that clung to his clothes. The acrid smell of burning flesh filled the air as he writhed in pain, his cries echoing off the stone walls of the dungeon. A resounding *boom*, the final sound before it all fell silent.

Fear replaced rage. What had I done?

27
KENNA

*I*ris snapped her fingers, using some form of magic to strip me of my gown and the other trinkets she had adorned me with. Slipping back into my tunic and leggings, I felt much more myself. I sighed and slid down the wall of my cell. Laurel, who had silently slipped back into the cell after I'd changed, and Iris watched me with poorly hidden concern.

"Are you well, Princess?" Iris asked.

"I'm tired, Iris. I want to go home. And I want Killian with me." The sadness permeated my voice, no matter how hard I tried to squelch it.

"Home is with the people you love," Laurel said gently. I looked up to see Iris sweetly place a soft kiss on his cheek. Laurel smiled at her with such love that it was palpable. I wondered if that was how Killian and I might look to others. I took a deep breath and sat up a little straighter.

"That may be true, but at least my cottage has a bed."

Iris turned to Laurel, a look of shock on her face. "She has no bed?"

"It's not my fault!" He held up his hands to the little woman who was shaking with fury.

"If I weren't afraid to lose my head, I'd roll the king's right off his shoulders," she grumbled.

Laurel chuckled. "Your dedication is admirable," he teased her.

I sat enjoying the banter between them for a moment longer before Iris gathered up the gown and other items and bustled off into the hallway, presumably to return home. I tried to relax in the little space and be at peace, knowing I was safe, at least for the moment, but something nagged in the back of my mind; something wasn't quite right.

I felt the tension in my body before I heard the resounding *boom* and screams from the general area of Killian's cell. I whipped my head toward Laurel and was met with his wide-eyed stare, which mirrored mine. A heartbeat later, he reacted, grabbing my arm and pulling me to my feet.

"Time to go, Princess. This wasn't my plan, but it'll do." The resolve in his face told me everything I needed to know. I nodded, unsure what exactly he meant by "his plan," and began to follow him out of the cell toward Killian.

The anxiety in my chest was becoming unbearable, but just as we left the confines of the quartz cell, I felt the bond strengthen, and my fears subsided slightly; Killian was alive, at least. Laurel stopped me, grabbed my arms where the magic-suppressing cuffs were, and turned them until the lock was visible. He hurriedly unlocked them and let them fall to the floor. I felt my magic rush through my body. I let out a sigh of relief.

"Why are you willing to risk your life for me?" I asked him in shock.

"Because the king has gone too far this time," he said sadly.

"What do you mean, this time?"

"The king is close-minded and power-hungry. He plots to invade the other realms in retribution. As you saw, many of the Fae are getting tired of how he rules. There is a small resistance that has begun, but your bonded just blew up the dungeon, so Plan B it is," he said, grinning.

"What's Plan B?" I asked suspiciously.

"Get you and that thick-skulled Hunter out of here so we all live to fight another day." Laurel's grin grew wider, and we climbed the steps.

"I am not thick-skulled," Killian interjected.

"What did you do?" I hissed as I pressed myself to the bars of his cell.

"He threatened you!" he whispered back loudly. I narrowed my eyes at him.

"Get back." I tightened my grip on the bars.

"No, Princess. The last thing we need is you drawing even more attention," Laurel hissed.

"Fine," I conceded, letting my magic fizzle out.

"Where are your pretty bracelets, love?" Killian mused.

"If you're going to get out of here in one piece, they, along with your talisman, have to go," Laurel said as he unlocked Killian's cell. Stepping aside, he motioned for Killian to exit. As Killian walked by him, Laurel grabbed his arm and plucked the talisman off it. Killian rubbed his wrist and grinned.

"Thanks, friend." Killian grinned before rushing and sweeping me into a tight hug. He picked me up off my feet and spun me around, burying his face in my neck. Over his shoulder, I could see Laurel good-naturedly rolling his eyes. Killian kissed my cheek as Laurel cleared his throat.

"Can we go now before we all get killed? Or would you rather twirl like court dancers in this burning dungeon?"

Killian and I nodded and followed him hand-in-hand down a dark hall. Killian squeezed my fingers reassuringly as we passed several offshoots to the main hallway and pulled me along to keep up with Laurel.

As I turned to look behind us, I heard the faint sound of footsteps. My breath caught, and my heart rate increased. The panic I had been trying to swallow began to swell. Laurel stopped abruptly, causing Killian and me to almost plow into him.

"I hear footsteps!" I hissed anxiously. Killian pulled me close and shushed into my hair soothingly. Behind him, Laurel was shouldering the door in front of us, trying to open it.

"Damn thing is locked from the other side!" he seethed. "We have to split up. Did you see the other hallways?" He looked at Killian and me. Killian nodded, but I was too stunned to respond. Laurel grabbed my shoulders and looked into my eyes. "Princess, remember what I said. A phoenix does not dull its flames for others. It's time for you to do the same. Can you do that?"

Something clicked in my head when his words sank in. A wave of calm washed over me, and my hands stopped shaking. I didn't accept my grandfather or his intolerant ways, but I was willing to help these people, especially if they were anything like Laurel or Iris and willing to risk their lives for mine.

I nodded and looked up at Laurel. "Tell me what to do," I said, squaring my shoulders. Killian grinned next to me and took my hand.

"Survive," Laurel said. "Get out of here in one piece, Princess. I will cause a distraction, but you two—" he looked between Killian and me "—need to live to fight another day," he said resolutely.

"You do, too. Iris would never forgive me if you didn't come home." I grinned at Laurel, who grinned back.

"Until we meet again, Princess." He took one more look between us before turning and running back down the hall we had come from. I stared after him, uneasiness settling in the pit of my stomach.

"We need to go, love. Don't let his choice be for nothing," Killian said gently as he started to pull me back down the corridor toward the cells. As we got closer to the fork in the hall, I could hear the sound of shouting coming from the direction I was sure Laurel had gone.

Killian pulled me along and held my hand tightly, guiding me in the opposite direction. As we ran, I heard a familiar voice cry out: Laurel. I skidded to a stop, and Killian forcefully stopped as well.

"Kenna, no. We need to go. Running into the battle is the exact opposite of what he wanted," Killian said in a steady, low voice.

I squared my shoulders and stood up straight. "That is where you are wrong. He wanted a princess to save the kingdom from my villainous grandfather, and I intend to do exactly that." Killian's eyes widened as I spoke, but he must have felt my resolve through the bond because he didn't say another word or try to stop me. I turned back toward the corridor from which the yelling was coming and murmured, "Goddess, be with me."

Killian's fingers wrapped around mine. "May she be with us both." He grinned before we took off running.

28
KENNA

As Killian and I reached the fray, we froze. Before us was a mishmash of what had to be twenty soldiers fighting a slew of what I could only imagine were everyday Fae folk—regular people without armor colliding fearlessly with heavy silver-clad soldiers. In the middle of it all was Laurel, yelling commands and doing his best to fight off a massive guard, who I abruptly realized was Jolan.

Watching these everyday people being forced to fight against the guards that should have been protecting them ignited something in me. My magic swelled, and the air around me vibrated. I was outraged. Killian must have felt it, too. I had no sooner turned toward him than he had grinned at me, let go of my hand, and launched himself into the fray. A smile briefly crept across my face. Even when he was being reckless, he was still endearing, and I loved him all the more for his dedication to anything that mattered to me. I followed his movements momentarily before I felt a looming presence behind me.

I turned to see the massive form of Jolan in full armor, looking down at me with a malicious grin. I felt more like prey than a savior. I took a wary step back and began to summon my magic.

"Princess. How nice of ye to join us," he sneered. The air around me began to feel cold, and I narrowed my eyes. If he wanted to play, I was game.

Remembering what Killian had said, I began to work to summon all my anger. Slowly, I felt the prick of the spark in my palm. It grew as I focused on the injustice before me. The scales might have been tipped in my grandfather's favor at this moment, but I was sure as hell going to tip them back.

Launching myself forward, I let out a frustrated string of profanities as I smashed my palm into the warrior's throat. The fireball seemed to seep into his armor for a second, and a brief look of shock crossed his face. Then, just when I thought I had won, the fire poured out of the cracks of his armor and dribbled onto the floor. I blanched as he began to laugh.

"Oh, come now, Princess. The granddaughter of our esteemed King Arrion must have more fight in her than that." His tone tweaked my already simmering anger and sent me into a flying rage. If ever there was a time to be compared to a banshee, that time was now.

With my cry of rage, the room around me began to shake, and the battle suddenly stopped. Everyone, warriors and everyday Fae alike, turned to look at me. Nothing would calm the storm burning inside my gut.

"Enough!" I screamed. The large Fae warrior let out a chuckle.

"I didn't know ye had it in ya." He mocked. "It seems even your dirty Witch blood couldn't cloud your Fae blood after all." I'd had enough of his arrogant, self-righteous nonsense. I was piping-hot mad, and he was my target.

I took a step toward him. He didn't bother stepping back. He only looked more amused the more furious I became.

"Kenna…" Killian's voice said. "What are you doing, love?" he yelled above the din. I could hear the mix of fear and amazement in his voice. Before I had time to ponder what he was talking about, Laurel's voice cut through the crowd.

"Princess!" As I turned my head to look in his direction, I saw a purple blur out of the corner of my eye. Confused, I reached for my hair, which was most definitely red the last time I had checked, and was shocked to see my entire arm encased in what looked like purple fire. I looked down at myself and realized it wasn't just my arm but the rest of my body, too. This should have terrified me, but once I recognized it, the amount of magic pouring through me felt *good*.

Jolan let out another chuckle as he stepped toward me. He reached behind his back and pulled out an intricately carved sword with an amethyst inlaid into the handle. My face scrunched in irritation. Great, a power-charging stone... He grinned at my expression.

"Now this—" he gestured to me "—is a fight." he said as he readied to strike.

"Kenna!" Killian cried. I saw him running toward me out of the corner of my eye. It was as if time had slowed down. Without thinking, I used my Witch's magic to weave a magical net around the warrior with one hand and send a pulse of magic toward Killian with the other. To my surprise, he flew backward, slamming into Laurel. I saw the hurt in his eyes and felt that pain stab my heart for the span of a breath. I would have time to feel guilty about that later.

Turning back to my intended opponent, I pressed the woven magic toward him, wrapping him in what I hoped would at least slow him down. Time seemed to speed up again, but the damage had been done. The warrior strained against my magic, and it was all I could do to hold him still. The other warriors began to advance on me, and the flames on my skin burned brighter with the fury I felt.

Laurel and Killian were methodically taking out warriors at the back of the bunch headed in my direction. I knew what I had to do, and I knew they, along with the Fae folk, needed to leave. Now.

"Killian!" I yelled over the sounds of battle. Using one of my hands, I strained to press back the advancing warriors while still holding the biggest one in my magical net. "Killian, get everyone out!"

"I won't leave you!" he yelled back. Briefly, I looked in his direction and was struck by just how beautiful he looked in the heat of battle. For a man with no weapon, Killian was certainly holding his own.

"You need to go!" I screamed at him, but he just shook his head. He would never leave my side willingly. Although I appreciated his dedication to me, to our bond, I needed him safe. I couldn't focus if he was here, in harm's way. Pain shot through my heart briefly. The man I loved was a distraction to me. Holding onto my magic for dear life, I turned toward Laurel.

"Laurel! Get everyone out!" My voice echoed above the sounds of swords and weapons clanging. He looked up at me and briefly contemplated his options before nodding.

"Everyone, follow me!" Laurel yelled. He had alerted not only the innocents in this battle, but also the enemy to his plan. I let out a strangled cry of pain as I stretched my magic farther than I ever had before, grasping the warriors around the corridor and holding them in place. I would burn myself out like a moth to a flame if it meant saving these people who had done no wrong, but most of all, I would die for Killian if it meant he was safe. I knew that now without a shadow of a doubt.

Killian looked up at me, dropped whatever object he had been using as a weapon, and started toward me. I shook my head at him, but as stubborn as ever, he continued to advance toward me. I silently prayed to the Goddess for more energy. I just needed more time. I needed Killian safe.

"Kenna, please, love. Stop this. You can't do this alone."

Tears pricked at my eyes when I saw the absolute love and

devotion mixed with fear in his eyes, but I blinked, forcing away the display of emotion. I looked into his eyes and shook my head. "Wait, Kenna," he started to say.

"Forgive me," I whispered, using my remaining excess strength to forcefully blow him backward toward the door Laurel was leading the others out of. Killian's face filled with surprise and pain as he flew toward the door. I knew in that moment I had damaged the bond, but I would take a damaged bond if it meant he would live. It wasn't that I didn't have faith in him; I did. I didn't have faith in myself to focus on my opponent instead of him, and I refused to leave the only person who had ever made me feel loved because of a stupid mistake.

Laurel grabbed Killian's shirt as soon as he landed and dragged him toward the door. Killian put up one hell of a struggle, but Laurel wasn't having it.

"She sent you away for a reason, boy! Don't you trust her?" he yelled at Killian.

Killian's eyes softened as he looked at me, but I could still see the pain he was trying to hide, the betrayal he was feeling. "I do. With all my heart," he whispered as he let Laurel pull him out the door.

29
KENNA

Pain washed over me, knowing I had hurt Killian, and then rage quickly burned out any traces of hurt. The fire around me swelled. I turned to the large warrior struggling in my magic net.

"Make no mistake, I may have my grandfather's bloodline, but I am nothing like him. I will not stand here and let you torment your own people any longer. I will not let you play a part in separating me from my bonded. Don't worry, though, I'll show you the same mercy I'm sure you showed all of the people whose lives you destroyed to get to where you are," I hissed.

Jolan let out a roar and pulled against my magic. "I'll kill ya, you little wench!" he yelled and ripped through the fabric of the net, freeing himself. Struggling to keep my hold on the other warriors, I focused my magic and sent a pulse of harsh energy around the room, effectively scattering them and slamming them against the corridor walls. The giant warrior came crashing toward me then.

"Is that all ye got, Princess?" his voice boomed across the corridor.

"Not even close." I hissed. Summoning my magic, I felt the familiar hum running through my system.

The giant warrior advanced on me like a lion stalking its prey. Unfortunately, I couldn't focus solely on him, as the rest of the warriors began to stand and stumble. I was running out of time.

He whirled his sword in my direction, and I managed to duck in time to save my head but let out a growl as a red curl fluttered to the floor. I had never been particularly vain, but I knew Killian loved my curls, and the loss of something tied to my bonded, no matter how trivial, was the spark I needed. I started to feel the fury coursing through my body. Something must have shifted because the warriors around me paused as I began to speak.

"First, he took it upon himself to send you bumbling idiots to kill my mother and father. Then, you burned my damn garden." I was stalking back and forth at this point. "Then, someone thought it was a good idea to lock me in a dungeon and try to destroy the Fae bond I have with Killian. And to top off this beautiful fucking fairytale—" I paused "—my goddess-damn grandfather wants to peddle me off like a prostitute to secure his claim to the throne! I'm fucking done!" I seethed.

The warriors around me grinned, as if my story amused them. What I noticed, which they had not, was that the purple fire around me had begun to glow brighter. The angrier I got, the brighter and more powerful the flames felt.

"Cry me a river, Princess," one of the other warriors chuckled.

Jolan grinned. "Your mother put up a good fight, but nothing like your father did. He had the same Fae fire magic you do. Come to think of it, so did Amabel." He shrugged. "Your mum and dad were no match for me, though. I thoroughly enjoyed watching the life leave their eyes." He gave me a malevolent, toothy grin.

In that moment, I snapped. The fire exploded around me, and the vibration in the air began again. Any weariness I felt was gone, replaced by pure, unchecked fury. I refused to let these heathens take any more from anyone else the way they had taken from me.

The fire around me swirled. The warriors stepped back, but Jolan wasn't deterred. He urged the others forward and swung at me with his sword. With a flash, my magic grasped his sword, heating it until it glowed. Jolan cried out in pain before dropping the red-hot metal with a clatter.

Some of the other warriors retreated, but I wasn't allowing that. Reaching out, I grasped the others with wisps of magic and dragged them back toward me. The remaining warriors stood frozen, their eyes bulging in fear.

"Don't just stand there! Attack!" Jolan bellowed. As if snapped out of their trance, the free warriors cautiously moved toward me while their leader cradled his burnt hand. My attention turned to my latest opponents, and my magic was distracted by holding onto the others.

As I readied for the oncoming attack, I was in no position to defend myself, and as the rock Jolan must have picked up crashed into the back of my skull, I let out a surprised cry. I hit my knees but refused to loosen my hold on the warriors I had within my magic.

"Just give up, Princess." Jolan grinned. "Your parents did."

The fire ripped through me and around my body. I felt the power of my magic growing, and the warriors closest to me were tossed back by the force. I let out a feral growl. "Enough!" I screamed, the flames growing brighter. "It's time to end this!"

As Jolan lunged toward me, I felt the fire shift. The flames lifted from my body, and the corridor shook. The ground rumbled, and the walls of the halls warped. A massive amount of energy built around me. Instantly, fire and pent-up rage erupted from me. The corridor exploded, and the warriors were scattered in the rubble and amongst the debris.

I looked up into the night sky from where I stood. Nothing in the dungeon section remained. Only flames and rubble existed around me. My own flames still burned but were rapidly fizzling out.

Exhausted, I stumbled in the direction Killian, Laurel, and the others had escaped. I needed to reach him. I needed to see that he was safe. Nothing else mattered.

As I climbed over a pile of rubble, I saw his face. Relief swept through my body, and I whispered, "Thank the Goddess," before the world around me spun, and I crashed into darkness.

30
KILLIAN

My whole body relaxed when I saw Kenna's form crest over the mound of rubble left behind after the explosion. I felt the tension from the fear of losing her begin to dissipate. Unfortunately, the massive headache I was sporting remained, although it had partially subsided. Not once had it crossed my mind that she might be dead; the bond had told me that was not the case. However, that didn't stop the painful ache of being separated from her.

She was beautiful despite being beaten and battered. Her hair blew in the breeze, tousled and charred in a few places. The purple fire that cloaked her before slowly fizzled out and only remained sporadically on her body. She looked like a warrior Goddess, and something so deadly had never been so damn attractive to me until that moment. Momentarily stunned by her beauty, I didn't register she was falling at first. As quickly as my battle-weakened body would allow, I rushed to her side, catching her just before her head hit the ground.

Having her back in my arms sent a shockwave through me that sent my heart into overdrive. I'd said it before, and I'd say it again: this woman would be the death of me. But if this was how I went, having her by my side would be worth it.

Pulling her close, I lifted her unconscious body away from the ground and began to walk back toward the crowd. Over the murmurs of the Fae folk, a horn sounded. I stopped in my tracks. I knew those horns. The king knew what had happened, and now he was coming.

Despite his old age, Arrion was a magnificent warrior. He had fought in the Fae Revolution and single-handedly defended the castle gates against invading creatures from the Wildlands. He had been protecting the most important thing to him: his family. Unfortunately for the world, his family had been torn apart that night when Queen Amabel died protecting Kenna's father.

It was said Amabel had placed herself between Prince Finnian and an unknown warrior trying to end the royal Fae line. Something broke inside Arrion that night, and he became the cold-hearted Fae king the world knew now. A king who was capable of ordering the death of his own son simply for "polluting the bloodline." I shuddered.

Laurel met me where I stood, staring at Kenna, concern etched into his features.

"She's just unconscious," I reassured him, "but I need to get her somewhere safe. We both know what those horns mean."

He nodded and turned back toward the crowd. "The princess is safe." His voice echoed over the rubble, and the crowd began to cheer.

"They shouldn't be here," I urged him, shifting Kenna's weight so her head rested on my shoulder. Laurel turned and surveyed the crowd of Fae folk smiling up at us. I assumed it had more to do with Kenna than with me.

"I agree, but they will follow their Princess anywhere after she defended them like that," he said resolutely. I looked behind us as the horns blasted again. We were running out of time, and I was unwilling to give up Kenna, the only person who had made me feel like I belonged. I held Kenna closely and stepped forward toward the crowd.

"Princess Kenna is safe for now, but I need to get her to safety. I know you all feel indebted to her and want to help her, but right now, the best thing you can do is blend back in. Don't let them know you are on her side, and I promise, I will bring her back to you," I boomed over the crowd. They fell silent before a man in the front looked up at me and nodded. I recognized Callum immediately.

Turning back toward the crowd, he bellowed, "Fall back! Protect the princess by protecting yourself!"

Immediately, the crowd began to murmur, but they did as he asked and began to disperse.

Laurel looked at me, a bit surprised, but nodded as well. "My wife will appreciate me coming home tonight. Although she might also clock me with a frying pan when she realizes I let you take the princess who knows where." He grinned. "Keep her safe, Hunter," he said as he glanced at Kenna. "The kingdom needs the princess now more than ever." And with that, he tore off into the night, blending into the darkness between the buildings. I looked down at the still-unconscious woman in my arms. Now what?

Steeling myself for what was to come, I took off in the opposite direction toward the trees. I knew at this point I was too weak to teleport myself and Kenna. Carrying her slowed me down, but I could still slip into the trees as the first wave of Fae warriors swarmed the explosion site.

King Arrion led the charge in silver armor with gold detailing. He looked utterly furious. "Kenna!" he bellowed in a fit of rage. "Get back here, you half breed wench!"

Kenna stirred in my arms, but I held her tight to my chest and whispered soothingly into her hair. "Shh, love. Stay still."

She quieted in my arms, but I heard a whisper escape her lips. "Killian?"

"I'm here, love. Shhh. I'll get us out of here," I whispered back and slowly stood. I felt Kenna go limp and realized she had passed out yet again. I refused to let anything happen to her, and that resolve bolstered my determination.

Drawing on my Fae bloodline, I urged the flora around me to clear a path for Kenna and me. The brush and trees before me spread apart, and I was presented with a clear path out of the area. As I began to walk forward, I pressed my magic behind me, closing the path and effectively hiding my escape. My grip on Kenna tightened, and my spine stiffened as I heard Arrion yell once again.

"Find the bitch and kill her. She's just like her father, supportive of all those who defy me! I'd rather have no lineage than one that would destroy everything I've worked for. Her life is no longer worth sparing."

My blood ran cold. It was bad enough that he had sent warriors after her before, but this was an entire army.

Cradling Kenna, I took off at a full run. All I could think about was keeping her safe, but I was exhausted, and she was beyond battered. I needed to find a place to rest, but there wasn't a single location that felt safe enough to bring Kenna, except maybe the coven.

Crashing through the brush and trees with no time to focus my magic, I silently prayed to the Goddess, apologizing for damaging her work. I didn't have time to worry about the plants I was destroying; I needed to save Kenna. That was the only thing I could focus on. I held her tight as I ran and willed myself not to pass out from fatigue.

After what felt like hours, I paused at the edge of the In-Between. The darkness of the night had wholly consumed the area, and I could hardly see where I was going. The moon didn't touch the In-Between, as if it feared what lay beneath the thick canopy, just as the locals on either side of the eerie forest did.

I heard the heavy crashing footsteps and the low growl before I saw the glowing eyes of whatever mountain of a creature stalked by the edge of the forest. Taking a deep breath and waiting for it to pass, I had no choice but to find somewhere within the In-Between to hide us for the night. Desperation to save Kenna outweighed all common sense and rational thought. If the Fae army did find us, I hoped that Kenna had gathered enough favor with the monsters of the In-Between to keep us safe from both the army and the creatures within these woods.

As the creature disappeared back into the darkness, I faced the entrance of the In-Between, my eyes adjusting to the shadows. The air was thick with magic, the tendrils of chaos snaking their way through the place's energy. We had to be careful; the longer we stayed here, the more likely we'd attract the unwanted attention of whatever creatures lived in this bleak and mysterious world.

With Kenna cradled in my arms, I cautiously stepped into the In-Between. The ground seemed to shift beneath our feet, and a chill crept up my spine as the darkness closed in around us.

I continued deeper into the darkness and, gradually, the atmosphere changed. The air became thicker, and an almost tangible sense of magic enveloped us. Kenna's body, still cradled against my chest, seemed warm and alive, a reminder of the bond that flowed between us.

As I walked forward, taking careful steps, I noticed a faint glowing that had to be Fae lights dancing in the distance, beckoning us forward. Knowing that Kenna and I needed protection, I didn't question it, and perhaps the Goddess had answered our prayers.

Approaching the area where the lights bobbed, I saw the small faces of two little foxes staring up at me. Violet and Poppy. As if a weight had been lifted from me, I felt a renewed sense of strength and rushed toward the little animals. They didn't shy away from me. Poppy approached me first, slinking through the darkness and sniffing Kenna's limp arm as it dangled from my grasp. She chirped, and Violet gingerly came to sniff Kenna's fingers. Both foxes seemed to heave a sigh of relief and began walking deep into the woods. They stopped and looked at me as if to say, "Come on, you bumbling Hunter."

"Alright," I said quietly. "I'm coming."

I followed the little foxes just a bit further into the darkness and came face-to-face with the mouth of a small cave. Violet and Poppy hopped down the rock ledge and disappeared into the cave. Assuming hiding in a fox den would be safer than staying out here, I carefully stepped down into the mouth of the cave and shifted Kenna so I could carry her inside.

The cave was small and cool but dry, and Fae lights danced along the ceiling. I lay Kenna down gently on a flat spot, and the two foxes scuttled over and curled up along her sides. She was breathing evenly, and I sighed with relief. Her eyes fluttered momentarily, and she muttered my name before easing back into what appeared to be a comfortable sleep.

Her head lolled to the side, resting against one of the foxes, and that was when I noticed the blood matting her red hair. Without the Fae lights, I wouldn't have seen it, and berated myself for not checking her more thoroughly. Poppy licked her hair, trying to clean the wound. I tried to shoo the little creature away, but she bared her teeth at me and made an aggressive, growling noise. Kenna stirred again but didn't quite wake.

"Shhh, Poppy. I want to check the wound and make sure she's alright. I need to clean it, or it might get infected," I cooed to the little animal. She made a sort of groaning noise and moved a little further down Kenna's body, allowing me access to the wound.

I palpated the area, careful not to touch the small cut. Head wounds always bled like a sieve, but this wasn't as bad as it looked. I carefully opened one of Kenna's eyes with my thumb and watched her pupils constrict when the Fae lights met her vision. At least she wasn't concussed. It was more likely she had used all of her magic and depleted herself so intensely from the battle that she would be out for a while.

"I should clean this," I sighed as I rubbed my hands across my face, only then realizing how dirty I was. Violet's ears perked up. "I need to clean us both up, but I don't have clean water or anything to patch her up." I gestured to Kenna. Violet's head cocked to the side, and in one smooth movement, she moved further into the cave. She stopped at the edge of the Fae lights and chirped once at me, as if asking me to follow. I looked at Poppy, who laid her head on Kenna's chest.

"Will she be safe with you? Just for a moment," I asked. Poppy made a snorting sound that I assumed meant she was offended that I would even ask such a thing. "Alright then."

I followed Violet back into the cave, just a few feet past the Fae lights, and stepped directly into a small moving stream of cold water. "Thanks for the warning," I chided. Violet made a slight chuffing noise, which I took as a laugh.

I wasn't sure how the Fae lights had come to be in this cave. Although some were naturally occurring collections of magic, they seemed to hold a presence that mirrored Kenna's. It hit me then as I started to wash my hands in the stream, that this was likely near where Kenna had found the foxes as babies, and these Fae lights must have been hers. It was incredible to me that she was powerful enough that these lights remained a year later.

One of the Fae lights from the main cavern of the cave drifted back toward me and provided just enough light for me to see that I was standing in a pool fed by a spring within the cave. The water would be safe to drink then. After rinsing my hands as best I could, I scooped up some water and drank hastily before assessing the area around me, hoping to find something to bring water back to Kenna. I thought for a moment I saw a glimmer of something iridescent in the water, but dismissed it.

My head snapped toward the mouth of the cave as heavy crashing footsteps passed by, and a thump sounded as a large object fell into the cave entrance. Violet and Poppy seemed unperturbed and kept doing their fox things. Cautiously, I stepped back into the main cavern and toward the lump on the ground. As I drew closer, I saw it was a soldier's pack. The purple embroidery on the grey bag showed it was from one of the king's soldiers. The blood on the strap gave me the impression that this soldier had met his end tragically. Abruptly, I realized the mountain of a creature had likely killed one of the royal guards who had tried to follow us and then had brought the bag here; it had brought the pack to Kenna.

"Thank the Goddess!" I cried in relief, knowing the pack would have basic survival and healing supplies. I looked back at Kenna's sleeping form and thanked the Goddess again that Kenna was loved by so many of these odd and beautiful creatures. Her dedication to respecting the world around her, as the Mother Goddess commanded, was awe-inspiring and made me love her even more.

Grabbing the pack by the strap that wasn't stained with blood, I rifled through it, searching for some water vessels and healing supplies. I found a small canteen filled with fresh water and a small felt roll containing tiny healing salve vials. Relief flooded through me.

I returned to her side, careful not to disturb the foxes curled protectively around her. Poppy raised her head and watched me intently as I cleaned Kenna's wound. After I cleaned as much of the blood away as I could, I checked the wound once again. The gash on her head wasn't deep, but it needed to be treated to prevent infection. Kenna stirred slightly in her sleep, a faint furrow appearing on her brow before she relaxed again. I uncorked one of the vials, carefully spreading the soothing balm over Kenna's wound. The cut began to close before my eyes, healing rapidly under the influence of the magical salve. It did not heal completely, but the bleeding stopped.

After ensuring Kenna was as comfortable as possible and giving her small sips of water from the canteen, I focused on the rest of the supplies in the soldier's pack. Amongst the basic provisions, I found a map detailing the surrounding areas and a small pouch of dried rations. The map showed several landmarks I recognized, hinting at a possible path to safety if we could navigate the treacherous woods.

I stood up and took the canteen to the small spring in the back of the cave to refill it. As I stepped down onto the ledge next to the water, I saw the iridescence again. This time, however, large blue eyes peered back at me. A water sprite. Local lore made them out to be mischievous creatures that could help you or drown you, depending on their mood.

I stared for a moment before remembering my manners and trying to emulate Kenna's dedication to showing respect to all creatures. I bowed my head. "I apologize if I am intruding," I said softly. "My bonded is injured, and I need clean water to sustain us until we can reach safety."

When I lifted my head, the sprite said nothing but gave a small nod and seemed to blend back into the water before a small blue flower floated to the surface. I had no idea what the flower might have been used for, but I had to assume it was a gesture of peace, letting me know that it was alright to take the water. I carefully filled the canteen. "Thank you. Your kindness will never be forgotten, and I will forever be grateful."

Giving the odd little pool of water one last glance, I stood and walked back toward the mouth of the cave toward Kenna. I settled the canteen in the pile of items on the cave floor and took a moment to collect my thoughts.

I was grateful it was a warm night, or this damp cave would have chilled us to the bone. I looked out into the night.

"Thank you," I called out a bit hesitantly. A growl came from somewhere outside the cave. I assumed that was the shadow creature's acknowledgment of my thanks —regardless of the disturbing sound— and appreciated that the creature had responded.

As I settled back against the cave wall, exhaustion began to seep into my bones. The day's events had taken their toll on me physically and emotionally. The adrenaline that had fueled me through the battle was now ebbing away, leaving me drained and vulnerable.

I glanced at Kenna, still sleeping soundly despite the commotion around her. Her chest rose and fell in a steady rhythm, a testament to her resilience even in unconsciousness. The Fae lights flickered around her, casting an ethereal glow that seemed to protect her slumber.

Outside the cave, the night was alive with mysterious sounds and movements. Shadows danced across the forest floor as unseen creatures moved about in the darkness. A feeling of unease crept over me, a primal instinct warning me of lurking dangers.

I closed my eyes, trying to push away my fears and doubts. Tomorrow would bring its own challenges, but for now, all I could do was rest and gather my strength for the trials ahead. With a silent prayer to the Goddess for protection, I settled beside Kenna, wrapping us both in a cloak from the soldier's pack. Violet and Poppy wiggled beneath the warm fabric and snuggled into Kenna's side. The scent of pine and earth surrounded me, lulling me into a fitful sleep filled with dreams of battles fought and victories to be won.

When I woke, the first light of dawn was filtering into the cave, casting a golden hue over everything it touched. Kenna stirred beside me, her eyes fluttering open as she slowly regained consciousness. She blinked up at me, confusion clouding her gaze.

"Where are we?" she asked, her voice hoarse from sleep and exhaustion. Her eyes fluttered, and she slumped into my hold again.

"We're safe for now," I replied, offering her a reassuring smile. "Your Fae lights found us a cave, and your little friends helped me tend to you. One of the In-Between creatures brought us some supplies, too." I gestured towards the soldier's pack that now lay empty beside us, its contents strewn about in our makeshift camp.

"Oh," she said sleepily.

"It's alright, love. Sleep. I'll keep us safe." A small smile graced her lips before she closed her eyes again, and her breathing slowed just a bit. I looked at Violet and Poppy, lying with their small heads perched on Kenna's stomach. "We have to move from here. I can't imagine the royal army will remain outside the In-Between during daylight." Both foxes chirped as if they understood.

I carefully moved out from under the cloak and began putting things in the bag. It wasn't much, but based on the map, I could likely make it to the coven by nightfall if I hurried. I was exhausted, though, and the likelihood that I'd have to carry Kenna the rest of the way weighed on me.

I secured the pack to my back, ensuring it was tightly fastened and well-balanced. I lifted Kenna into my arms, attempting to avoid jostling her too much. She felt so small in my grasp. Harnessing my strength, I resolved to get her to the coven if it was the last thing I did.

I stepped outside from the safety of the cave as the golden light of dawn slowly crept over the dark and shadowed landscape. The air was cool and crisp, the remnants of the night's chill still lingering in the forest. I took a moment to gaze at the horizon, trying to determine our bearings from the map.

Despite the calm of the morning, my heart raced at the thought of leaving the safety of the cave and venturing back into the woods. We needed to move fast. The sun was rising quickly, and I could already hear the faint sound of distant footsteps and clanging metal. The army must have been closer than I thought. My heart pounded against my chest as I knew the soldiers would be approaching soon, and I couldn't afford to be caught unaware.

I looked to Poppy and Violet, who sat calmly where Kenna

had been lying. "Are you coming?" Both foxes laid down, tails wagging, and whined. Acknowledging that they were not going to be joining us, I nodded my head to them. "I'll keep her safe."

On leaving the cave, I noted the massive patch of flattened grass and foliage. One of the shadow creatures from the In-Between had likely slept outside the cave. Again, I felt a sense of gratitude for the love this terrifying and dangerous forest felt for Kenna.

A roar sounded in the distance, and I heard the clang of metal. The hair on the back of my neck raised, and a sense of anxiety skittered down my spine. There must have been a shadow creature keeping the army at bay. From the sounds of it, we had few precious moments to get out of here. With that realization dawning on me, I ran, crashing through brush and vines.

31

KILLIAN

I didn't know how long I ran, and honestly, I would have been lying if I'd said I cared. The only thing I cared about was getting the suddenly frail and seemingly fragile woman in my arms to the only people who could potentially heal and save her.

The forest blurred past me as I carried Kenna through the dense undergrowth, my heart pounding with fear and determination. The soldier's pack bounced against my back, the weight a comforting reminder that allies were hidden within the shadows. Behind me, I could hear the sounds of pursuit growing closer, the shouts and clamor of the soldiers driving me onward.

The soldiers relentlessly pursued, their armored footsteps pounding against the forest floor like a war drum. I knew we couldn't outrun them for long, but I refused to give up without a fight. I would not let them take Kenna.

A piercing howl echoed through the forest, causing my steps to falter. Catching my balance again, I chanced a glance behind me. A massive shadow loomed in the trees, blocking the army's path with its imposing presence. It was a creature unlike any I had ever seen, with dark fur and glowing eyes that seemed to pierce through to the very core of my being.

The soldiers came to an abrupt halt, their expressions shifting from aggression to uncertainty as they faced this unknown threat. The shadow creature stood its ground, a silent guardian protecting us from harm.

Taking advantage of the distraction, I quickened my pace, determination surging. The path ahead was treacherous, but we could reach safety with the shadow creature holding off our pursuers. Kenna stirred in my arms; her warmth and weight were comforting even amid the chaos. Squeezing her to me just a little bit tighter, I pressed onward.

I ran until the forest began to thin and more sunset hues filtered through the shadows. I ran until the tower of the coven school came into view. I ran until the gates around the coven lands were before me. My mind was frantic with thoughts of Kenna's injuries and I pushed myself harder than I ever had before.

The coven tower loomed before me, a massive stone structure rising high into the sky. Its ancient walls were etched with intricate runes and symbols that seemed to pulse with power. As I approached the imposing structure, I could feel the energy in the air shift, a palpable hum of magic surrounding the keep like a protective barrier.

Abruptly, I felt a tingling sensation on my skin, alerting me that if I didn't slow down, I would smash both of us directly into a ward. At this hour, there were no guards as the wards hadn't been opened yet, which meant getting in would be a feat all its own.

"Kenna. Kenna, love, I need you to wake up." I gave her a gentle shake. Her green eyes cracked open, and she peered at me, unable to focus. Good Goddess, she was a mess. "Kenna, how do I get through the coven's ward?" I asked a little impatiently.

"Only love shall enter, only love shall leave…" she managed to whisper before succumbing to unconsciousness again.

"Kenna. Kenna, I don't know what that means, love!" I cried, distraught and fearful that I couldn't protect the one person I needed most in this world. She pulled in a shuddering breath but didn't open her eyes before repeating herself.

"Only love shall enter…" She struggled for another breath. "Only love shall leave…" She breathed the last word so quietly, I had to press her lips to my ear to hear her. I was starting to panic. I didn't have time for riddles if she was struggling this much.

With Kenna still clutched tightly in my arms, I began pacing. What the fuck could she be going on about? My mind was whirling, and I was starting to feel like I had angry bees buzzing in my brain instead of thoughts.

Suddenly, I stopped. A memory of my mother surfaced, of her once telling me about Witches she had been charged to kill but couldn't reach. She had told me that their protection ward included an incantation that denied any negative energy or intentions, and thus, she hadn't been able to touch them.

That was it. I loved Kenna, and I would never hurt her or her coven. *Only love shall enter; only love shall leave.* My intentions were pure, and I wouldn't cause them harm. That would work, right? It was all I had, and I believed it would let me through the ward. I could hear the Fae warriors in the distance and knew I was running out of time.

Steeling myself, I took a deep breath and held Kenna tightly to my chest. I stepped forward, one foot in front of the other, waiting for the electric shock of the ward to send me ricocheting backward. I could only hope Kenna would make it through without me.

When I met no resistance, pain, or shock, I looked up directly into the face of Mrs. Lancaster, coven leader and the woman who had raised Kenna.

"Hello, Hunter. You're late, and we don't have much time. Come along," she said briskly before turning on her heel and striding away toward a large stone building surrounded by smaller stone structures. My jaw dropped.

32
KILLIAN

I hustled to keep up with the headmistress, still cradling Kenna. Mrs. Lancaster looked at me and raised an eyebrow.

"Ask your questions now, Hunter, while I'm still in a good mood," she said.

"How did you know we were coming? How do you know me? Can you save Kenna?" The questions tumbled out.

"I have the gift of foresight. I know a lot of things. Yes, I can save Kenna, but we must hurry. There isn't much time. Unless you want to feel excruciating pain or insanity, I suggest you pick up the pace, Mr. Cambell," she said coldly.

I followed her into one of the smaller stone structures, where I was greeted by three other women, bustling about with bunches of herbs and other plants. One woman laid a blanket on what looked like a large wooden table.

"Lay her there, Mr. Cambell," Mrs. Lancaster barked out. Snapping out of my stupor, I placed Kenna on the blanket and brushed red curls away from her face. Refusing to let go of her, I held onto her hand, which suddenly felt so small and fragile.

"You need to go elsewhere. You are in the way," Mrs.

Lancaster said bluntly. She glared at me, annoyed I was still in the small structure. The women continued their bustling, but their ears were clearly tuned to the conversation.

"No. The only way I'm leaving her is if you kill me, and that would most likely kill her too, considering I'm her bonded, so I'm pretty sure that would defeat the purpose of all of this." I glared back. One of the women covered her mouth in what I assumed was shock and tried to suppress a gasp. I could imagine that not many people said no to the coven leader.

"Stop staring, Maeve," Mrs. Lancaster scolded. She turned to me with an intense stare. She looked to be assessing me, and I internally began to prepare for a battle. "Maybe you are worthy of this Fae bond after all…" was all she said before turning and taking a poultice from one of the women behind her. "You may stay, but if you get in my way, I will make sure you pay for it dearly." I knew the threat was empty. Kenna was like her daughter, and she would never put her life in danger. But the cold stare she gave me still sent shivers down my spine.

I stood at Kenna's side, watching the women spread salves and creams on her burns, poultices on bruises I hadn't had enough salve to treat, and set what I assumed were likely a few broken bones. Mrs. Lancaster raised an eyebrow at me but said nothing as she studied the wounds, stopping to inspect the semi-healed location where I had used the salve on Kenna's scalp.

The women in the building moved in silence, dancing around each other while Mrs. Lancaster whispered under her breath, her eyes closed and her hands hovering over Kenna's body. I felt the energy pulsing through the small space as she worked. It was tangy like lightning, and it tasted like sour grapefruit.

Kenna began to groan, and her body began to shudder. Holding her hand tighter, I whispered soothingly, "Hush, love, you're safe." Kenna seemed to calm down, and her body stopped trembling.

I looked up to see Mrs. Lancaster, with one eye cracked open, continuing her whispered chant, studying me. When she saw I had noticed her, she snapped her eye shut, cleared her throat, and continued chanting. A small smile spread across my face. I was sure this woman, who cared greatly about Kenna despite her cruel outward presentation, could heal the battle wounds she had sustained. That was something I would never be able to formulate an appropriate thank you for.

As the headmistress continued her healing work, a soft golden light emanated from her hands, enveloping Kenna in a warm glow. The air in the room seemed to hum with magic, and I could feel the tension slowly melting away as Kenna's injuries started to heal before my eyes. It was both mesmerizing and comforting, a testament to the power of the coven leader.

Kenna's wounds began to close painfully slowly. Kenna's labored breathing had just started to even out when I noticed the glow dimming. Mrs. Lancaster's face was etched in concentration and pain.

"Your magic... it's almost gone, isn't it?" I asked cautiously. I knew Witches only had so much power to draw from and couldn't imagine even the coven leader had much left.

"Yes." She sighed. "And we're running out of time... Unlike your other half, I cannot draw my magic from the world around me. I deeply regret it, but I once allowed the other coven girls to use her like a source of power so they could practice, and so she would toughen up. I knew she would always surpass them, regardless. It seemed a good idea at the time, but I know now that is not the case. She harbors a darkness, and I believe I am to blame. If I cannot save her, I will have failed her in more ways than one..." She trailed off, looking utterly defeated.

"Use me," I said with conviction.

"What?" She turned to look at me, shock registering in her tired old eyes.

"If you can use Kenna as a source because she can draw from the earth, then you can use me. I am half Fae, too. Use me. You said it yourself: we're running out of time, and I refuse to let her die."

Mrs. Lancaster looked at me and shook her head while a small smile crept onto her face. "Yes, you are quite a match for my little spitfire, aren't you?" she mused. "You must let go of her, or I will draw her energy. Give me your hand, Mr. Cambell. Let's save your beloved." I released my grip on Kenna, and the old crone grinned as she took my hand and resumed her chanting.

As Mrs. Lancaster intertwined her magic with mine, a surge of power unlike anything I had ever experienced coursed through me. It was as if the very essence of the earth itself was flowing into my veins, mingling with my Fae heritage to create a potent force of healing energy. I focused all my willpower on channeling this power towards Kenna, willing her wounds to close and her strength to return.

The room filled with brilliant light, swirling around Kenna and me, intertwining our beings in a dance of magic and energy. I could feel a powerful tether coursing through me, connecting me to Kenna in a way I had never imagined possible. Mrs. Lancaster's voice rose in a melodic chant, resonating with ancient power as she drew from the depths of my Fae heritage.

I closed my eyes and focused on Kenna and the unbreakable connection that bound us together. Despite the overwhelming sensation of magic flowing through me, a sense of peace settled over my soul, a certainty that we would emerge from this trial stronger than before.

As Mrs. Lancaster continued her chant, the wounds on Kenna's body began to heal at an accelerated rate. The burns faded, the bruises vanished, and even the broken bones seemed to knit themselves back together before my astonished eyes. Color returned to Kenna's cheeks, a rosy hue replacing the pallor of death that had haunted her features. Her breathing steadied, becoming strong and steady once more. It was a miracle unfolding before me, a testament to the indomitable power of love and magic intertwined.

As the last injuries faded away, Mrs. Lancaster's chanting ended. The room fell silent, the only sound the soft rustle of fabric as Kenna shifted on the makeshift bed, still not fully conscious. I turned to look at Mrs. Lancaster, gratitude and awe shining in my eyes.

"Thank you," I whispered, my voice full of emotion.

Mrs. Lancaster nodded, a weary but satisfied smile on her lips. "She will need time to rest and recover. The healing magic will sustain her for now, but she needs to regain her strength."

I nodded, my gaze returning to Kenna's face, peaceful in repose. I brushed a strand of hair away from her forehead, feeling an overwhelming wave of relief.

33

KENNA

I awoke in a small stone structure with damp fabric draped over my eyes, and a familiar herbal smell floated through the air. I reached for the cloth but found my hand encased in someone else's fingers. Fear washed through me, and I tensed, trying to pull my hand away.

"It's me, love. You're safe." Killian's soothing voice filtered through the fog encasing my brain.

"Where am I?" I asked, my voice was raspy, and my throat dry. The action caused me to cough, which jostled the damp cloth from my face. The light in the room was bright, and it took my eyes a minute to adjust. My eyes widened. I was in a healing hut at the coven. I whipped my head to the side, looking at Killian and giving myself the spins.

"I didn't know where else to go, love. I couldn't lose you, and this was the only place I could think of to go." His eyes were full of pain and fear, and I couldn't help but reach out and touch his cheek with my fingers.

"I'm here. I would never leave you," I said softly.

He pressed his face into my hand and kissed my palm. "You almost did, love..." He choked out his nickname for me as if the memory caused him physical pain. I slowly pulled myself to a sitting position, allowing my body to adjust to the movement.

"Never," I said with absolute certainty. "I love you."

Killian beamed. "I love you, too." He placed a gentle kiss on my lips.

"Ahem."

I knew that voice and sprang away from Killian like a maiden who had just been caught kissing her beau after curfew.

"Mrs. Lancaster!" My voice came out much shriller than I would have liked.

"As adorable as your little reunion is, the healing hut is not a place for lovers' trysts," Mrs. Lancaster said with a hint of amusement. She approached us, her eyes full of fondness and exasperation. "You gave us all quite a scare, Kenna. It's good to see you awake and among us again."

I tried to stand, feeling shaky, but determined not to show weakness. Killian moved to support me, his arm wrapping around my waist protectively. Mrs. Lancaster watched us with a knowing smile before her expression became serious.

"I must warn you, the danger is not over yet," she said, her voice low and grave.

Killian cleared his throat and stood up straight, suddenly looking every inch the respectful gentleman. "Thank you for saving her, Mrs. Lancaster. We are forever in your debt."

The old crone waved off his gratitude with a smile. "It was not only me, but the power of your bond that brought her back from the brink. Love is magic all its own, one that cannot be underestimated."

I shifted on the bed, embarrassed and grateful for Mrs. Lancaster's words. "Thank you, both of you." My eyes met Killian's with an intensity that spoke volumes.

Both Killian and Mrs. Lancaster shared a glance and a smile. The headmistress abruptly turned and headed out the door, motioning for us to follow her.

"Come along. I have foreseen the Fae army's arrival. They will not be here until tomorrow. I will show you to a room you may share for the night." We skidded to a stop as she turned to face us with a stern look. "Please use the room to rest. I expect you—" she motioned at Killian "—to be a respectable gentleman and keep your hands to yourself."

Killian blushed furiously at Mrs. Lancaster's pointed remark, but he nodded earnestly in response. I couldn't help but chuckle at his flustered reaction before turning my attention back to Mrs. Lancaster. She led us through the winding corridors of the coven manor, her long skirts swishing with each step.

As we walked, my mind raced about the impending Fae army's arrival. I couldn't shake off the foreboding that lingered in the air. The Fae army's imminent arrival meant our time to prepare was limited, and the stakes were higher than ever. But with Killian by my side, his presence a steady reassurance, I felt a measure of courage kindling within me.

Mrs. Lancaster stopped before a wooden door adorned with intricate carvings depicting spell markings. She turned to us, her expression grave yet determined.

"This room will offer you safety for the night." She opened the door to reveal a small, modest room with a bed, a desk and chair, a large armoire, and a small washroom in an alcove on one side. "Rest while you can, for tomorrow will bring challenges that will test your resolve," she said cryptically before turning to walk away.

"Mrs. Lancaster." My voice was sharp, and she stopped before slowly turning back toward me. Killian stiffened beside me, picking up on the shift in my demeanor. "I need to rest, that is true, but you owe me an explanation." Her shoulders slumped, and she took a few steps toward us.

She sighed and motioned for us to enter the room. As we stepped inside, the warm light of candles illuminated the space, casting shadows that danced along the walls. The room was simple yet elegant, with tapestries hanging from the walls and minimal furniture.

She closed the door behind us, her eyes holding a mixture of weariness and wisdom. Taking a deep breath, she began to speak.

"You are right to demand an explanation, Kenna," she began, her words measured and deliberate. She motioned for us to sit on the bed as she pulled a chair closer to the bedside. "It has been a long time since I've allowed myself to think of your mother." She looked into my eyes. "I assume that is what you are asking about."

"What happened to her? Who was she? Did you know my father?" My mind churned with questions, and I struggled to sort them. Mrs. Lancaster hesitated momentarily, her gaze far away as memories seemed to wash over her. She took a deep breath before beginning her tale.

"Your mother, Elara, was a powerful Witch with a kind heart and a fierce determination. She was one of the most gifted seers our coven has ever seen, and her magic was unparalleled. She also possessed an affinity for gardening, which I believe you inherited." She raised an eyebrow at me, and I smiled softly. "She was well-known by many within the different realms, and people from all over the continent came to see her. One of her visitors was your father. He was troubled with his royal lineage, the loss of his mother, and the expectation that he would take the crown and rule a land full of the distrust that his father had created."

"You knew..." It felt as if the floor dropped out from under me.

"I did what I thought was necessary to protect you. If the king ever found out who you were or what you were capable of..."

I shook my head, my heart breaking as the realization dawned on me. I understood why she had not told me the truth, but it did not soften the sharp edge of pain. "You lied. You knew who my father was all this time..."

Killian sat silently on the bed, not daring to interrupt. "I won't lie and say that I did not despise him. As the Fae prince, he was the embodiment of everything I hated, especially after the queen died. His kind treated the Witches with immense disrespect, and if a Witch wandered into the Fae territory, they often never returned. I did not trust him, and once I realized they had become quite close and he was visiting her privately, I banned him from coven lands. It was too late at that point; your mother had already become pregnant with you." She sighed and looked into my eyes. "I am not proud of my choices; please know that." I gave no response, and she solemnly continued.

"When I banned him from entering the coven lands, and your mother learned of my actions, she threatened to leave. Instead of trying to reason with her, I was so angry that I told her to go. I took my own anger toward the Fae prince out on a woman I considered akin to my own child. I had raised her here when her own mother and father were killed in an accident." Tears began to stream down her face.

I felt my own eyes blur, but said nothing. Killian wrapped his arm around me and pulled me close. "She immediately ran to your father, and they began building that little cottage you love so much in the In-Between. I was terrified your mother would face a fate worse than death in the dark woods, but somehow, she tamed the wild in that small patch of land you call home, and the monsters seemed to leave her be. I resolved to watch her from afar and trust my visions that she would be well and your father would care for her."

Mrs Lancaster smiled then, a new memory washing over her as she wiped away stray tears. "I was so happy the night you were born. I'd seen it the day before and knew how beautiful a baby you would be." I wiped a tear from my cheek. "I stayed out of their life at that point, resolving that your mother had made her choice and seemed happy and healthy. You were growing, and your father adored you."

"What was he like?" I sniffled.

"Oh, he was quite handsome, I suppose, and didn't act like a prince at all; in fact, he acted quite commonly despite my expectation that he would be a spoiled brat. He was tall and thin with bright red hair like yours and lilac eyes. He was fair, compared to your mother, with her dark hair and deep green eyes. He was a happy man, but he carried the heavy burden of his realm. You didn't need to be a seer to know that." She sniffled and wiped her nose with a handkerchief she had produced from somewhere hidden within her skirts.

"What happened?" I asked hesitantly. I wanted—no, needed—to know, but I was also terrified of the answer.

"The Fae king must have finally tracked down your father, despite his and your mother's attempts to cover their location with magic. The Fae king is notoriously unfond of outsiders."

"Oh, I am well aware." I grimaced at the memory of the forced matchmaking.

Mrs. Lancaster lowered her gaze, acknowledging what I had endured. "You were only three months old, and your parents were so in love with you they didn't see the attack coming. The Hunters tracked your parents and led the guards. They snuck up on the cottage at night. Your father was killed trying to hold back the attack while your mother escaped. He had no weapons. He did not think he would need any."

She shuddered as the memory overtook her. I felt my heart shatter as she spoke. "Your mother ran through the woods of the In-Between to the coven. A thunderstorm began, and you both were drenched as she banged on the coven doors. It was quite late, and I was slow to open the door. When I did, I was met with your frantic mother, who pushed you into my arms, screaming, and told me to take care of you and raise you as my own. She took off into the woods again before I could question her or bring her inside. I had a vision then of the guards catching up to her and killing her. I knew then she had sacrificed herself to save you. Both of your parents had." Tears fell freely from her face as she recalled the horrific memories.

I sobbed, and Killian tightened his grip on me, enveloping me in his warmth.

"I'm so sorry, Kenna. I should have done more. I should have been honest with you from the start. I should have been better to you from the beginning." Her remorse was evident as she began to cry.

"You did what she asked," I choked out between sobs.

"Kenna, love, breathe," Killian soothed.

We all sat silently for a moment, trying to absorb the gravity of the story she had just shared. My sadness and confusion grew with each detail, my mind struggling to process this newfound history. Eventually, my sobs subsided, and only the echoing hiccups and a few stray tears were left. Killian kissed my temple before releasing me from his grip.

"I'll run you a bath, love," he whispered as he stood and walked to the tub on the other side of the room. Mrs. Lancaster stood and smiled sadly.

"You are a lot like Elara, you know. You chose your own path as she did, and you found true love just as she did." She placed the chair back at the desk and moved toward the door. I heard the water fill the tub as Killian moved around the room. "I will leave you two to rest. Food will be brought up to you, and there are clothes in the cabinet." She pointed to the armoire across the room. She turned to look directly at Killian. "Take care of her, Hunter."

"Yes, ma'am," he replied with resolve.

I moved toward Mrs. Lancaster and embraced her for the first time in many years. The warmth of her body against mine was comforting, but I couldn't shake the feeling of emptiness. The revelation of my parents' sacrifice was overwhelming and still felt so far away. I inhaled and whispered, "Thank you for everything, Mrs. Lancaster."

She hugged me tightly and whispered, "You are a strong woman, Kenna. You will get through this."

As she left the room, I turned to Killian, who was already undoing the belt on his pants. He looked at me, his eyes filled with concern and love. I wanted to forget about my past, but the reality was that I couldn't. The past was a part of me, and I would have to learn to accept it.

I stepped toward him, beginning to pull up the hem of my dirty, torn tunic. Killian replaced my fingers with his.

"Let me, love," he cooed. Killian peeled the tunic from my body, careful not to bump into any remaining bruises. His fingers brushed along my ribs and the underside of my breasts as he reached around me to untie my undergarments. "Are you okay, love?" he whispered, pulling me to him.

"I think so," I said with a slight nod as I snuggled closer to him. I pushed thoughts of my parents to the back of my mind and directed my attention toward the man in front of me, trying to stay present in the here and now. "Although," I noted with a wrinkled nose, "you do have a bit of a ripe scent." A bath would benefit us both.

Killian chuckled. The deep sound of his laugh reverberated through me as he held me. At this moment, for the first time in days, I felt safe. Slowly letting go of the hold I had on his waist, I began to finish the job Killian had started and slid his pants down to the floor. He stepped out of them and lifted his gaze to mine.

"Are you sure? If you want to rest, that's fine with me," he said with concern.

"Killian, I might die tomorrow. You might die tomorrow. If that's the case, I'm living my life tonight, right here, with you." I moved my hands to his chest and traced the lines of muscles and the map of scars across his abdomen. He tensed in anticipation at my touch. His manhood lengthened and hardened against my stomach as I moved my hands lower and lower.

Killian stepped out of my grasp, his desire visible by the bulge in his drawers. He reverently removed my leggings and panties, all while worshipping my skin with kisses.

A shiver ran down my spine as my bare skin touched the cool air. Killian's warm hands moved over me, igniting a fire smoldering within me. His lips trailed kisses up my body to my neck, sending waves of pleasure through me. I pulled him closer, wanting to feel every inch of him against me.

Removing his remaining article of clothing, I took his length in my hand, easing my hand up and down his shaft. He hardened even further and moaned against my neck.

"Goddess, Kenna. I've missed your touch," he groaned.

With a hunger that matched my own, Killian lifted me effortlessly and carried me towards the tub. The water was warm and inviting, welcoming after the day's turmoil. He lowered me into the bath, his eyes never leaving mine. His gaze pierced through me, reaching parts of my soul that had long been hidden.

I reached for him and pulled him into the tub with me. Our bodies tangled as we sank into the warm water, our love and desire for each other palpable. The warmth from Killian's strong arms and the water enveloped me and eased my sore muscles.

Killian poured soap onto a cloth and brushed the fabric over my shoulders, then my neck, and down to my chest. He tenderly scrubbed away the dirt from the last several days with practiced care. He motioned for me to sit forward so that he could slide behind me. There were no words, only the gentle caress of Killian's fingertips as he massaged soap into my hair, careful not to irritate the still-sore patch of my scalp. I tipped my head back, and he rinsed my hair with the pitcher next to the tub. With my eyes closed, I focused on the feeling of his touch, the expression of profound love he felt for me.

Once Killian removed his fingers from my hair, I fluidly turned and began to wash away the filth and grime from his body. After rinsing away the soap from his skin, I kissed his neck before turning to pick up the water pitcher. Seated in Killian's lap, with his hard length still pressing into my belly, I washed and rinsed his hair as well. The scent of the herbal cleansers washing over us both filled the air.

I reached for Killian's neck and pulled his mouth to mine. He kissed me deeply, our tongues dancing together, our passion growing with each touch. I reached between us, taking his cock in my hand again, guiding him to enter me. He groaned into my mouth as he slid inside me, filling me completely. The stretch was so delicious, and all my senses narrowed to the sensation of him.

Killian began to move his hips, and I was distantly aware of small sloshes of water spilling out of the tub as he captured my moan with his lips. There would never be enough of these moments, pure, unadulterated love between us.

Grasping at him with desperation, I pulled my body closer, allowing myself to sink even further down his length. Throwing my head back, I released a moan that I have no doubt others heard, but I couldn't be bothered to care.

Killian smiled into my neck and pressed gentle kisses to my breasts before taking one nipple into his mouth and rubbing the other with his thumb. I moaned again, arching into him, chasing the ecstasy that came when he hit that deliciously sensitive spot within my walls.

Killian lightly bit my nipples, causing a shockwave of pleasure to rock through my body before he pulled his mouth away. I whined in protest.

"I know, love, but we're making a mess." He gestured to the water that had sloshed onto the floor. I pouted before hastily grabbing his shoulders as he lifted us both from the water, carefully pulling himself from my center as he stood. "I didn't say I had plans to stop." He grinned as he stepped out of the tub.

He set me down, and we dried each other off until the towel was forgotten. His fingers danced along my skin and found their way to my entrance. I let out another moan as he pressed his fingertips into the sensitive bundle of nerves there and worked my body like an instrument he played professionally. Waves of ecstasy flowed through me at his touch.

"Killian," I whispered, my voice thick with desire, "please, I need you."

He smiled at me, his eyes filled with pure adoration. "You have no idea how much I need you, too, love."

Taking my hand, he led me to the soft bed. I lay down, my body malleable to his touch. Killian knelt between my legs; his eyes locked onto mine as he positioned himself at my entrance. He ran the tip of his cock up my slit and teased the overstimulated bundle of nerves, causing me to buck my hips forward. Then, with a single swift motion, he thrust himself into me, never breaking eye contact. I cried out in pleasure, the sensation of fullness taking my breath away.

I clawed at his back in a silent plea to be even closer and whimpered as he pulled himself free of me before sliding back in. He set a torturously slow pace, pulling out and pressing into me with restraint. I could feel his muscles bunching as he held himself back.

"Killian," I breathed his name, "let go."

He lost all restraint at that point, my words breaking the dam holding him back. He slid in and out of my wet walls at a dizzying pace. I dragged my nails down his back, and he moaned as he thrust into me hard. I let out a breathy gasp as I felt him bury himself deep inside me.

"Yes," I cried out, encouraging yet another deep thrust from Killian. Our bodies moved in perfect synchronicity, the love and passion between us manifesting in every stroke. Our breaths became ragged, matching our movements. My nails dug into his back, desperate to be as close as possible. Killian groaned, his name falling from my lips with every thrust. His pace quickened, pushing me over the edge.

I wrapped my legs around his hips, pulling him deeper into me. His mouth left mine to find my sensitive nipple, and I arched my back, my second climax building quickly. Killian released my nipple from his lips after biting down and sending intoxicating torrents of sensation through my body. Killian's eyes locked onto mine as he plunged into me one more time. A wave of euphoria engulfed me, and I screamed his name, clutching him tightly.

I bucked beneath him, feeling my orgasm crest as his body shuddered above me. He wrapped his arms around me, drawing our bodies even closer, and continued to thrust as I came again, shivering in pleasure—the room filled with the sound of our lovemaking, the force of our passion filling the air.

Killian released his tight grip on me to kiss me, our tongues darting and mingling, tasting each other as our bodies moved in rhythm. I tightened my legs around him, pulling him deeper into me, feeling him explode inside of me with a final, fiery thrust.

As we lay entwined in the aftermath of our lovemaking, I felt a deep sense of contentment wash over me. Our bodies still pressed together, I whispered his name into the candlelit room, savoring the moment. Killian's eyes locked onto mine, filled with a depth of emotion.

"I love you, Kenna."

"I love you, too," I whispered.

Killian kissed my temple before slowly extracting himself from me. I felt his seed drip from my opening and shifted to get up from the bed to clean myself up.

"No. Let me," Killian whispered. He stepped away from the bed, holding up a hand to remind me to stay put. I lay back on the pillows, and he returned with a damp cloth. He gently removed the remnants of our lovemaking before offering me a hand and helping me stand. I made my way to the washroom alcove again, carefully sidestepping the pool of water on the floor. Waving my hand, I helped the water float up from the floor and back into the tub.

After cleaning myself up the rest of the way, I padded back to the bedroom and found Killian, still wholly nude, trying to figure out how to open the armoire. I gave a breathy chuckle as I pushed him away from the giant wooden doors engraved with spell-casting symbols. I placed my hands on the intricate carved spider center on both doors.

"The Goddess will give us what we need. You just need to know how to ask."

Killian watched as the door glowed with energy as I asked for some nightclothes. "Should you be doing that, Kenna? Aren't you tired?"

"I'm fine." I smiled at him as the armoire shuffled and the door clicked. Swinging open the doors, I found various men's and women's nightclothes hanging within. I reached in and picked out a soft white nightshirt for me and a pair of cotton trousers for Killian. As I handed them to him, I couldn't help but notice the way his eyes lingered on my body, still flushed from our lovemaking.

"You look stunning, love." Killian's voice was low and husky, sending a shiver down my spine.

"Thank you." A blush crept up my neck.

I sat down on the edge of the bed and slipped into the nightshirt, the silky fabric caressing my skin as I did. Killian joined me, effortlessly slipping on the bottoms.

"Would you like something to eat?" he asked. It was only then that I remembered Mrs. Lancaster promising food earlier. I nodded vigorously. I had eaten very little over the last few days and was famished. My stomach growled in agreement, earning a chuckle from Killian. He stood and moved across the room to open the door. He picked up a small covered tray and returned to the bed.

Uncovering the tray, my eyes widened as I saw a spread of delicacies arranged on it: fresh fruits, cheeses, and herbed bread. A small bottle of the coven's signature blackberry wine sat beside two silver goblets. My stomach rumbled in anticipation.

"I'm starved," I admitted, my eyes never leaving the food.

Killian chuckled, sitting down next to me on the bed. He poured a glass of wine for each of us and handed me mine. We sat silently momentarily as I indulged in the treats before me. Once we'd filled our stomachs, Killian set the tray on the desk and returned to the bed.

Snuggling in under the covers, I curled into him. I couldn't help but feel a sense of inseparable connection to this man. Killian wrapped his arms around me, pulling me close and nuzzling his face into my hair. He whispered, "I don't want this night to end, Kenna. I want to keep you here, in this moment, forever."

I smiled, feeling the warmth of his love enveloping me. "I feel the same way, Killian. This is a night I will never forget."

Lying in his arms, I traced a few of his scars with my fingertips. The fear I felt of losing him still rattled around in my skull. Killian must have sensed my racing thoughts and turned his head to look at me.

"I can practically hear the gears turning in your head, love. What's bothering you? Aside from the obvious…"

I sighed before trying to organize my thoughts. "How are you so calm?"

"Calm? Kenna, I was just told by a woman with foresight that a Fae Army is coming to try to rip you away from me again, and Goddess knows what they want to do to me… I'm not calm. I'm just better at hiding it than you." I gave him a withering look.

"I'm terrified to lose you." The words slipped from my lips so quietly, I wondered if he'd even heard me. Killian rolled onto his side, pulling me close.

"I will never leave you willingly. I have every intention of rebuilding the life we had started in your tiny cottage. You are my future, Kenna. Only the Goddess herself could keep me away from you," he soothed. The corners of my mouth pulled up just a touch as his words settled over me.

"You're my future too." I nuzzled into his chest. "I hope our friends are alright. Do you think Laurel and Iris are safe?"

"I think Laurel loves his wife as much as I love you, and it would take more than a Fae army to take Iris from him. I'm sure they're tucked away somewhere safe."

"If we are to fight a war tomorrow, we'll need all the allies we can get." The thought of fighting alongside others gave me some peace, but I still felt as though the worst was yet to come.

"I don't think we'll be alone. You had no trouble making people love you while we were stuck in that dungeon." He chuckled. I nodded and hoped that all those who seemed on my side would be safe; Iris, Laurel, the coven Witches and guards, even Elicas, though I still wasn't quite sure why he seemed to be in favor of me. "Sleep, Kenna. You will be utterly useless tomorrow if you stay up worrying all night."

"That's easy for you to say. You sleep like the dead," I teased.

"As long as I don't join them, that's fine by me."

I rolled my eyes but settled back into him, trying to push away the fear of what tomorrow would bring.

We lay there for a while, simply enjoying the afterglow and the comfort of each other's embrace. Eventually, as the candles flickered low and the night grew calm, I drifted off to sleep, lulled by the rhythm of Killian's breathing and the beating of my own heart.

34
KENNA

I was jarred awake by someone banging on our door. I heard Maeve's muffled voice frantically screaming that the Fae army had been spotted and was nearby. My heart raced as I sat up in bed, startling Killian awake. He immediately grabbed me in his sleep-induced haze.

"Killian!" I hissed. "The Fae army is close. We need to get up!"

His eyes shot open, and he sat bolt upright. "Bloody hell!" he said, standing quickly and almost tripping over the bedding that fell to the floor. He looked at me with sadness in his eyes. "I was having such a nice dream."

"You can tell me about it later, okay?" I forced a tight smile. Killian's eyes reflected the fear I felt. At that moment, I knew I would go to the ends of the earth for this man.

I turned to the armoire, hoping for protection from the Goddess. As the shuffling sounds ceased and the doors creaked open, a matching set of silver and gold armor with additional leathers hung inside. The morning light illuminated the armor, giving it an almost mystical aura. Each piece was intricately designed and molded to fit the body perfectly.

I thanked the Goddess as I grabbed the leathers and slipped

into them before putting on the breastplate and securing the buckles. Surprisingly, it was lighter than I had anticipated, but still felt sturdy. When I turned around, I saw that Killian had also donned a similar outfit.

Just then, the door burst open, revealing a flustered Mrs. Lancaster on the other side. "It's time," she said solemnly.

I clutched Killian's arm tightly as the chaotic sounds outside grew louder and more urgent. The distant thud of marching feet and the clanking of weapons filled the air, accompanied by shouts and cries that echoed through the streets. I could feel my heart racing. An army was approaching, their intentions clear.

We followed Mrs. Lancaster down the hall and out the main entrance without hesitating. As my eyes adjusted to the bright light, I took in the scene before me. To my left, Killian stood stoically beside Mrs. Lancaster.

In the distance, a swell of armored bodies appeared over the crest of the hill below the coven gates. Like a rippling, multicolored tide, they advanced towards us with purpose. Adorned in ornate armor and wielding weapons that glinted in the rising sun, they were a formidable force that seemed endless in number. My pulse quickened at the sight, my mind racing through possible strategies to defend against them.

As time seemed to slow down, I focused on their approach and how they might attempt to breach our defenses. They could not pass through our coven wards easily, but I knew they would attempt to wear them down over time. If I could reach Arrion before that happened, there was a chance of ending this threat once and for all.

Despite the fear gnawing at my gut, I forced my voice to remain steady as I addressed Killian and Mrs. Lancaster. "We must prepare for battle. The Fae army will not easily breach our wards, but we cannot underestimate their tenacity. We must focus on holding them off for as long as possible."

Mrs. Lancaster's agreement was swift, and she wasted no time organizing the coven members. They worked feverishly to fortify the walls, station archers on the ramparts, and devise a retreat plan should our defenses fail.

Quickly, I sketched the shape of the land around the coven in the dirt at our feet. I outlined the river to the far side, the In-Between, and the coven's keep itself.

"That river might be a problem." Killian pointed at the winding line delineating the river. Mrs. Lancaster looked down at us as we squatted on the ground.

"This is not the time to be cryptic, Hunter. Spit it out," she demanded.

"With the In-Between on one side, and the keep here–" he dragged a finger along the line I'd drawn depicting the walls around the keep, "–the river offers one of the safer retreat points. If we're going to win this, they can't just run away if we get the upper hand."

I looked around us at the faces of the Witches, the coven guards, and even some locals who had planned to attend the market as they worked out their own strategies. My heart ached that these people would have to put themselves in harm's way to protect their land.

"Unless your travels made you fluent in water sprite, I think that is a risk we have to take." My words sounded distant as I concentrated on the crudely drawn map.

"I did meet one in that cave in the In-Between. She didn't talk much, though," he said with a grin, obviously trying to lighten the mood. Although I appreciated his attempt to help me manage my fears, the timing was off.

"You have time to eat," Mrs. Lancaster stated flatly. "Nothing good comes of an empty stomach." I stood from the map and looked at her.

"Mrs. Lancaster, now really isn't the time," I said quietly.

"Yes, Kenna, it is. You and your Hunter are about to fight a battle against a ruthless king. The least you can do is eat something before you charge into battle like the little spitfire you are."

Internally, I wanted to scream. The army was close enough to see in the distance, and I found it hard to relax and enjoy domestic things when not only my life, but the life of my bonded, and the lives of all these people were potentially on the line.

"I, for one, am always hungry," Killian chimed in.

"Of course you are." Mrs. Lancaster's face twitched a bit as she tried to hide her smirk. "Come along then. There's bread, fruit, and I bet I could find you some cheese," she said as she turned, her skirts swishing around her legs.

I groaned faintly but allowed Killian to take my hand and lead me along behind the headmistress.

We followed her into the dining space of the coven, and she brought out a small wooden platter of food as well as a carafe of water. Killian wasted no time digging in and mumbled a garbled, "Thank you," as he munched on a piece of bread.

"Delightful," Mrs. Lancaster said sarcastically, and I couldn't help but chuckle.

I plucked a piece of cheese off the platter and popped it into my mouth. My mind wandered to the events of the last few days. I had learned so much about myself, my family, and yet, I still felt like I didn't have the entire picture.

"Eat, Kenna," Killian instructed.

"I am eating," I said, my mind still racing. "I just like to taste my food, unlike you."

Killian cracked a grin at that. "You going to eat that?" he gestured to a piece of cheese I picked up.

"Yes, Killian. That's why I picked it up." I arched an eyebrow at him.

Mrs. Lancaster chuckled as she left us to our small breakfast. We spent a bit of time enjoying the silence as we ate. Despite trying to focus on the man before me, the food, and the water, my mind continued to reel. I knew we didn't have much time for this, and forced myself to remain present in this glimmer of peace as long as I could.

As the sun climbed higher in the sky, the approaching Fae army roared with a cacophony of battle cries that shook me to my core. Each step they took felt like a pounding heartbeat, a relentless march toward destruction.

With determination burning in my chest, I prayed to the Mother Goddess for strength and forgiveness from Killian.

"I love you," I whispered to him, knowing Mrs. Lancaster understood the gravity of my words and the unspoken meaning laced into them as she gazed at me over his shoulder. I braced myself for what needed to be done, knowing it could change everything. But if it meant saving the ones I loved, I was willing to make the ultimate sacrifice. My only hope was that Killian would survive if I did not.

"Kenna, I love you, too. What—" I cut him off with a fierce but brief kiss.

"Don't try to stop me," I said firmly, my voice shaking with determination as I locked eyes with Killian.

He grabbed my arm, his fingers digging into my skin. "What the hell are you on about? You're not going out there alone!" he snarled, a mix of fear and anger flashing in his eyes.

"I need to do this."

"Do what? Get yourself killed?" Panic filled his voice as his grip on my arm tightened even more.

"End this." My words were barely above a whisper, but my body was ablaze with power that threatened to consume everything in its path. The fire spread along my skin as it had during the battle in the dungeon. Killian's eyes widened, but he didn't let go.

I turned away from him, pulling my arm free, ignoring the sharp pain that shot through our bond as I marched towards the gates. With each step, the ground seemed to tremble beneath me as if it knew the gravity of what was about to happen.

I couldn't bear to see the anguish on Killian's face, but I glanced over my shoulder one last time before turning away for good. At that moment, I saw Mrs. Lancaster pushing him back, her magic preventing him from following me.

Killian dropped to his knees, howling my name and frantically raking at the earth below him, trying desperately to claw his way to me as tears poured from his eyes. But I couldn't allow his desperate cries to weaken my resolve. This was a war that only I could wage.

With unshed tears stinging my eyes, I whispered an anguished apology and again turned towards the gates. A fierce wind tore through the landscape, whipping up a frenzy of dust and debris, as if nature herself was preparing for the battle. The air crackled with anticipation.

"Goddess be with you." Mrs. Lancaster's solemn voice rang out behind me. I braced myself and took a deep breath before stepping through the gates into the unknown.

I heard nothing, felt nothing, knew nothing but determination as I walked through the wards and directly into the path of the oncoming army.

35
KILLIAN

Rage flared inside me like a storm unleashed, a whirlwind of fury I could not control. Every beat of my heart was heavy with the weight of betrayal—Kenna had abandoned me. My bonded, the one person I had trusted with everything, had turned away. It stung deeper than any blade, sharper than any wound I had ever endured.

The old crone's magic gripped me, but this was nothing more than a distant nuisance. My mind was a blaze of thought and emotion, too far gone to care about her magic. I barely felt the bind tightening around me; all I could feel was the overwhelming need to run, to find Kenna and shake her, then kiss her senseless for being such a bloody infuriating woman.

How could she leave me like this? How could she turn her back on everything we were, everything we could be and do together? And yes, that included naked things. Lots of naked things. Maybe on a table. Or against a tree. Preferably soon.

As my frustration grew, the ground beneath me began to shake as if it, too, was having an emotional breakdown on my behalf. My skin prickled with energy, and with a cry that felt as if it came from the very depths of my soul, I released the fire within. It roared to life, searing through my veins, a force of nature. If I had to burn the world to find her, I would.

"You have Fae fire? I thought... only the royal Fae..." Mrs. Lancaster gasped.

I ignored her. The crone's magical grip faltered, and shock registered on her face. She looked as if she'd seen a ghost or one of the In-Between creatures. She covered her mouth with one of the hands she had been casting with and shakily pointed at me with the other.

I began to stalk toward her. Her eyes widened with surprise—fear? I wasn't interested in her fear or her magic. She was nothing. My world had shrunk to one thing, one single purpose: Kenna.

"Why?" I growled, the words thick with the weight of my despair and fury. "Why did you let her do this?" My voice was eerily calm, too calm for the torrent raging inside me.

She didn't answer. Her trembling finger pointed behind me. "Hunter. Look," she said.

"Answer me!" I bellowed. She strained to maintain control over what was left of my binds.

"Look behind you, boy!" she yelled back. Still pulling against the lingering hold she had, I again ignored her.

"Kenna!" I screamed. The fire coating my hands grew.

"For the love of the Goddess! Turn your thick skull and look behind you!" Mrs Lancaster shrieked. Her magic pressed my head sideways like I was an unruly child refusing to say sorry.

There, behind me, two pools of lilac fire had appeared on the ground, dripping from my fingertips, smoldering with the energy that had once only been Kenna's. My heart stumbled as I saw them take shape, twisting into something familiar—two wolves, their bodies carved from fire, their eyes gleaming with the same fiery intensity that burned in my chest.

A fragment of my mother's teachings stirred in my mind—the Hunter's wolves. But this... this was no legend. These were *real*, made of me, made of *us*. Our souls—bound in fire, in magic, in something far beyond anything I had ever known. The hair on my neck rose as all eyes in the courtyard turned to me, their fear palpable.

"These are—" Mrs. Lancaster's voice faltered. "A manifestation of a Hunter's soul... but there hasn't been a Hunter chosen in millennia," she whispered, as if speaking to herself. A what? I had no idea how to respond to that. Hell, I had no idea what was happening. It didn't matter. I wasn't looking for definitions—I was looking for *her*.

Frozen by both shock and awe, I remained in place, no longer focused on trying to fight the magic bindings. The wolves padded over to me, one on each side of me, their fiery teeth bared, and heads lowered. Their energy coursed through me, fueling my need to reach Kenna. But as the wolves nuzzled against my hands, I noticed something—the fire that burned through them wasn't just mine. It was *ours*. The essence of Kenna was within them, woven into the very flames. I couldn't explain it. I didn't need to.

Without hesitation, I ripped away from the last remnants of the crone's magical hold and ran. I didn't think, I didn't stop to question. I just *ran*—because she was out there, and she needed me. I needed her.

The wolves surged ahead, moving with purpose, guiding me like they knew what I sought, like they knew the way to her. I followed, lungs burning, every step fueled by the single, reckless desire to reach her, hold her, and demand answers I probably wouldn't like—but would beg for anyway.

"Kenna," I whispered, breathless. "I'm coming for you, love. Like it or not."

I pushed through the chaos around me, the sounds of battle fading into the background as my every sense focused on the pull

I felt deep in my chest, the pull toward her. The wards loomed ahead, but I didn't care—I would tear through them if I had to. Nothing would stop me.

The wolves shot out before me and flew through the ward gates with an elegant leap. I followed as quickly as my legs would carry me.

The air around me was thick with magic, and for a moment, I lost myself in the chaos—the clashing of steel, the shouts of warriors, the whoosh of magic, the cries of pain. But none of it mattered. None of it could drown out the call of her presence, the way the fire within me burned with the need to reach her.

Where the fuck was Kenna?

The wolves surged forward again, pulling me along, urging me onward. But then, a sharp pain raked across my arm, pulling me back to reality. I whirled, and there, grinning with malice, stood a Fae guard. Blood dripped from the wound, but I barely felt it.

My eyes narrowed, and the fire within me surged. "Get out of my way," I snarled, my voice rough with fury. I wasn't going to let him stop me, not when I was so close.

The battle raged around me, but I barely noticed. I dodged a blow, my focus entirely on the fire coursing through me. Clenching my fists, I summoned the flames coiling around me, the heat intensifying until they crackled like a blazing furnace. The wolves gnashed their teeth beside me, ready to lunge.

The guard met my gaze, his eyes widening in fear. He saw the combined spirit of the Hunters and the power of the Fae awakened within me.

"Half breed," he whispered the slur shakily.

He tried to strike again, but I was already moving. The flame that had once felt like a whisper was now a roar, a force of nature that I couldn't control even if I wanted to.

I swung my sword, but it wasn't just my strength driving it now. It was the fire, the magic, the bond between Kenna and me.

In that moment, I didn't care about anything else. I couldn't. The guard fell, any lingering words dying in his throat.

The air around me crackled with magic, and I felt the power surging through me. I became that which they all feared—the half breed with too much power, rage, and determination. My senses were heightened, and I felt more alive than ever.

But still, my thoughts were with her. *Kenna.*

The wolves tugged at my soul, pulling me forward, toward her. I moved faster, pushing through the battlefield, but I couldn't see her. I couldn't feel her in the chaos. My chest tightened with panic. *Where was she?*

Then, the wolves darted forward, and I followed. Ahead, I could see a large rock with the In-Between to the right-hand side. It was a decent vantage point. If I could get to it, I would be able to climb up on it, and I hoped I would be able to survey the battlegrounds for Kenna's fiery form.

The wolves followed at my side as I crested a small hill. Stopping short, I came face-to-face with a massive mountain of a man. Jolan.

"Fuck," I muttered.

The bastard stood like a mountain in armor, grinning as if he'd been waiting for this exact scene in his dramatic little dreams.

"Hunter, how nice of you to join the fun," he crooned before swinging his massive battle axe at my head.

I ducked just in time to feel the edge of his blade scrape across the metal armor on my shoulder. I could feel the heat of it, the force of it, but it was nothing compared to the force inside me. The force of my need to find her. Thanking the Goddess for her gift, I tensed my muscles and stood ready with my sword raised.

Holding the weapon above my head, I prepared for the blow. He swung with such force that I felt the reverberation from my fingertips to my toes. It took every ounce of my strength to hold the sword up. I knew without a doubt in my mind that should he gain the upper hand, I would die here on this hill, and Kenna would likely die with me.

Summoning the fire, I envisioned it climbing up the sword onto the warrior's axe. I prayed to the Goddess that it would slip down his weapon like molten rage and consume him. I was nowhere near as strong as Kenna, though, and my focus jumped from the Fae fire to the wolves, disrupting my efforts.

Out of the corner of my eye, I could see the wolves charge forward, their teeth bared. Jolan must have seen the oncoming creatures as well. He released his attack on me only to swing the axes at the wolves. Their fiery paws skittered in the dirt as they tried to stop, but it was useless.

The blade swung through their flame bodies, and they burst into embers, falling to the ground like red, sizzling snow.

"No!" I screamed. Now, I was truly alone. I had no idea if I could re-form them or if that was truly their end.

Jolan turned his big body my way and grinned. The light caught his armor, and I noted the charging stones inlaid in the handle of his weapon. I was truly, utterly fucked.

He raised his axe once again. "Say goodbye, boy. I think we're done here," he sneered. I raised my sword, readying myself for the impending blow, fully aware that I was rapidly losing strength from wielding the Fae fire.

In that last breath, I saw her. Kenna. She was there, cutting through the Fae with the fury of a Valkyrie. The sight of her nearly stole my breath. She was a sight to behold, a warrior goddess in the flesh. She was *everything*.

Goddess above. Her body moved like a promise I'd never be worthy of. Every swing of her blade, every flash of her eyes was a reminder of what I'd fight and bleed and die for. And gods, if she didn't look *good* doing it.

I could feel the tears of relief prickling in my eyes, but I didn't let them fall. I couldn't. Not now. Not when she was finally here.

The pain, the rage, the fear—it all vanished. There was only her. My heart ached, and I silently prayed to the Goddess. *Please don't let Kenna see this.*

"Kenna," I whispered, my heart beating loud enough to drown out the chaos. But then, the pain in my side flared. The world blurred in my agony just as Jolan's axe began to descend.

36
KENNA

I saw the wolves before I saw him. Killian. He strode across the battlefield like he owned it—fire trailing his steps, sword flashing, eyes burning with that infuriating, magnetic intensity. Of course, he made battle look like some sort of promenade. Were those wolves running with him?

"Goddess damn it!" I hissed, barely lifting my sword in time to parry a blow. My breath caught—not from fear, but fury. And alright, maybe a little bit from the way he looked like an avenging god made of fire and bad decisions.

He wasn't supposed to be here.

My focus frayed as I caught the movement of another guard circling behind me. They were trying to box me in. How quaint. I wouldn't be caged. Not again. Not when Killian was within reach —and apparently too busy playing hero to *not die*.

My magic answered my call. Lilac flames erupted over my skin, seething with heat that mirrored the churn in my chest. The guards recoiled at the sight of them. Good. Let them be afraid.

"Come on, then," I said, voice low and steady. "Let's end this."

My sword in one hand, a pulsing flame in the other, I stepped into the fight—not just with rage but with purpose. I was done watching people I love pay for someone else's ambition. If Killian got us both killed trying to protect me, I would find him in the next life just to kill him myself.

A guard lunged. I spun, my blade finding the soft spot beneath his ribs. He crumpled. Another raised his sword. I answered with a lash of fire. Lilac flame arced through the air, searing him into ash.

"Anyone else?" I spat, lifting my chin. "You want the princess? Come get her." It wasn't pride that fueled me. It was desperation; sharp and reckless and real.

My limbs moved on instinct. I couldn't afford doubt, couldn't let the pain beneath my skin slow me. This wasn't just about a throne or legacy. It was about *him*. About making sure he lived to make more idiotic, noble decisions that drove me insane in the best and worst ways.

The guards faltered. One stepped back. I surged forward, my fury breaking like a storm over them.

And then—pain.

A flash of steel caught me at the seam of my armor, just above my hip. My body jerked. The battlefield blurred for a breath. I staggered, blinking away the red edging into my vision.

I stumbled again, and the Fae guard took advantage of my wobbly stature. As he swung his sword again, it was all I could do to parry the blow and take a defensive stance. I knew I was losing too much blood and could not continue fighting like this.

Swinging my sword, I clashed with the guard once again, a resounding clang filling the air. My red hair flew around me as I whirled my body, courtesy of pure adrenaline, and caught the guard in the knee. He fell to the ground, clutching his leg, which was now bloodied and bent at an unnatural angle.

I let out a strangled cry of pain and clutched my side. My scream echoed through the air, a raw, guttural sound that gave voice to the agony coursing through my body. I could feel the warm, sticky blood pooling beneath my armor, a stark reminder of my mortality as well as Killian's. I knew I had mere moments to do what needed to be done.

Hiking up my armor as best I could, I summoned a flame to my hand. Having no idea if this would work, I pressed the flame to the wound. Searing pain tore through my side as the Fae fire cauterized the wound. Some level of shock settled into my mind as my healer abilities and Fae bloodline combined.

The fire crackled against flesh. The scent of char met my nose. I was shaking now—magic and instinct the only things keeping me upright. The wound knitted, barely.

The guard I had injured watched with wide eyes, his gaze never leaving the wound that now began to knit back together. "You're a half breed," he stammered.

"Very astute," I panted. "Want a prize?" I hissed sarcastically before I began moving again. Clearly, the king had not told all of his men what I was.

More guards advanced. My magic flared again, got brighter, hotter, more volatile. The fire obeyed, not because I demanded it, but because it shared my fear. My grief. I hurled it forward, and the world lit up in lilac light.

Again, I began forcing my way forward to Killian. He remained in the same spot atop the hill, with Jolan towering over him. Even from here, I could see his arms shake as he raised his sword over his head. I could see the flames flickering out on his hands *Fae fire. My* fire. *His* fire. My breath caught.

Hope bloomed—and then shattered as Jolan raised his axe.

"No," I whispered. Then louder: *"Killian!"* My cry cracked the air.

Before the weapon could hit its mark, though, the earth beneath my feet began to shake. Jolan, thrown off balance by the quake, missed Killian by a mere hair's breadth. Stunned, he looked around.

Before my eyes, cresting the hill and emerging from the forest was a massive collection of common Fae, Witches, coven guards, and creatures I had never seen before, all led by a towering mountain of a shadow creature. Its enormous feet crashed through the battlefield to Killian's right, each step shaking the surrounding ground.

The creature stood tall enough to peek in through the coven's third-story windows if desired. Its mountainous shape, covered in what appeared to be thick, shaggy, dark fur with glowing ice-blue eyes, was a sight to behold.

Before I could register what was happening, the creature took one more step forward, reaching Jolan in a single stride. I watched in stunned silence as the creature picked Jolan up like a rag doll, and tossed him into its mouth with a sickening crunch as it bit down.

It seemed to grin at me as it released a sound between a roar and a chuckle. I saw then a chunk of something shiny stuck in its teeth. A shiver ran down my spine; this was a creature of the In-Between. This monster had just eaten a massive Fae male in one bite and now had armor stuck in its teeth. This creature had been my silent neighbor for years, and I had never been so thankful for its terrifying presence in my life.

Killian looked up, eyes wide with disbelief. He mouthed something—*thank you*—and stepped away from the monster's path.

Behind him, a horde of smaller shadow creatures emerged from the darkness, their sinuous forms slithering and crawling onto the battlefield with eerie, fluid movements. The air was alive with the flickering light of their glowing eyes, a kaleidoscope of colors that pierced through the souls of all who made eye contact.

I heaved a sigh of relief and made my way slowly to Killian. Cresting the small hill, I fell to my knees at his side. Between labored breaths, I leveled my stare at him.

"Why couldn't you just stay behind that wall where you were safe?" I ground out; my anger palpable.

"I'm fine, love. Thank you for asking," he said with a sly grin and a gaze that I couldn't help but notice dipped to my lips.

I smacked his arm before whispering, "You could have been killed." I touched my forehead to his.

"Kenna, I would go to the ends of the earth for you. I would gladly burn in hell for you. Where you go, I go. Where you fight, I fight. You are not alone anymore, and you never will be again."

As a tear slipped down my cheek, I moved my hand to touch his face before gently kissing him in thanks. He was right, of course. I was so used to being alone, I forgot I no longer had to be. What he failed to recognize was that I had been protecting him the way I had never been protected because I loved him. I did not leave him behind because I ever wanted to be apart from him, but in a futile attempt to prevent losing him.

I felt the heat surrounding Killian before I pulled away and opened my eyes, a shock of fear running through my veins. To my surprise, though, it was not enemy flame or even my own, but the ghostly apparition of a wolf's head made of Fae fire decorating Killian's head. I gazed at him in shock, every bit the Hunter he was born to be.

I'd never seen anything like it before. Like the traditional garb of the Hunters, the lilac flame headdress of a wolf was perched upon his head, with its snout and fangs protruding over his forehead, and a fiery lilac pelt draping down the back of his neck.

"Killian," I breathed, lifting a shaky hand to point at his head, where a helmet might have sat.

"Do I have something on my face?" he asked, looking genuinely concerned.

Giving him a bewildered look, I touched the snout of the wolf's head. "Not quite..." I trailed off. How would I even explain this? "You have a wolf headdress made of flames?"

"I what?" He touched his head and felt the fiery shape adorning him. His eyes widened as his fingers danced over the flames.

"I hate to break up this touching moment, but this is a battlefield," a sarcastic voice said above the din around us.

A massive smile broke out over my face as I laid eyes on Laurel in full guard armor, grinning at me, with Iris wielding a butcher knife beside him. Iris gave me a small wave. Behind them both, many more Fae followed, armed with what appeared to be anything they deemed a usable weapon, including frying pans and irons. Trotting alongside the makeshift army atop a Kelpie, of all things, was Elicas in full armor, a smile plastered on his face.

"I thought I said two phoenixes, but a phoenix and a flame wolf will do, I suppose," Laurel quipped.

I grinned at him before rising with Killian to stand before him. "I'm glad you are unharmed."

"It'll take more than a few guards to keep these people from aiding their princess. You are the only hope they have." He smiled uncertainly, as if knowing the pressure that was placed on me.

Taking a deep breath, I nodded. "We need to find the king."

Laurel nodded before turning behind him to address the Fae militia, awaiting instructions. "Find the king! But do not engage! The decision of what comes after will be up to our princess!" His voice carried over the crowd, and they raised their makeshift weapons in a cheer.

"And please stay safe!" I cried out over their cheers. "I need people to lead, or there will be no Kingdom of the Fae Realm at all!"

More cries rang out from the crowd. Witches, coven guards, and other commoners joined the crowd. Various Fae guards who had come with Laurel began breaking up the crowd and providing directions. Although untrained and unprepared, the factions that had broken away were not afraid as they engaged the king's army head-on.

I turned to my right and caught sight of Elicas leaning forward on the back of the Kelpie and whispering in the ear of the great beast he rode. Water dripped from its seaweed-laden mane, and it tossed its head and made a sound that I assumed was the creature's version of a whinny.

To my shock, more Kelpies and various other water creatures rose from the small river beside the battlefield, forming a barrier that would hopefully prevent the escape of any of the king's men should they try to flee. Water glinted off the scales and slick bodies of those coming to our aid. I'd never seen something so haunting, yet beautiful.

Elicas winked at me as he rode down the line of water beings and shrugged, adding, "My mother was a water sprite!"

Wait. What? Did that mean…? I didn't have time to ponder that at the moment and would come back to that later.

Adrenaline coursed through my veins as I felt the power surge within me. Killian took my hand, and a gust of wind swirled around us. My flames flared, and his face lit with violent delight. "Shall we?" he said as his eyes met mine.

Nodding, I squeezed his hand before we raced into the fray.

37
KILLIAN

Kenna released my hand before adjusting her grip on her sword and rushing into the battle before us. Her determination and courage were more than admirable, and I took a whisper of a second to appreciate that she was, in fact, mine.

I raced in after her, my senses heightened. I assumed it was the wolf headdress I now wore, allowing me to tap into the abilities of the Hunter's wolf spirit that had so long ago become a part of my people. I silently thanked my mother for her teachings and my heritage. Hoping that message would reach the other side of the veil, I sent her my love before ducking below the sword of a Fae guard. As I stood back up, wielding my sword and preparing for a fight, Kenna sliced her blade through him. He dropped like a sack of rocks.

Kenna pulled her sword free as he fell, wiping it on the edge of her tunic. She blew a piece of loose red hair from her face and grinned at me. "Keep up, Hunter."

I gave her an appreciative smile before she turned and began to skirt around more of the fight. Despite my desire to satisfy the violent urge to eradicate anyone who might threaten Kenna's safety, I followed her as she carefully navigated around smaller shadow creatures that seemed to absorb whole Fae guards into their dark bodies. She dodged spells cast and thrown by the Witches and ignored the sickening crunch and gurgling sounds coming from the direction of the larger shadow beings. Again, I gave thanks to the gigantic dark creatures that had saved us in the woods and were now defending us once again.

Kenna stopped at the edge of the woods bordering the battlefield and spun in a circle, her eyes searching for something.

"What is it, love?" I asked, trying to follow the path of her gaze.

"He has to be here somewhere," she murmured. "He wouldn't put himself in the middle of the fight. He's too selfish to defend his own people."

"So, you think he's in the forest?"

"He'll be on the edge of it all. I just wish there was a way to track him." She flexed her hand at her side and adjusted her grip on her sword again, clearly agitated.

Without a second thought, I began to focus on the noises around me. If my fire wolves could track Kenna, maybe I could track the king. Narrowing my focus, I attempted to channel the soul of the Hunter. I recognized this was what Mrs. Lancaster had referred to, and I hoped the old crone was right.

I took a deep breath, I felt it almost immediately, and I almost tripped in shock. As if there was a magical tether to that which I was hunting, I saw the way forward. "This way," I said as I focused on maintaining the tether.

"How do you know?"

"The wolf," I said. Kenna stared at me in wonder for a brief moment before nodding.

I took off in the direction of the pull. Kenna had been correct in that he was not in the main battle, but instead of hiding in the woods, it appeared he was hiding behind a small hill just before the coven wall.

I could feel the wariness of the wolf within me, so I held out a hand, trying to keep Kenna back as we approached. To our left, the battle raged on, and the sounds of the dying echoed in my ears. I would mourn their loss another time, though, as the only way to end this was to end the king's tyrannical reign.

"Is he over there?" Kenna murmured. Despite being on the outskirts of the fight, we both appeared to be making an effort not to draw attention to ourselves.

"Over that hill.".

"Are you sure?"

"Yes?" I said uneasily.

"Well, that's reassuring," she mocked before striding past my outstretched hand. I grabbed her left hand and pulled her back to me.

"We go together, or we don't go at all," I demanded. She nodded, acceptance gracing her battered but beautiful features. By now, her wild red hair had escaped most of the braid and was whipping around her head. It gave her the appearance of a warrior goddess in the flesh.

Together, we crept closer to the hill, all the while checking for possible traps or guards. Kenna, true to her word, stayed by my side, much to my relief. I had half-expected her to run off again.

The closer we got to the anchor the tracking tether had found, the more an eerie feeling prickled my skin. There was no way this could be this easy. I looked around me, scanning the surrounding area for any sign of a threat. It was oddly quiet, and the sounds of battle lessened and became muffled.

In my confusion at the strange change in sound, I turned to look at Kenna, only to be swept into the grip of a guard. Fear flashed across her eyes as she screamed, "No!"

The guard stood immobile, one arm clamped around my neck, slowing the entrance of air to my lungs, while the other arm held my sword hand twisted behind my back, forcing me to drop my weapon. Kenna moved quickly, lifting her sword as if to slice the guard.

"I wouldn't if I were you, child," came the king's icy voice from atop the hill.

"Let him go!" Kenna shrieked.

"Kenna," I wheezed. "I'm fine, love."

"Yes, the Hunter is fine. For now," Arrion said, bored. "As much as I appreciate your fighting spirit, let's end this, shall we? Come with me, and I'll call off my guards, and we can all go home." He remained so self-assured, he hadn't even bothered to make eye contact with Kenna or take her sword.

"Let him go!" she screamed again, stalking closer to her grandfather. "Let him go, you monster!"

"Ah, see, I am not a monster. Those dreadful things you brought from the forest are monsters. I am simply a man trying to manage insolence and keep what's left of my control over these petulant people," he said as he picked at his nails. "And don't bother yelling for any of your so-called 'allies.' They can't hear you. If you haven't noticed, you are within a ward of my making. Actually, I'm quite surprised the Hunter could penetrate the barrier to even find me." Arrion turned then, looking at me with disgust. "Maybe you aren't as useless as I thought. Shall I keep you as a pet after this nonsense is over?"

Given my lack of air supply, I snarled at him the best I could. "I'd rather die."

"Well, that's unfortunate," he said as he turned back to Kenna. "Granddaughter, accept that this is not a war you can win, and it is time to go home and do as you are told. I will overlook this little temper tantrum."

Seething, Kenna advanced on him, her sword lifting as she walked. "I will never submit to your plans, *grandfather*," she spat.

"Very well then. I tried to do this the easy way, but just know that anything that happens from here on out is your own fault." He motioned for the guard to drag me toward him.

As the guard approached, Kenna growled and tensed. "Don't you touch him!"

Arrion ignored her and placed a hand on my shoulder. Raising his hand, he made a snapping motion, and another guard holding a short sword stepped forward from behind him.

"If you hurt him, you hurt me," Kenna seethed.

"Ah, yes. What an unfortunate side effect of this blasted bond, but it can be survived. I'm living proof of that." Arrion rolled his eyes. Despite the gravity of the war and the situation at hand, the king seemed uninterested.

"You wouldn't want to hurt your granddaughter, would you?" Kenna said sweetly, clearly trying to play the situation to ensure my safety.

"Kenna, love, run," I wheezed. Anger flashed across Arrion's face before he turned to glare at me as the guard moved the sword to my throat.

"Say another word, and my guard will slit your throat and let her watch you bleed out on this very hill," he growled.

"If you kill him, you'll kill me, too!" Kenna screamed, the desperation evident in her voice.

"Again, another possible unfortunate side effect. Not to worry, though. I have at least a couple of hundred years left to ensure another heir if you don't survive." Looking utterly disinterested in the discussion, Arrion added, "I would have just named Jolan my successor, but your disgusting forest pet had to eat him. That had been the plan all along, to be honest." Arrion picked at a cuticle as he spoke dismissively.

I watched in horror as Kenna tensed, and I knew she was planning to launch herself at the king any second. I felt her rage swelling in my bones, and at that moment, I was willing to accept my death if it meant Kenna would live.

I prayed to the Mother Goddess that she would let Kenna survive. I had never prayed consistently to the Goddess, never blatantly asked for help before, but I had seen how Kenna revered her and loved her, and if anyone would be able to save Kenna, it was the Goddess herself. There would be no regrets, no fear, no pain. I had found the love of my life, my bonded, and I would gladly die for her.

Kenna's furious eyes shifted from her grandfather's face to mine just as a tear slipped down my cheek. No, I would not regret this decision if it meant she would be safe.

"No!" she screamed as if she knew what I was thinking.

Ignoring her pleas, I prayed once more that the Goddess would save her. I looked into her eyes and mouthed; *I love you. Now run*, before using the rest of my strength to slip my free hand under the elbow of the guard encasing my throat and slamming my head back, freeing myself from his stunned grip. I turned to the king, determined to protect Kenna. I made it one step before the other guard stepped in front of the king, and his sword lodged in my gut. "Go!" I screamed to Kenna. Tears ran freely down my cheeks, and I felt the warmth of my blood pooling beneath my armor as I sank to the ground.

"No!" Kenna screamed before falling to her knees. She began to crawl toward me.

"What a mess," Arrion mumbled before stepping around the guard who was pulling his short sword free.

"What have you done?!" Kenna's voice pierced the haze beginning to cloud my vision. She was still yelling, so she was still breathing. I thanked the Goddess for that, but prayed Kenna would escape with the chance I had given her.

"Get up, girl. You're still alive, although I'm not sure what good that will do. You are returning to the Fae Realm whether you like it or not," Arrion growled.

I felt Kenna's hands on mine, but I was losing focus, and my legs were going numb. I knew I didn't have long. I mustered my strength and whispered to Kenna, "Love, please go. Live to see another day." Through the haze, I could see her tears flowing freely, and despite the rushing in my ears, I could still hear her sobs.

"I will not leave you! If you die, the Goddess had better take me with you! I will not live without you!" she screamed. "Don't leave me, Killian! Everyone else has, and I need you!"

"As touching as this is, it's time to go," Arrion said in a blasé tone before reaching for Kenna.

"Don't you dare touch me!" she wailed. My vision was darkening, and I could no longer feel her touching me, but I felt her in my soul and knew she was still there, still holding me.

"Do not let my death be in vain," I croaked. I felt heavy and could no longer fill my lungs.

"No! You can't die! You can't leave me!"

I thought for sure I was hallucinating, maybe a trick of the Goddess to ease my death, but a soft light began to materialize around Kenna. Unlike her usual lilac fire, this appeared to be a soft golden color. Then, everything went dark, and I fell into the blackness.

38
KENNA

So much pain. Anguish and rage filled my entire being. I kneeled there in the grass, covered in Killian's blood, shaking him, trying to bring back the light in his unfocused eyes. Somewhere in my consciousness, I knew the king was watching, completely unfazed by my agony, but I did not care. If he were to kill me now, I would gladly go, for I knew I would not live without Killian. How could I live with only half of my heart and soul?

"Killian!" I screamed. "Stay with me!" I shook his limp body, trying to bring him back, but his eyes remained vacant, and his chest did not rise. "Killian!" I screamed his name so forcefully, it was as if a shockwave rippled out from where I lay on Killian's chest, weeping.

Much to my surprise, a soft gold glowed through my tears. Praying it was the Goddess herself who had come to take me with my bonded, I opened my soul to her, begging for release from this torment.

"I cannot do that, my child," an ethereal voice echoed in my head. "It is not your time, nor is it your Hunter's." I was dumbfounded, and momentarily, the tears stopped before anguish ripped through my soul once more; the bond was being severed. "Open your heart and soul to me. I will end this. If you do not, your elder will kill you both, and this world will suffer a great loss. You are the light which will lead this world through the darkness and into a new era."

Briefly, Elicas flashed in my mind as he said something eerily similar to me in the past. Without speaking a word, I silently questioned what I assumed was a hallucination.

"I am not a hallucination. I am the Mother Goddess, and I will decide when your time has come, not this tyrant. You have done well, remaining faithful to me, and now it is my turn to help you. Open yourself, child. I have no body with which to end this, but you do. Allow me this small favor, and I will bring your Hunter back to you."

That was all the answer I needed. I would do anything to bring Killian back and heal the bond. It didn't matter if this was truly the Goddess herself or a demon come to borrow my body; I would do whatever it took to save my bonded.

Yes. I consent, I thought.

"I grow bored with this," Arrion said before raising his hand as if to snap and summon his guard to end my torment. I was reminded briefly of the courtyard outside my dungeon window, where he had, without hesitation, had two lovers murdered.

I felt her then, the Mother Goddess. Her presence in my mind was warm and comforting, like a ray of sunshine on a summer afternoon. I felt her take control of my body, and there was nothing I could do but watch as time seemed to slow. The goddess turned me to face the king, who appeared frozen in place, mid-snap. My body stood, my own hand raised in his direction, and time appeared to speed up again.

"Enough!" A melodic voice that was not mine left my body. I could see the king's eyes widen as he took in my form. My outstretched hand was radiating a soft, pulsing golden color. "You have gone too far, tyrant king. You have taken far too many lives that you had no right to take. The deaths of others will never bring your Amabel back. She would be so disappointed," the ethereal voice echoed.

Arrion stood still, panic rising in his eyes. Although it appeared he could move his head and mouth, he did not speak. His hand remained frozen in the air, and he looked terrified. He began to shake and mouth the word "no" over and over.

In my head, I heard the Goddess once again. "It is time to end this. Would you like me to shield you from what is next?" Although I understood that she was making this offer to protect me, I knew that I needed to see this war end. Without my even voicing this, she conceded. "Very well."

My outstretched hand closed into a fist. "Tyrant king, you have taken so much from so many, and regardless of your motivations, you can no longer be trusted to rule. And so, I will do you a kindness you have not given others, but you will still be punished. You will remain trapped in your prisons, but very much so alive. I sentence you and your most loyal guards to spend the rest of time here on this hill as trees, forced to watch others live their lives, but unable to live your own."

Arrion's form, as well as the two guards next to him, twisted into gnarled trees atop the hill. Somewhere in my mind's eye, I was aware of other trees twisting up from the battlefield as those guards who had supported Arrion met the same eternal end as he did. Both shock and gratitude rolled through me.

Before I could thank her, the presence of the goddess was no longer there. I was snapped back into control of my own body and fell to my knees beside Killian's still-lifeless body. I gripped the edge of his armor and tried to pull him to me, but he was so heavy.

"Killian," I pleaded. "Please, Killian. She said you would come back to me. Please!" I wept as I slammed my fists down on his breastplate.

"Princess?" a horrified voice called. I shrank away as Laurel touched my shoulder. He came around the side of me and dropped to one knee when he saw the body I was holding.

Touching Killian's neck, he looked at me with sad eyes. "He's gone, Kenna. The war is over," he said, gesturing to the newly formed trees on the hilltop. "Do not let the Hunter's sacrifice mean nothing. Your people need you."

"No! She said he would come back! Please!" I screamed as I collapsed onto his lifeless form. I did not care about the battle that began to slow around me. I did not even register that the ward the king had placed around himself had shattered with his punishment. I did not care that more of the friends we had made had begun to surround us. I did not care about anything because the only person who had cared for me was gone, and I had nothing left to live for.

I lay there on the bloody grass next to Killian's limp body and kissed his cheek as tears poured down my face. "Leave me," I said in the most commanding voice I could muster.

"I cannot, Princess. It is my sworn duty to protect you," Laurel said.

"I am not your princess. I am nothing without my bonded," I whispered. I laced my fingers with Killian's and closed my eyes, silently praying that if the Mother Goddess was not going to bring Killian back that she take me with him.

Laurel shook me and tried his best to pull me away from the body of the only person I had allowed myself to love. Violently, I pulled out of his grasp and refused to leave my place beside my bonded. I was unwilling to accept a life without him, and despite the efforts of Laurel, Elicas, Iris, and even the old guard, Sal, I remained next to Killian.

Only when I heard Mrs. Lancaster's voice did I open my eyes. Tears flowed freely down her face as she lowered her old body to my side and began stroking my hair.

"I am so sorry, Kenna. I never wanted any of this for you." I felt her shake beside me as silent sobs wracked her aged form.

"All I ever wanted for you was for you to feel loved. Although it was short-lived, I am forever grateful to the Hunter for loving you as he did. I owe him a great debt with no way to repay him," she said solemnly.

"I'm sure I can think of something you can do," a raspy voice whispered.

"Killian!" I shrieked as I shot up, hopeful I was not hallucinating.

"Hello, love." He smiled weakly. "It's good to see you again."

Throwing myself onto him, I kissed him fiercely despite all of the gore and debris covering us. "Don't you dare leave me ever again," I chided between joyous sobs.

"Never," he said between kisses.

"Let the boy breathe," Elicas said with a chuckle.

"Are you alright now?" I questioned as I tried to peel off his armor to see the wound.

"Can we save the undressing for later, love? When we don't have an audience?" He smirked.

Rolling my eyes, I looked to the sky and said, "Mother Goddess, I will never be able to repay you."

"I am not up there, child," her melodic voice chimed from the woods to the right of us. "I have never understood why everyone thinks I am floating in the sky when I am here all around you, in the rocks, the trees, the water, and everything in between," she said as her glowing figure emerged from the forest.

Everyone froze.

A small smile lit up her otherworldly, beautiful face as she said, "You can repay me by living the life you were meant to have. Usher this world into a new light."

"Mother Goddess, I cannot thank you enough," I whispered, unsure what else to say.

"You do not need to thank me, Kenna. You trusted in me to end this, and so I will now trust in you to prevent this from happening again in your lifetime. Unfortunately, as you are not full-blood Fae, that will not be quite as long as those who came before you, but it should give you plenty of time to create many heirs," she said with a conspiratorial wink.

I blushed, and Killian chuckled before we both moved to stand. Laurel helped Killian stand and stood at his side. The Mother Goddess smiled at us then.

"Weary warriors, it is time to rest. You have my blessing and my thanks."

We all inclined our heads in reverence before she simply vanished.

Killian turned to me then, taking my hand and kneeling before me with slow, wobbly movements. "All hail Kenna, Queen of the Fae!"

The same words echoed from those around us as they kneeled. Row upon row of soldiers, guards, commoners, Witches, and other beings began to kneel and cheer, "All hail Queen Kenna!"

Tears flowed down my cheeks, not in fear or heartbreak, but from the overwhelming love I felt for this man. This man, who had done as he said he would and sacrificed himself so that I might live. So that our people might live. So that *we* would live.

EPILOGUE: KENNA

"I'm fine, love," Killian said, chuckling as he swatted my hands away.

"I just need to make sure," I protested, pulling at the buckles of his breastplate. I wanted the damn thing off. I needed to see with my own eyes that his wound was healed. I needed to know he would be safe.

Back in our room at the keep, he conceded to my persistence and allowed me to carefully remove the armor and pull his blood-soaked tunic over his head. His entire torso was coated in sticky, drying blood, and the tangy smell of copper filled the air as I turned to the small wash basin in the corner and wet a rag with warm water.

"I think you'll need more than a rag," he said, gesturing to his torso.

"Oh. Right." I shuffled over to the bath with shaking hands, still clad in my armor. I reached for the pump on the tub at the same time Killian reached for my hands.

"Kenna. Stop. I'm fine," he whispered in my ear as he came up behind me.

I spun around and looked into his eyes, tears forming in mine. "You died today."

"And I would do it again. I would die in every lifetime, in every way, if it meant that you, my beautiful Kenna, would live."

I stared at him in disbelief that this man would willingly sacrifice himself for me. I didn't think I had truly known what love was until that moment.

As tears freely ran down my face, Killian gently tucked a piece of my fiery hair behind my ear and kissed me gently. Leaning his forehead against mine, he softly said, "It'd be nice if you actually listened to me next time, though."

"Next time?" I squeaked. Fear rose in my throat, and my heart rate increased.

Killian pulled away from me and looked into my eyes. "Kenna, if I ever have to sacrifice myself for you, I will, but please run the next time I tell you to run." His face was serious, but his eyes held a touch of that cheeky humor I enjoyed so much.

Swatting him, I stonily replied, "If you die, I'll go with you. There is nothing here for me without you. There was nothing before you, and there would be nothing after you. The Goddess would have to accept us both."

His mouth quirked and he moved closer to me, unbuckling each clasp of my armor one by one. The fire in his eyes lit something in my soul, and I suddenly felt too warm. My heart raced for a very different reason, and my knees shook from anticipation instead of exhaustion.

As the last piece of my armor rattled to the floor, his mouth met mine in a fierce, all-consuming kiss. As if he needed me to breathe, our lips sealed, and his tongue danced against mine. I breathed a soft moan into his mouth before my hands began exploring his body.

I carefully unhooked the remaining armor covering his lower half and allowed it to clang to the floor. I felt his grin against my lips before he pulled away to maneuver my tunic over my head and slide my leggings down.

Killian kneeled before me, looking at my now naked body with reverence. The evidence of his arousal protruded against his blood-stained trousers. His hands slid from my ankles up my calves and to my thighs as he whispered, "Long live the queen," before his fingers dipped between my thighs.

I moaned as his fingertips made contact with my most sensitive area. The overwhelming nature of the day slipped from my mind as he worshipped me.

Despite the intense euphoria I felt building in my core, I gently pulled his fingers from inside me and leaned down to kiss him. When our lips parted, he gave me a quizzical look.

"We're covered in sweat, dirt, and blood. Your blood, to be exact," I said, gesturing to our bodies.

Killian smiled and stood, kissing me again and pulling me against his chest. My hands wandered to his waistband, and I began to untie the laces at the front.

"I suppose we should take care of that," he whispered as he kissed my neck. His breath hitched as his trousers hit the floor, and my hand wrapped around his member and stroked him gently. Instead of answering him, I used my free hand to cast in the direction of the tub, causing the pump to pour steaming water into the copper basin below.

I released my soft grip on his manhood and turned him toward the bath. He made a small noise of protest before he started moving toward the tub.

"Ladies first." He gave a small bow as we reached the edge of the tub. He held out a hand to me as he straightened, and I smiled, sliding my hand into his. Killian helped me step into the still-filling basin and then quickly followed after.

The water immediately began to turn a rust color, and Killian turned the water off. We said nothing as we rinsed the majority of the blood from our bodies and hair before he allowed the tub to drain and then started the pump again.

I reached over the side of the bath as it began to fill with steaming water once again, and poured a soap and herb mixture into the bottom of the basin. The herbal smell filled the air with sweet, healing steam, and I relaxed as the water began to pool around me. Killian moved to settle in behind me.

Using a small pitcher, he poured some of the water over my hair and silently began massaging the soap into my tangled mess of curls. I sighed in pleasure and leaned back into his chest.

After he had rinsed and conditioned my hair, I turned in place. The tub, now nearing full, sloshed with my movement. I quickly stopped the flow of hot water before turning back to examine Killian.

"Like what you see, love?" he said with a cheeky grin.

"I need to make sure you're alright," I said determinedly. He rolled his eyes but sat up straight, allowing me to run my fingers and then a soapy cloth across his body, cleaning the remaining grime and blood away as I checked to make sure he was truly healed.

I gave a relieved sigh when I saw that where Killian had been stabbed was only a pink scar now. Killian shivered and closed his eyes as I ran my fingers along the raised edge of the scar.

"Satisfied?" he asked.

"Am I satisfied that you were stabbed and died? No. Am I satisfied you were healed and are not still dead? Yes," I replied.

My fingers trailed over the myriad of other scars along his torso and followed one down his hip until the water covered my hand, and I could no longer see the shape I was tracing. Killian sighed softly as my hand feathered over his member and then back up his chest.

"My turn." He shifted, making sure not to slosh water from the tub. He reached for a clean cloth and more soap. He wiped my body clean of any trace of battle he could find while carefully avoiding any small scrapes.

When he reached my side, where I had cauterized my own wound, he saw the palm-sized patch of angry skin, which appeared to be far more healed than I had expected. He looked into my eyes before adding, "Well, that explains that searing pain I felt."

I gave a small laugh and shrugged. "I suppose so."

"You burnt your own skin?" he asked.

"I cauterized a stab wound. I was trying to get to you when a guard I hadn't seen attacked me, leaving me this." I gestured to my side.

Killian looked at me then, studying my face and then studying the wound. "If I felt you get stabbed, why didn't you feel it when Arrion had me killed?"

"I'm not sure." I shrugged. "I think the Goddess had something to do with it. I did feel the agony of the bond severing," I said with a shiver as I recalled the hollow sensation. "I won't pretend to understand how she took over my body or what happened at that moment, but I am grateful nonetheless."

Killian nodded, clearly contemplating the chain of events. "You can tell me what happened another time. Right now, I have a duty to worship my queen," he said with a mischievous grin.

His mouth met mine in a searing kiss, as if he needed to claim me. My fervor matched his as I tried desperately to tamp down the fear I had felt when I thought I had lost him. I met his passion with a fierceness all my own as I proved to myself that he was there, real, and alive.

Killian broke away from the kiss long enough to step from the tub and reach for towels. He dried himself quickly before pulling me to my feet, helping me out of the basin, and drying me with such tenderness that I thought I would melt.

He picked me up, carried me to the bed we had shared the night before, and perched me on the edge of the mattress.

Kneeling before me, he lifted my right leg over his shoulder and grinned. "Now, where was I? Ah, yes," he said before he pressed his face between my thighs. His tongue traced my opening and then up, before he swirled it around the sensitive bundle of nerves. Grasping his hair as my head fell back, I let out a strangled moan. The pleasure of feeling his warm, wet tongue lapping at me so diligently threatened to take over my senses.

Killian slid a finger inside my core and continued his efforts to worship my body. I felt the coil of pleasure building in my core, and it was not long before I fell back onto the bed. I let out a cry of ecstasy as I crested the ledge of my release. My body buzzed with the aftershocks of the orgasm, and as I lifted my head to look down my body at Killian, he winked before placing a gentle kiss on the over-sensitive bundle of nerves there. I shook involuntarily as he stood from kneeling and motioned for me to slide up the bed.

I moved back until my head reached the pillows. Killian, towering over me, climbed between my thighs. He leaned down to gently kiss my lips, then my cheek, down my jaw, and finally, the pulse point on my neck.

I gasped as Killian slowly slid his manhood into my core. The sensation of him filling me so wholly was momentarily overwhelming. I grasped at his back, pulling him closer.

"Thank the Goddess for bringing you back," I sighed.

"I've never felt so alive," he said as he bottomed out inside me before pulling back and slowly sliding back in.

"I love you," I whispered as he began to pick up his pace. I gripped his shoulder and back with my hands and wrapped my legs around his waist, determined to be as close as I could be, desperate to feel him alive and well and to convince myself that we were safe now.

"I love you, too," he said into my ear. "In this life and any other, I will always love you."

The intensity of his love overtook me, and I, again, fell over the edge of my release and cried out in pleasure. Killian groaned at the feeling of my body tensing around his and began to move faster, pumping in and out of me harder and harder. The headboard began to slam into the wall, and I released my grip on his back, placing my hands above my head to steady myself.

Killian moaned as he straightened his back and gripped my hips, sheathing himself to the hilt with each thrust before he, too, fell over the edge and filled me with his essence. His grip on me was relentless, and I knew he was feeling the same intense emotions I was.

Collapsing beside me, he pulled me to his chest, and I pressed my lips to his neck before lowering my head to his shoulder. I relaxed into his hold and smiled, finally feeling safe once again. He gently stroked my hair and pulled the blankets over our spent bodies as I drifted off to sleep in his arms.

"Kenna!" several voices called as I entered the dining hall of the coven's keep, Killian by my side.

"She's a queen now!" Laurel chided the entire room before bowing to me. Abruptly, everyone in the space scrambled to do the same.

"Kenna is just fine," I said with a giggle.

"Hello to you lot, too," Killian said with mock irritation.

Elicas lifted his gaze first and grinned at Killian. "Good morning, Hunter." A few mumbled voices echoed the phrase as the room moved back to their seats.

"That's better." Killian grinned before stepping from my side to clasp Elicas's shoulder. "I believe I owe you thanks for bringing your water friends to battle."

"I believe we owe *you all* a great deal of thank yous," I said over the mumbled voices of all in the room. "We would not be here without you. I am forever in your debt. And I am forever grateful to those who lost their lives. May we all live in honor of their sacrifice." A cacophony of cheers rang out in the crowd, and I smiled at their good spirits despite the deadly battle they had just fought the day before. Although many appeared wounded and exhausted, they did not seem to have lost their joy.

Laurel, the old guard, Sal, and Iris bustled over to my side to stand with Elicas and Killian. Mrs. Lancaster also made her way to the group, but not without scolding a few large Fae warriors who were making a mess of her dining tables. I couldn't help but chuckle as memories of her scolding the Witches in the coven when we were children came to mind.

The room was filled with laughter and talking. The calm in the space was comforting, but I still felt uneasy when I peered out the window nearest to me and saw the gnarled trees scattered about outside the coven walls. Was it really that simple?

I turned my attention back to the room, smiling as a few people waved in my direction. Everyone genuinely seemed happy. Healers handed out salves and bandages as breakfast was eaten and smiles were shared. The war was over, and they deserved this calm for a moment. Whatever came next would have to wait.

"Well, what now?" Laurel asked.

"Now, we eat breakfast," I said with a grin.

SNEAK PEEK OF BOOK TWO

KILLIAN

I stared out the window at the gnarled trees that protruded from the coven grounds, not truly present in the conversation around me. I couldn't fathom the amount of magic the Goddess had used to trap the king and his followers in those trees. It was as if they still pulsed with the magic of the soul trapped within. It was faint, but my newly awakened wolf senses picked up on it. It was entirely distracting.

Kenna and the rest of those who swore to protect her sat around one of the large tables in the coven's dining hall, discussing what came next now that the Fae King had been defeated.

"Killian?" Kenna's soft voice dragged me from my thoughts. "Hmm?" I turned to face her. "Sorry, love. What did I miss?"

She smiled knowingly. "Lost in your head?'

"A bit, yeah." I looked at her sheepishly. She had been so determined and driven since the king's reign had ended. I owed it to her to focus, but something nagged in my brain whenever I looked at those trees.

"We're planning what's next. You're the most traveled, so I was hoping to hold your attention for just a bit."

I gave her an inquisitive look. "Why do my travels matter?"

"You're rather dense, aren't you, Hunter?" Mrs. Lancaster's voice was sharp.

I looked at Mrs. Lancaster, who was sporting a disapproving look. She shook her head with a huff. I had thought I'd won the old coven headmistress over when I saved Kenna's life, but apparently dying for the woman she raised still wasn't enough.

Kenna reached out, touching my face, and gently turning my gaze to hers again. "It's my duty to try to fix what my grandfather broke. I can't do that from here."

"You want to travel the territories?" I looked at her with disbelief.

"I'm queen of the Fae now, whether I like it or not. If I'm going to protect my people, I need to reestablish allies. Otherwise, the Fae realm is a target," she said quietly but resolutely.

ACKNOWLEDGMENTS

This book was written in the quiet chaos of life — in the moments between sleepless nights, diaper changes, a pandemic, editing sessions, and the thousand responsibilities no one sees. If you're holding this book, then you're holding a piece of a dream that survived all of that.

To my readers:

Thank you for stepping into Illucidia with open hearts. Thank you for letting Kenna and Killian's story take root inside you. Your support, messages, enthusiasm, and kindness kept this book alive through every hard day. You are the reason I write.

To my Street Team and ARC readers:

Your excitement lit the path forward. Thank you for reading early, supporting this world, and treating this story with such care. This magic exists because of you.

To my editors:

Thank you for seeing the heart of this book, protecting my voice, and strengthening every page.

To my husband:

Your unwavering support, your patience, and your belief in me made this possible. You are my safe place and my constant.

And to my children:

You won't remember the nights I held you in one arm while writing with the other, but those moments built this world. This book is proof that we can be mothers and creators, gentle and powerful, tired and still full of magic.

ABOUT THE AUTHOR

Imogen Kay writes sweeping tales of love, magic, and danger, where fierce heroines and morally gray men collide in worlds you won't want to leave. A lifelong storyteller with a love for all things creative - from sewing her own wedding gown to 3D printing and painting - she's fueled by the belief that a good book should make you *feel*. She lives in New England with her husband, kids, pets, and a TBR pile that could probably qualify as a safety hazard.

JOIN THE NEWSLETTER!

Subscribers receive:

- Bonus scenes
- Early art reveals
- ARC opportunities
- Behind the scenes updates on future books
- Special announcements

Subscribe to Imogen's newsletter:
www.authorimogenkay.com

IF YOU ENJOYED THIS BOOK

Reviews help indie authors more than anything. They make stories visible, help other readers discover new worlds, and support the continuation of series like this one.

If *Half Breed* touched your heart, thrilled you, or left you a little breathless, I would be honored if you left a review on:

- **Goodreads**
- **Amazon**
- **Storygraph**
- **Pagebound**
- **Fable**
- **BookBub**
- **Anywhere else book reviews are welcome**

Thank you for supporting independent publishing. Your voice carries this world forward.

www.ingramcontent.com/pod-product-compliance
Lightning Source LLC
LaVergne TN
LVHW091706070526
838199LV00050B/2298